I0539421

Taking Tennessee To Hart

A NOVEL BY
JOE STOCKDALE

Hyphenates Books

Published by Hyphenates Books^{sm}
A division of Hyphenates, Ltd.
P.O Box 3771
Danbury Connecticut 06813

First Printing, October 2011
10 9 8 7 6 5 4 3 2 1

Copyright © 2011 Joe Stockdale
All rights reserved.

ISBN: 0983882509
ISBN 13: 9780983882503
Library of Congress Control Number: 2011936953

Hyphenates Books, Danbury, Connecticut

Hyphenates Books is a service mark of Hyphenates, Ltd.

Printed in the United States of America

Without limiting the rights under copyright reserved above, no part of this publication may be reproduced, stored in or introduced into a retrieval system, or transmitted, in any form, or by any means (electronic, mechanical, photocopying, recording, or otherwise), without the prior written permission of both the copyright owner and the above publisher of this book.

PUBLISHER'S NOTE
This is a work of fiction. Names, characters, places, and incidents either are the product of the author's imagination or are used fictitiously, and any resemblance to actual persons, living or dead, business establishments, events, or locales is entirely coincidental.

The publisher does not have any control over and does not assume any responsibility for author or third-party Web sites or their content.

The scanning, uploading, and distribution of this book via the Internet or via any other means without the permission of the publisher is illegal and punishable by law. Please purchase only authorized electronic editions, and do not participate in or encourage electronic piracy of copyrighted materials. Your support of the author's rights is appreciated.

For Robin,
who took the trip with me
And happy 100th birthday, Tennessee

Contents

Taking Tennessee To Hart

Prologue

An elderly man drank red wine and picked at his food. The same two young waiters in white aprons who regularly served him stood in a corner and laughed—at him, he knew. This single, unsubstantiated thought brought on the panic, the heart palpitations which he had experienced most of his life. He called for the check. "And may I have a sheet of paper?"

As he waited he thought of his present condition. He no longer could stand at the end of the Second Avenue bar checking the clock, its bawdy hands now upon the prick of midnight, and frantically search the line of faces hoping to connect. When he was young and the fleet was in, he and a companion would cruise 42nd Street for "fresh sea food," and it was as Hart had written..."*Oh, life's a geyser*! The gob explained." Now his sole companion was a hired young male who, for a few hundred dollars a week, slept in the room *next* to his.

He would go back to The Easy Lay, get into bed and would read to prolong turning off the light. When his left eye, taxed from long ago cataract operations, could no longer make out the words, he would take the ritual Seconal, or Ritalin or Nembutal, and wash it down with white wine in order to stun consciousness into submission. Then, laying a sleeping tablet in the bottle's cap, as something in reserve in case sleep did not come, he would finally turn off the light.

Of late, sleep was especially difficult in this near-death time of life. In the dark, his mind alternated between light and shadow, the clear and the cloudy, a consciousness which paralleled his long-ago troubled vision. In the dark he would see ghosts: his sister Rose, whom he truly loved; his lover, Frank "Little Horse" Merlo; Gran; and his reverend grandfather, who would never again return to Memphis; and the ghost of his agent, Audrey, whom he had thought of as dead since their quarrel and with whom he had never reconciled, a relationship needing healing, never healed, apologies left unsaid.

Finally, unable to deal with his ghosts, he would reach out in the dark, remove the sleeping tablet from the bottle's cap, place it on his tongue and take a last sip of white wine. Then lying back on the pillow he prayed to God for sleep ("blind and eternal hope with its broken lyre") but he would hear only The Grim Reaper's rattling of the window's casement there in The Easy Lay.

∽

When the young waiter had brought him paper and pencil, he wrote for some time. When he had finished he signed the credit card receipt, added a generous tip, and walked unsteadily into the lobby where he asked the desk clerk for the location of a public phone booth.

The clerk moved the desk phone to the counter, "You can use ours, Mr. Williams."

He rejected the offer, preferring a private booth. The clerk rang for the bellhop who respectfully ushered him to a booth, opened its door, and helped him be seated before moving away to wait at a respectful distance. Tennessee closed the door, found the number in his wallet, and dialed.

∽

At the Charles Hotel, Walt Wordsworth, in his worn bathrobe, was seated in the big overstuffed chair. Pen in hand, and by the light from the lamp with the faded fringed shade, he read and revised pages he had written during the day.

It was a Monday. Billy was home from work and in the shower, preparing for bed.

The phone rang.

"Hello?"

"Walt?" said the whispered voice.

"Tennessee?"

"Yes."

"Are you all right?"

"I've just finished dining *au solitaire* at the Plaza, my secretary-companion having found something better to do. I am now headed back to The Easy Lay. I have no one else to turn to and I'm about to check out."

"Of the Elysée?"

"No, Baby, *check out*. I'm having palpitations. The Grim Reaper is hovering and I'm told the *New York Times* has my obituary written and waiting and they're putting me second to O'Neill."

"Tennessee," Walt said, attempting to keep the concern from his voice, "do you think you should go to the emergency ward at St. Luke's?"

"No, no, no! Not that! Never, never that! I have no one to depend on. I can't count on the one who committed me to Friggins' Division of Barnacle Hospital in the city of St. Pollution, or my executor. So would you please come to The Easy Lay at once?"

"Of course."

"And bring two people with you to witness a document, people we can trust." His voice took on a secretive tone. "People of a revolutionary nature. Take a taxi, I'll pay. It's *En Avant*, Baby, ya hear?"

⟡

Annie drew water into the kettle for another cup of herbal tea. She was reading John Naisbitt's *Megatrends* which the *Times* had described as predicting that ambitious young people would not continue to be happy in the northeast. The idea interested her because she was thinking of heading to the Pacific Rim and starting afresh in L.A. God knows, the major attractions on Broadway were no longer straight plays.

The phone rang.

"Hello."

"Sorry for calling so late but . . ."

"Walt! I've been hoping you would call."

"I must ask a favor."

"Anything."

"Tennessee Williams just called. He needs witnesses for some kind of document. Can you meet me in the lobby of the Elysée Hotel on East Fifty Fourth Street in half an hour?"

∽

The desk clerk called Tennessee's room to announce their arrival, hung up, and informed them of the elevator's location. Walt introduced the two as the doors closed.

"Ann Laurel," Billy repeated as the elevator rose. "Great name." He held out his hand which was awkward since they were so close, but she shook anyway and noted that he was not a bone crusher like guys who seemed to think they proved their masculinity when they squeezed her hand. But the name! Billy? She had never known a Billy. Bill, yes. William. But Billy? It was like naming your kid Junior or Willie. She smiled, "Billy Lamb's a nice name."

∽

They sat quietly as Tennessee unfolded a sheet of paper. "I'm grateful," he told Walt, "that you found two such good-looking companions to witness this. Putting on his glasses he read: "St. Valentine's Day, February fourteenth, nineteen-eighty-three. This irrevocable last testament, written as a codicil to my will, concerns the disposal of my remains." He paused a moment, to take a sip of wine. "I, Thomas Lanier (Tennessee) Williams, wish to be buried at sea as close as possible to the American poet Hart Crane, who leapt to his death from the deck of the *Orizaba* on his return from Mexico in nineteen thirty-two. I wish my body to be sewn up in a clean white sack and after the Episcopal burial service, dropped overboard. The burial is to take place under the . . ." He glanced at Walt and gave a high piercing giggle, ". . . under the *tutelage* of Professor *Emeritus*, Walter Wordsworth, and carried out by his young poet-advocate colleagues recruited to sign this, my last testament." Removing his glasses he asked, "Do you understand?"

"Yes." Walt said, "I understand."

"Yes," Annie said when he turned to her.

"And you?"

"Yes, Sir," Billy replied.

"Good. I'm depending on the three of you. Now bear witness to this codicil with your signatures. Tomorrow I'll take it to my lawyers, Southern and Southern."

Unfortunately Tennessee's wish wasn't granted and he was buried in the family plot in St. Louis.

What follows is the story of how an aging theater professor and two young, willing acolytes went about righting this wrong.

Chapter I
Monday, 12 September 1983

Billy Lamb woke to the early morning chirping of birds. Bounding out of bed, he went to the window and pulled the blind. The sun was just below the horizon and in the distance, over the docks across the West Side Highway, was the Hudson River and the dimming night lights of the Jersey shore.

"What's it like?" Walt asked in his full rich voice, having been too wired about the trip to get any sleep.

"It's a beautiful, no humidity, no-workday morning; one of them cool, clear early September days with not even a small lazy cotton-white cloud."

It was after seven when Annie drove them across the George Washington Bridge and Billy observed that the GW's suspenders were similar to those of the Brooklyn Bridge, but not as beautiful—he actually used the word beautiful—noting that the GW lacked the slight curve of Brooklyn's arc.

"Aw, shut-up and get out the map," she growled in her New York cabbie imitation so he would know she was kidding. But her tone of voice indicated more of what she really felt than she cared to admit. She had not slept well. She kept wondering why she and Billy were not connecting. Last night after they had packed the van, she had done everything she could, short of tying him to the

Castro, to get him to bed down at her place rather than going back to Walt's apartment where he'd been living recently.

"Where's the map we marked?" Billy asked.

She remembered instantly. She had left it on the coffee table under Sunday's New York *Times*.

"That's okay," Billy said. "I can remember the route, and if we need a map we've got the road atlas."

Drumming out a rhythm with his hands against his thighs he went over the route they had planned: "Go left over the George Washington Bridge on highway 95-80. Go north on 80, to Patterson, Allamuchy, Hope. Then cross the Delaware Water Gap Toll Bridge to Stroudsburg, Pennsylvania."

A smiling Walt, wearing a planter's hat, sat in back and finger-combed his beard. "I hear America singing," he murmured.

Monday morning traffic was backed up going into the city, but they were headed in the opposite direction. Once over the Bridge, the highway's shoulders were littered with beer cans, papers, and garbage. Through the van's open windows came the smells of pollution from New Jersey industries. But nothing could dampen the excitement they felt in anticipation of what lay ahead.

As Billy rapped out the names of the towns and villages they passed, Walt repeated the names as though tasting America in his mouth: "Hackensack, Little Ferry, Mountain Head, West Parsippany, and Hibernia—I hear America singing, each singing what belongs to the day." He knew better than the young people that what he was going to experience was a rebirth—"A positiveness, which generated an energy, a creation, a vibrant love of life, that in a dying world, was itself, revolution"—Frank Waldo's prescription to Hart Crane for the rediscovery of America.

They had planned to make the trip in eight days, starting out on Sunday the eleventh of September and getting back in a week, but when Billy asked Tony for a week off, his boss had frowned and wanted to know why. Billy hemmed and hawed and finally said it was a personal matter.

Tony grinned. "You kids getting' hitched?"

"No," Annie said.

"You...?"

She knew he was going to say "knocked up" so she let the question hang. Embarrassed, Tony laughed, and to show he was a good guy tucked a nickel bag into Billy's shirt pocket. "Just enough for a couple of days to put lead in the old pencil," he winked. "So you're coming back...?"

"Sunday, the eighteenth."

"Okay kid, I'll let you go, but on one condition. You gotta work this Sunday because I got a party of old ladies coming in."

So their plan had been changed. They had to reach Garrettsville, Ohio, by the end of the first day, and now that they were underway Annie was not sure the goal was attainable. When she said so, Billy answered, "Sure we will." She looked at him and smiled—his fair skin, the blue eyes, shaggy dirty-blond hair—and her heart seemed to stop. Whether they would be able to follow the schedule or not was an open question but for the moment there was the joy of passing bumper stickers: "Honk if you believe in Jesus." "Honk if you're Elvis."

Walt, who liked Elvis, proclaimed that in bumper stickers he could hear America singing.

∽

The buzzer sounded in actors' agent June Saffron's office. Venetia said that it was an urgent call from producer David Lesco. June was more than half expecting it but at the same time hoped that Annie had taken the advice she'd left on the young woman's answering machine on Saturday and would report to work as usual.

"Where is Ann Laurel?"

"Why, David," June purred into the receiver, sounding bewildered, "isn't she at the studio?"

"Would I be asking where she was if she was here?"

"Well, I have no idea. Did you call her at home?"

"Of course!"

"This is not like Annie. She's never been late before, has she?"

"Never."

"I'm heartsick, David." June tried to modulate her usually strident tone. "Something awful could have happened to her. You know the crazies who hang out in Central Park, and Annie's an early morning jogger."

"If anything has happened to her," David said, enunciating each syllable, "we stand to lose a bundle."

"Let me run over to her apartment and see if I can find out anything." June feigned fright.

"Get back to me!"

"Yes, David. I just pray to God that she's all right."

Ann Laurel had been problematic right from the start. June had gotten her a sustaining part on a soap right after she graduated. It was a three-year contract, but she would not sign, demanding a year and a half because she was "determined to be an actress in the theater." June had eventually gotten her a two year deal because she was extremely talented, but when the contract was up she had actually refused to renew for another two years.

During the mid-seventies June had sent her out on casting calls, and she had gotten jobs—not very often, but a few in the major regional theaters plus voice-overs—but nothing on Broadway. After five years, June was going to drop her. But then this new writer, Brian, an old school chum of Annie's, had talked to the behind-the-scene-powers-that-be and they had accepted his fresh story line that reintroduced Annie's character on the soap.

The previous Friday, Annie had come to her office and said she needed to be gone for a week. June told her that she was out of her mind and to not even think of such a thing, and had called on the weekend and left a message reinforcing what she'd said.

Now this!

❦

An hour later, June got out of a cab in front of the brownstone on 76th Street, went inside and buzzed Annie's apartment. When there was no answer, she rang the super's apartment.

A heavily accented Puerto Rican woman's voice came over the intercom. "Is a delivery?"

"No, it is not a delivery. I must speak to the super, in person. At once!"

"My husband be right up."

The super appeared, as slow of gait as of speech, and introduced himself as Juan.

"I'm Mrs. Laurel, Ann Laurel's mother," June said, managing to mingle authoritarianism and motherly concern in the same breath.

"Oh, yes, Annie."

"I have reason to believe that something dreadful may have happened to her."

"Oh, I hope not, such a nice girl. Have you talked to police?"

"Do you have a passkey?"

"I do, but…"

June flashed a roll on top of which was a twenty dollar bill.

"Passkey, yes, I have."

"And bring along a crowbar just in case."

June was exhausted and short of breath when they arrived on the fourth floor and could hardly control her persistent smoker's cough. When Juan opened the apartment door, she wheezed past him into the room. "Check the bathroom," she ordered.

The sofa-bed was made. Everything looked normal. There was no evidence of a quick exit. Sunday's New York *Times* was on the coffee table. She picked it up. Under it, she saw a road map marked with a magic marker. Hearing Juan say, "Everything in order in here," she slipped the map into her bag.

Downstairs, she peeled two bills off the role, closed them into the super's outstretched hand, and was quickly out the front door.

Juan watched the departing figure before he un-clinched his fist and looked down at the two one-dollar bills. Putting a thumb to his mouth, he bit and snapped it as the woman entered a cab. "*Hija de perra!*"

∾

For Walt, there was the beauty of the fog-shrouded Delaware Water Gap, which really was a gap between two mountains; the Poconos and the barn country of Pennsylvania with its vibrant red sumac, green firs and the reds, yellows, and oranges of turning poplars and maples; and later, the yellow patches where wheat had been harvested, contrasting green pastures. And inside himself, as well as the youngsters, were the relived feelings of past Septembers, with their special promise of beginnings.

Later in the day, just when the country began to flatten out, more mountains appeared in the distance and a sign proclaimed, "The highest point on highway 80, east of the Mississippi, 2,250 feet." Then one hundred miles east of the Ohio border, again the land flattened to start the great Middle West. They crossed the Allegheny River, "Ohio Welcomes You to the Heart of it All" the sign read, and then there was the town of Ashtabula.

It was nine p.m., time to rest, but Annie felt only exhilaration and energy. "How do we get to Garrettsville?"

Billy drummed out the directions on his thighs. "At Girard, turn north, highway eleven, then west on the by-pass to eighty-two. Keep on eighty-two through Warren, then Braceville and on up to Garrettsville."

They drove past the Deep Pit. Sand and gravel. Ohio peat! Potato patches. Queen Anne's lace. And Billy beat out the rhythm.

∾

"Garrettsville, Founded in 1803." The van crossed a bridge onto Main Street and they parked across from the Farmer's Bank. "Let's have a drink in celebration," Annie said.

"I didn't think you drank," Billy said, remembering that first night they'd met after meeting Tennessee and signing the codicil; Walt had encouraged him to walk Annie home.

"I don't. But after driving four hundred and ninety miles, I think I can use a beer."

"All right," Billy replied, bounding out and stretching like a dog after a long sleep.

"Yo!" Walt cried, carefully lowering his ancient body onto the tarmac and cautiously walking in circles to get his land legs back.

The bar in the Silver Crik Saloon was well toward the rear of the large rectangular room; on its walls hung old fashioned, sepia-colored pictures.

"Must be Garrett, the founder," Annie said, pointing to the framed portrait of a distinguished gentleman.

"There's Leadbelly," Billy said, pointing to another.

Young and old men talked at the bar. The bartender limped slightly as he moved toward them and leaned into his only female customer. "What can I get you?" he asked. He was muscular through the chest with good strong arms and a well developed torso and Annie felt a sudden attraction for the fine male face and brown eyes. Making no attempt to hide what she felt, she looked him over and told him with her eyes. "I'll have a draft beer."

"Bud?"

"Yes."

"I'll have the same," Billy said.

"And I'll have an Old Grand-Dad." Walt announced, "Make it a double."

"Are you from around here?" Annie asked when the drinks were served.

The bartender smiled, "All my life, except for one year at Ohio State."

"Do you know about the poet from here named Hart Crane?"

"A poet?"

"Yes."

"No," he said, without hesitation.

"There's supposed to be a marker in the Garrettsville cemetery," Walt told him. "Where would that be?"

"We've got two cemeteries."

The thought that there would be two cemeteries had never entered their minds.

"Did she die...?"

"He," Walt corrected.

"Did he die recently?"

"Nineteen thirty-two."

"Well, the Baptist cemetery is very small so I think who you're looking for must be in the Park Cemetery. At the red light, turn left and go out, oh, about half, three quarters of a mile. The cemetery is on the left. You can't miss it."

"Were you in Vietnam?" Annie asked as he moved away.

He turned. "No."

"I noticed the limp."

"A car accident. I've got a metal rod in my hip. It should be out by Christmas."

The thing that struck Annie was that this guy had never heard of a great American poet who was born in his home town. "If you're in town awhile, you ought to visit the old grist mill," he said, motioning with his head. "It's just to the right of the bridge. Been going since eighteen oh four, oldest operating grist mill in the country."

"Thanks. We will," she smiled.

ᘒ

The cold beer had made her a little high so she drove slowly under a bright slice of moon.

"Hart," Walt said in a hushed voice as they drove by the moonlit cemetery, "is not buried here but his father is and his father's second wife, and his father's father and his father's father's wife, all the seeds of the past that led to the birth of an American poet."

At the far end of the cemetery, Annie turned left on a side road and found a place to park, ignition and lights off. Walt unrolled his bedroll at the end of the van behind the stack of paraphernalia for the dig and was asleep almost instantly with rhythmic snores. The windows were left open and Annie and Billy's sleeping bags were spread out just behind the front seats. Billy removed his shirt and lay on his back, body tired, but mind still moving with the van. Reaching out to say goodnight, he heard her deep breathing. Rising on one elbow and aided by a shaft of moonlight coming through the window, he saw that her eyes were closed. A mass of red hair framed the milk-white skin, the swan's neck, the broad shoulders and beneath the blue denim shirt, the outline of her hand-cupping breasts. His tongue involuntarily slid over his lower lip as he looked at her slightly parted lips and she seemed to smile softly in her sleep.

Chapter II
Tuesday, 13 September, 1983

She woke at dawn to the sound of raucously cawing rooks and looked at her watch. Only six hours of sleep but she was wide awake. She looked at the sleeping Billy, a sweet smile on his parted lips. She had not been asleep last night when he propped himself on his elbow and looked at her. She saw his tongue move over his wet lower lip and she wanted desperately to reach out and pull him to her but she was dead tired, and there was the Professor in the back of the van not six feet away.

Sleeping, Billy Lamb looked like a boy, except for the thinning blond hair and the very beginning of a bald spot on the crown of his head. The sight of him made her so incredibly open to all sorts of feelings, tenderness and wonder, and she didn't know what-all, churning away inside, making her feel very close to her skin.

She was hungry and in need of a shower. She rose silently, so as not to wake him, took the towel and washcloth from her bag along with her shirt and jeans. Outside, she washed with the drinking water they carried. As the wet cloth touched her skin, she felt the coldness of the morning breeze. The breeze turned the maple leaves, blowing maple leaves, underside silver. She knew Billy's rhythm.

After she finished her ablutions and dressed, she moved to examine a spider web reflected in the sun's rays in a nearby bush: a long, lacy intricate pattern of webbing and in the middle, the spider, with orange spots on her black back, not moving, still. The grass was shiny and wet with dew and smelled sweet and morning-fresh. She listened to the cawing rooks as she moved her body, bending down and up, stretching. In a moment she would have to wake Billy and Walt, but for now she wanted this moment of dawn for herself. Soon enough they would start another day.

They drove the short distance to the cemetery, which was paralleled with one-lane dirt roads. "You look on that side and I'll look on this," she told Billy.

It was toward the back that she spotted the name, "Crane!" She was out of the van before Billy could open his door. "Sorry, false alarm," she called. "Read the description once again."

Walt read from the Unterecker biography, ". . . Crane family plot in the Garrettsville Cemetery where, now, near the graves of Arthur Edward Crane, Frederick Jason Crane and Cassius Crane, on the face of the small granite block that marks Hart's father's grave is cut in three short lines: HAROLD HART CRANE, 1899-1932, LOST AT SEA."

As they searched the graveyard the sun begin to climb in the early morning sky. Walt kept repeating the three names Arthur, Frederick and Cassius, as he moved from stone to stone. When he had exhausted the section Annie had assigned to him, he moved to another. No matter how hard he tried, the names ran together and finally the only one he could remember was Cassius. When the back part of the cemetery had been searched, without success, Annie, sounding discouraged called, "Let's go to town. Maybe the stone's in the other cemetery."

They were about to pull out onto the country road when Billy sang out, "There it is!"

Annie turned back into the first parallel road. At the top of the slope, to their right, was the large family monument. How could they have missed it? Twelve small markers evenly spaced and engraved with the name of a Crane, and a thirteenth for Bess Crane Madden.

They stood looking directly down at the name of Arthur, but as they moved along the line of headstones there was no Frederick, Jason or Cassius. They walked back and forth several times to look down at the granite stones but not one was inscribed "Lost at Sea."

"Damn," Annie said. "It must be the other cemetery."

"Let's get some breakfast," Billy suggested.

☙

Mr. Wright's hardware store on Main Street was perfect, a place for everything and everything neatly in its place. At its back, Mr. Wright was talking on the phone. A fairly young man, he matched his store's neatness, no hair out of place, voice modulated and even, and dressed with extreme care. Even his sleeves were rolled to the same height above each elbow. Smiling in their direction, he continued talking until all questions were answered before he hung up. "May I help you folks?"

"The waitress in the restaurant said if anyone in town would know, it would be you, sir," Walt said. "We're looking for a small granite marker in the cemetery with the poet Hart Crane's name on it."

"We just put up a stone over by the bell tower commemorating him. It's around the corner next to our civic building."

"Was the stone moved from the cemetery?"

"Oh, no, this is a nice new one."

"What we're looking for is a granite stone in the cemetery on which is written, 'Harold Hart Crane' on one line, '1899 to 1932' on another, and 'Lost at Sea' on the third."

"As far as I know there is no such stone. That's why we put the one up by the bell tower last spring, so there would be a memorial."

Walt showed him the evidence in Unterecker's biography.

Mr. Wright shook his head, "Well, if there is, it's news to me."

"Could it be in the other graveyard?" Annie asked.

"The Baptist, no, all the Cranes are buried out at the Park Cemetery. The reason I'm so certain there isn't is because, as head of the Chamber of Commerce, I had to give the speech for the one we put up by the bell tower; took a lot of reading. I must confess I could hardly understand any of his poems."

Outside Walt said, "Maybe Unterecker is wrong."

"Didn't you say he was a professor at Columbia?" Billy asked.

"Professors can be wrong," Walt answered.

At the bell tower was a small reddish-white stone with a plaque inscribed:

GARRETTSVILLE, OHIO
BIRTHPLACE OF
THE INTERNATIONALLY KNOWN POET
HART CRANE
BORN JULY 21, 1899
LOST AT SEA APRIL 27, 1932
SON OF GRACE HART AND CLARENCE A. CRANE

Returning to the graveyard, they walked toward the large Crane monument. As they did, they saw a white-haired but sprightly woman, accompanied by an elderly man with a walking stick.

"Excuse me," Walt called, "have you folks lived around here for any length of time?"

"Well, I should think so," the woman laughed. "I've lived here all my life, and that's a length of time. John," she said, indicating the man, "is originally from Michigan, but I was born and raised right here in Garrettsville. My first husband is buried right over there."

"Then perhaps you can be of help." Walt explained what they were looking for by showing her Unterecker's book.

"The Crane monument is right there." She pointed to the marker near the highway.

"We've been there, looked at every headstone. On none is written 'lost at sea.'"

She re-examined the book, "Seems to me I've seen that. She turned to John. "Why don't you go on back," she suggested.

"I think I will."

"John's leg is bothering him and he can't do much walking."

As they approached the Crane monument, the woman smiled, pointing to a marker. "It's right there!"

"Where?"

"The last one, closest to the highway."

They were standing about fifteen feet from the stone. The woman was right. There it was.

HAROLD HART CRANE

1899-1932

LOST AT SEA

Annie was incredulous. "How could we have missed it?"

"Maybe the fall leaves," the woman observed. "Or you may have been too close."

"You're right. We were standing above it, looking down," Walt exclaimed. "'Face' refers to the front of, not the top."

"Often," the woman said, "one has to see things at a distance to see them clearly."

"And I kept looking for Frederick, Jason and Cassius."

"What was in your mind were the unusual sounding names," the woman said. "One can usually find more in the familiar."

A few dried early autumn leaves blown by the slight morning breeze were lodged against the stone's face. Although it was difficult for him, Walt knelt down to clear them away. Who had decided to have this, the only marker in the world—at least up until last spring when the stone was put up in the village—engraved? Who in nineteen thirty-two had thought to have carved out on the *face* of the father's headstone this remembrance of one of America's great poets? To have had inscribed "lost at sea" took a certain sensibility in light of what actually may have happened. "Lost at Sea" was exactly the right phrase to cloak the reality of Hart's life and death. It was obvious that this remembrance had been done by someone, perhaps his stepmother, a woman not a great deal older than he and of whom he was very fond, who cared for the poet.

"One last thing," Walt said, producing a paperback book from his bag. "Here's a picture of the house Hart was born in. Do you know where this is?"

"The woman pointed to the building left of the house in the picture. "That is St. Ambrose. Just go back to the center of town, and at the red light go straight. It's in the first block."

It was a big house on Freedom Street. It had green shingles and the trimming was painted green. "Ah," Walt mused, "yet another connection with Tennessee. Hart, too, was born in the very shadow of the church."

༄

June was on the phone to Doug, the director of "One Woman's Family." "How valuable is she?"

"She's damn important to the show's plot right now because Brian has featured her in future episodes and she's beginning to get fan mail."

"Okay, so can you possibly schedule shooting around her for the rest of the week?"

"Yes, but more than a week and we can't do anything but bust a gut changing the story line."

"Between us, Doug, I think I can find her and get her back here."

"Between us, if you can, and she's got a damn air-tight alibi, I think it will be okay. The only person who wants her fired is David Lesco. He never wanted to rehire her in the first place, but he wouldn't know talent if he tripped over it. We all love her work. I think she's got a real future on the show with the way Brian is writing for her."

"I'll do my best at this end."

June buzzed Venetia. "Get Cindy Adams at The Post."

⁓

As they drove west and were passed by a truck, the side of which read, C.D. Casket Distributors, something set Billy to thinking out loud. "How long do you think a body will last once it's been buried?" he mused.

"'A tanner will last you nine years'" Walt said.

"A tanner?"

"A person who tans hides. That's what the gravedigger tells Hamlet."

"What I'm asking is what will a body *look* like after it's been buried six months?"

"I played Cleopatra in a class project," Annie offered. "Of course, in ancient Egypt burial was a whole other ball of wax."

"And there's Yorick's skull," Walt offered. "But of course he'd been buried some years."

"'Three and twenty years,' the first Gravedigger's line," Annie said. "You asked us that question on our Theatre History final."

"I may have," Walt confessed, "but I've struck all such trivia from my mind. I'm at a loss to think of other examples in dramatic literature of exhumations."

"Where do you suppose we could find out what the corpse might look like after we dig him up?"

"A library," Annie offered.

"No," Walt scoffed. "If one is in a hurry one can seldom find anything like that in a library."

Annie giggled. "Well, how about a funeral home then, professor?"

"Good idea," Walt acknowledged. "Oh yes, I just remembered. There's Robert Louis Stevenson's short story, 'The Body Snatcher.' It's based on a real life incident in which two men turned from body snatching to murder in order to provide bodies for dissecting purposes to the story's thinly disguised prototype, Dr. K, who was based on the real life Scottish anatomist, Dr. Robert Knox. This famous case resulted in laws making body snatching a crime punishable by imprisonment."

"Imprisonment," Billy exclaimed.

"Well, of course."

Annie and Walt behind bars? He could never let that happen.

༄

The Canadian prison in which Billy had been incarcerated was a genuine fortified castle with turrets, angel towers, outer walls with parapets, and flags.

"What's the answer?" Billy had asked from the top bunk.

His cell-mate, Omar, was looking at a Playboy centerfold by the light from a high-up fluorescent bulb in the passageway.

"To what?" Omar's was a black voice, rich and deep.

"To life," Billy answered.

The activity under Omar's blanket increased and there was deep breathing and toe curling before he confided, "Persistence, persistence and imagination."

Outside, in the spring, were masses of canaries, yellow breasted, tiny birds. Where they came from, Billy had no idea. But he got to know the songs of these tiny birds zipping around like crazy. "Kinda like hummingbirds. You know humming birds?" he asked Omar. "Beat their wings so fast they make a humming sound. Can't even see 'em, they go so fast; freedom, only a blur."

"A canary don't fly as fast as a hummingbird," Omar said.

Judy Garland had died during his first year of incarceration: "Somewhere over the rainbow." His mother remarried and she and her new husband operated an organic fish farm outside Roswell, Georgia.

He saw a lot of sights, heard a lot of sounds, in prison. Men just out of solitary; Dobermans running in the moonlit yard; a sign reading, "Don't Serve Time, Make Time Serve You," like eating a sugar donut's worth of thought food at the end of a late night, morning letdown. But Billy got to the point where he thought prison might be a good idea. He got clean: drugs, booze and cigarettes. Maybe a light tour of prison duty should be required of some of those college kids he'd seen at the U of Washington where Maeve went.

The guards kept getting one of the inmates on the charge of "silent insolence." They got Omar on "abusing government property" when they caught him beating off in the shower. Jimmy Hendrix and Janis Joplin both died during his second year in prison. He was treated well behind bars because he was an object of curiosity, a real American flower child who preached love, peace and nonviolence. "Walls," he comforted long-term inmates, "do not a prison make," which provided them with the best laugh they'd had in years.

Omar got him into the prison jazz band, the Cariboo Ramblers, which the old warden called a "swing band." Billy had time to read. He was a model prisoner; no dope, straight.

Richard Nixon resigned and Billy was released in 1975. The amnesty law worked for him and he crossed the border to the U.S. of A. Someone said it was "a time of healing," but the wounds were too deep to heal. He had been a defector, and as angry as the public was about the war and those who served in it, they were just as angry with those who defected. Seattle seemed like home and it was closer than Georgia, where his mother was, so he went there and played in Maeve's band.

With his record, it was hard to get any kind of job. He met a woman, Clara, with two sweet kids and got married. She had a good job and he turned out to be a good house-husband and babysitter. And he listened to a lot of music: The Beatles, The Who, Bob Dylan, Led Zeppelin, Simon & Garfunkel, The Doors, Paul Simon, Jim Croce, Jefferson Airplane, and Paul McCartney. John Prine was one of his favorites.

Drummers Keith Moon of The Who and John Bonham of Led Zeppelin died of ODing. People put out yellow ribbons for the hostages held in Iran and sold T-shirts with a "Fuck the Ayatollah" caption under his picture that sold for twenty-five bucks; and the U.S. put a shuttle into space. There were attempts to assassinate Reagan and John Paul II, and the Brits under iron maiden Margaret Thatcher kicked the stuffing out of Argentina in the Falklands, so like John Prine sang, things were: "Pretty good, not bad, I can't complain."

Actually, everything was just about the same.

∽

June dialed the number. After three rings the answering machine kicked in: "This is the residence of Julie Laurel," came the sweet voice. "I'm sorry, but I can't come to the phone right now. But if you'll leave your name and number, I'll get back to you just as soon as I can. Have a lovely day."

June slammed the receiver back into the phone's cradle so hard that Venetia, listening in from her desk, was afraid for a moment that she had lost hearing in her right ear.

"Mothers," June hissed. "Spare me!"

∽

It was a bright morning as the van tooled along highway 70 west. Annie attempted to pass an Arizona-plated Chevy Silverado camper with silver silhouettes on the mudguards of naked girls with ten inch waists and uplifted D cup breasts. When she was parallel with the camper, the thick-necked driver gave her the finger and sped up. She was about to pass him when ahead, she saw the cop car on the roadside. In her rear view mirror she could see Billy sitting surrounded by all their grave digging equipment. She slowed down and got back into the right lane behind the camper, on the back of which was a bumper sticker which read simply: "The Boss."

Billy was fascinated by the spray-painted signs that rimmed the lips of the overhead passes they drove beneath, "Jimmy, love you always, Mom." Had Jimmy's mother come to the overpass, hung over the side and spray painted that message?

Along the sides of the road were electric power lines held aloft by what looked like steel erector sets. Annie said the flowers in the fields were bachelor buttons. In the distance, at an exit, on top of a gas station was a plastic statue of a buffalo under a gigantic flowing-in-the-wind American flag. And forever, as far as the eye could see, the land lay flat.

"It's a great road," Annie said.

"It has to be," Walt said, without enthusiasm. "It's Ohio's Appian Way, built with no expense spared to transport Buckeyes to their favorite sport at the Coliseum every Saturday afternoon in autumn."

"Oh, come on, football's great fun," Annie chided.

"Of course," Walt said, "When it comes to Big Ten football you gotta provide the best roads."

"You gotta have the best team," Annie countered. "And the Buckeyes are."

"Don't argue with her," Billy told Walt. "Annie's a fan."

"Did you know that Ohio State has played in more Rose Bowl games than any other team in the Big Ten?"

She was lecturing him. Walt wheezed a sigh.

Highway 70 west to Indiana was heavily traveled by truckers. A door on the back of a truck had printed in its dust, "Pass and show your legs, ladies."

Billy was thinking of the way Annie had looked in her sleep last night. He had to talk to her, tell her who he was, what his life had been.

"Ohio thanks you for visiting the heart of it all."

A baby blue sign across the highway proclaimed, "Welcome to Indiana."

Back a hundred miles east of the Ohio border where the land flattened out, Walt had begun to realize that, at his age, unlimited space was more confining than a confined space. All he saw now was gigantic sky and flat land in all directions. He preferred an enclosure with a protective hill on both sides, down in a hollow such as the Delaware Water Gap. In the vast space of the Midwest, one had to be very secure in oneself.

A sign atop a water tower in the distance read: "Richmond, a Great All-American City."

"Let's try to find an undertaker here," Annie said.

"Okay," Billy agreed.

"But we'd better settle on a plan of attack with a list of questions."

"Welcome to Richmond – the City of Roses."

⚬∾⚬

Mr. Herman Willis wore a constant smile on his face. In his youth he had desperately wanted to become a writer. But instead of following his dream, he had opted for security, capitulating to his father's wishes and taking over the family business.

He was lamenting this choice for the thousandth time while he inspected the new "half-couch" with its two lids which had been shipped overnight by C. D. Casket distributors. He was testing the coffin's crank to see if it lowered and locked the lids when he heard the front door chimes. Placing the crank on the plastic that covered the coffin's interior, he glided toward the front door where he expected yet another in a series of dewy-eyed females mourning the death of Jock Warren, manager of the Kroger Store, who had dropped dead two days ago.

"Hello," the young man stammered in a half whisper. "I'm a writer. I'm writing a story and I need some technical information."

A writer! It was one of those moments you live for. "Won't you come in?" Behind the boy, Willis saw the young, redheaded woman and in back of her a bearded and very large African-American gentleman who, had he been white, would have looked amazingly like the picture of Walt Whitman on the dust jacket of the new Justin Kaplan biography. "My name is Willis, Herman Willis," he said, holding out his hand.

"My name is, er, Ramm, uh, Phil Ramm," The young man spoke as if he wasn't quite certain. "And this is Mr. Gault Wadsworth and his daughter, Frannie."

"So pleased," Mr. Willis said, indicating the sofa and ignoring that a black man had a white daughter. "Now then," he asked when his company had been seated "what kind of technical information do you need Mr. Ramm?"

The boy took a list from his shirt pocket. "If you were to dig a person up who'd been buried six months, what condition would the body be in?"

"Let's assume," Willis said, "that the 'person' is, one, embalmed, two, inside a casket, and three, the casket is inside a vault."

The older man nodded his head. "Good assumptions," he offered.

"I hadn't thought of a vault." The young man spoke as though the matter troubled him. "What's a vault's size?"

"An average vault would be thirty-eight inches deep, with the same width and seven feet long to hold the casket which is thirty inches deep, six foot long with a width of between twenty- six and twenty-eight inches, which leaves the corpse...a little wiggle room."

"What's the average grave size?" the boy asked.

"Eight by four feet."

"And six foot deep," the girl said.

"Mostly five."

"Is a vault sealed?" the boy asked.

"Oh, yes," Mr. Willis said. "Vaults are sealed by...well, the concrete vaults we use in this section of the country–where is your novel?–it *is* a novel?"

"Yes."

"A mystery novel?

"I guess."

"Where is it laid?"

"It's laid in St. Louis," the boy said.

"Well we prefer to use a, oh, it's like an epoxy, a very thick epoxy, not like your common thermosetting resins, but very thick. Eventually it cures and the weight of the lid–six hundred pounds– and the earth pressing down on it makes it so hard that the only way you can open it is with a jackhammer."

At this the youth blanched.

"Does the fact that you need a jackhammer to open the sealed vault throw a monkey wrench into your story?"

"Well, I didn't know the lid would weigh that much and I didn't know we'd need a jackhammer."

The young man seemed disturbed.

"The lid is sealed onto the vault's base, of course, to keep the body dry," Willis explained. "It must be thoroughly sealed because moisture is what causes the body to decompose. The natural bacteria within the body helps digest food but once a person dies, bacteria starts to self-digest, what we call autolysis. The chemicals we use in embalming today are preservative. The primary reason for embalming is the same today as it was in ancient Egypt, to restore the body to a lifelike appearance."

"How long does the body last?" the young woman asked.

"Well, it depends on the cause of death."

"He choked to death on a cap," the young man answered.

"You know, like a cap off a small medicine bottle," the girl explained.

"Ah, yes! How old was the deceased?"

"He would have been seventy-two on March twenty-sixth," the older gentleman said.

"And he drank."

Even as the words left the young man's mouth, Mr. Willis saw the apologetic look the boy gave the older gentleman, as though his remark was somehow inappropriate.

"Well, with someone with a history of alcoholism, you get this tremendous drainage. The blood just gushes out. With alcoholics their preservative power is excellent but the liver might be damaged. In which case you can't use a formaldehyde-based fluid because if the liver is damaged and the corpse is jaundiced, the bile pigments, bilirubin, biliverdin, back up and when that happens, the corpse turns green."

"Are you okay, Walt?" the boy asked.

The old gentleman nodded his head yes, although Mr. Willis could see that he looked queasy. But why had the young man called the old one, Walt? Herman was certain he had been introduced as Gault thinking at the time that it was an odd name. "Could you use that in your novel?" he asked.

"Maybe."

"And, incidentally, after six months or so, you might find a bit of mold or mildew on the corpse if there is any dampness in the casket, and you would also find a certain amount of dehydration."

"Would the body be stiff?" the young man enquired.

"Oh, yes, formaldehyde and glutaraldehyde coagulate the proteins. You see, the longer the preservatives are in, the longer it sets, the more rigid the body becomes. And you must remember that three feet below the ground's surface it is always sixty degrees."

"This body is buried in St. Louis," the young man said.

"The frost line in St. Louis is the same as it is here, three feet." Mr. Willis could hear his voice rising. "And the point I'm making is that sixty degrees is not ideal for bacteria."

At this point the older gentleman's face had gone slack and the young man rose suddenly. "Well, thanks, Mr. Willis. I think that about covers it."

"Oh, yes," Herman said quickly, "with dehydration, an eye might be open just a little bit. Or maybe the corner of the mouth might..." He opened his mouth slightly, letting one corner droop down. "Do you think you could use that bit?"

"Well, possibly." The boy turned to the door.

Mr. Willis placed his hand on the boy's arm. "And after a few months, maybe there would be a little mold on the necktie."

"This sure is a wealth of information." The young man took a step toward the door.

Willis grabbed his arm and guided him to the half-couch. "You know, of course, the top of a casket can be made in two different styles?"

"No, I did not know that."

"Chances are, if your story's laid in St. Louis, the top is all one piece. With a one-piece lid the family sometimes orders a blanket of flowers that covers the feet..."

"Okay. Well, thanks." The young man removed Willis's hand. "That about does it."

"Oh, yes!" Mr. Willis said, "Another point of verisimilitude. The caskets are also sealed."

The young man turned. "Sealed?"

At last one detail had taken root in the boy's mind, Willis thought, something he could incorporate into the story. "Yes, sealed, with a crank." Mr. Willis ran back to the new half-couch, on which the old gentleman was leaning. "See, this crank locks the lid down on the rubber gasket."

The young man moved with sudden interest and watched the demonstration.

"Do all caskets have their own unique crank?" the girl asked.

"Oh, no, one crank usually fits all. And, at the top, just inside the closed area, is a catch which allows you to open the other lid, if the coffin is a two-lidder."

"Where would you get one of those cranks?" the young man asked.

"Only in a funeral parlor," Mr. Willis smiled confidentially, placing the crank on top of the casket.

∽

Later, Willis would remember that at that very moment the young man had looked past him in the direction of the old gentleman and an odd, or perhaps it was a startled, expression had crossed his face.

"Okay!" the young man said quickly—too quickly—Mr. Willis realized later. "I think that answers all the questions. You've been very helpful."

"Thanks, Mr. Willis," the girl added, heading for the door.

"We are forever in your debt," the old man said as he hurried past, one hand in his pocket.

They were out the front door and already descending the steps when Mr. Willis came running. "Another detail...if there were flowers in the casket, the moisture would most certainly cause a little mildew."

"Good-bye," the young lady called from the driver's seat of the van.

"Thanks," the young man waved, helping the old gentleman into the back and barely being seated before the van sped away.

Something, Willis could not explain, perhaps the speed of their departure, made him take note of the van's New York license plates.

∽

Information gained in the interview from Mr. Willis greatly increased the self-doubt Billy had on his ability to think the thing through. His father, William "Billy" Lamb, Sr., had always told him,

"Look before you leap, boy. Think the thing through." And his father was not always pleased with him when he was growing up, especially when Billy marched to the beat of a different drummer in his high school algebra class. Billy Sr. was good at mathematics, so anything to do with figures Billy naturally backed off from. But his dad never outright called him a loser. When Billy flunked algebra all Billy Sr. said was, "Very little survives failure."

"I wonder if we've thought this thing through," Billy said.

"'Thinking the thing through' marks the difference between professionals who do not go to prison, and rank amateurs like us who possibly could," Walt lectured. "Professionals 'think the thing through' and are prepared for all eventualities. That's why they don't get caught." He added with great conviction, "I'd rather be an amateur."

"Why, if amateurs get caught?" Annie inquired.

"Because amateur in French means lover," Walt answered. "Professionals are whores."

⁂

"There are only two kinds of people in this world, man," Maeve had said to Billy and the other band members, "the power people and the lovers. And lovers is what you guys have gotta be tonight. Even though Lucy's ain't a union house, which for some fucked up capitalistic reason means professional, and even though there ain't many people out there, just remember that amateur, in French, means lover."

Then, well into the back side of that Sunday night gig in this grimy little pocket of integrity, where he did not feel like a 'six time loser,' Billy started with seven beats on the drum and Maeve gave out with her favorite.

"Cry Baby, Cry Baby, Cry Baby
Honey, welcome back.
And when you walk around the world, Babe
You said you'd try to look for the end of the road."

The "Olympic" in Maeve's "Full Tilt Olympic Rock & Roll Band" in which Billy drummed, was named for the mountains west of Seattle, and Lucy's was in the skuzzy part of town. A lot of downtown Seattle was depressed in December 1982, but putting a positive spin on it, Billy told himself he could always look up and see the mountains.

Rainier and Olympic weren't what he liked most. What he liked most was being inside Lucy's where the dark was broken by odd arcs of light which came from fluorescent bulbs that spelled out the names of beers in reds and blues and greens, the forever-moving light in the old jukebox, and the light that filtered through stained-glass hanging globes. And swirling through the light—though everyone knew of the surgeon general's declaration that it caused cancer—was cigarette smoke as thick as the fog that rolled in off Puget Sound.

Maeve was vocalist and Billy played drums and he and Curtis, who stroked a mean electric guitar, were Maeve's vocal back-ups. Morrese was on bass guitar, and Rod played the keyboard, organ, and piano. Maeve divided the hundred and fifty dollars Lucy paid for the weekend by five so each band member got thirty bucks. Business was always slow before Christmas but Sundays before Christmas were downright dead. Billy guessed it was for this reason Maeve called all of them together backstage in her dressing room, a tri-fold screen at one side of the kitchen, and gave a pep talk while she dressed in her new threads from the Salvation Army.

"That Henry Luce rag, *Time* magazine, came out with a story that Rock-and-Roll is dead on its ass. Seems the eighties is more interested in bubble gum Muzak 'cause it goes more with their delights which is makin' money and talkin' *me*. In short, we are in the Reagan Administration, which means The Beach Boys, sun-and-surf shoobie-doobie-do-bop-she-bam, Muzak. And Nancy wants them to spread that shit around the Rose Garden." Maeve stepped into her tight black satin skirt. "But to hell with that," she said, using a brush and brown liner to enhance the line of her cleavage before she slipped on a low-necked sequined blouse. "No one's gonna tell me Rock-and-Roll is dead."

When the band first started, Maeve imitated Janice Joplin so close you'd swear it was a lip sync. The only difference was the band didn't sound like Big Brother and the Holding Company or the Full-Tilt Boogie guys who backed Janice. Then, as time went by, Maeve found her own way with the songs. They came out of her from the way she lived, which was in one room over a store down a gritty block; a room with a water bed and only beer in the fridge.

Maeve could read music right off the page. Billy couldn't. But then most drummers can't. But what Maeve did uniquely was sing each song like she was giving a gift of herself. Her voice was a cry with air screaming and vibrating through the strings and the sound was a shrill gut-buster and harsh, and then again, sweet and soft as when she sang "Summertime." And off stage she did everything she could to toughen her instrument. She smoked cigarettes and marijuana, yelled at things and sometimes people, snorted Coke, and, when she could afford it, shot speed, and sometimes horse, and did as many guys as she could.

She was killing herself in order to feel the songs, the words, the story the songs were telling, and to make them honest and true to her own life. A *Seattle Post Intelligencer* critic, who wrote about sports, restaurants, and night clubs, wrote that although she wasn't a great singer, her singing had "integrity," which didn't exactly bring crowds flocking to Lucy's. But as Lucy said, philosophically, integrity wasn't a word to spell out over the club's marquee because no one in that part of town would read it anyway since they were so damn busy looking up at the mountains.

⁂

As they drove across the flat-lands of Indiana Billy now knew that not only had he not anticipated a vault, he had no idea that a vault's lid was sealed or that it weighed six hundred pounds. And, based on their experience in Garrettsville, they might not be able to locate the marker. When Walt had first proposed the transfer—Billy didn't really like the term body-snatching—he had envisioned a rather small cemetery, and now...

The major question was where in hell were they going to get a jackhammer? And a jackhammer made a terrible noise so wouldn't someone hear it? What if the grave site was right next to the road like it was in Garrettsville? How would they ever be able to dig the body up without being apprehended? And would they ever be able to place the sod back over the grave so that no one would notice?

One double-meaning word, *leverage*, kept coming back to him from the past. In prison he seemed to have an advantage because other inmates were curious about him. Omar claimed it was because he was a real American flower child, and the fact that he was white gave him "leverage" which Billy translated as an advantage.

"The only way I know we're going to lift six hundred pounds is rent, or maybe carjack, a truck with a hoist on it."

Annie had been thinking of her experience in summer stock when the director didn't allow time spent on thinking negatively. "If I say I need a fucking pink elephant," he had enunciated every syllable, "don't expend precious energy with debilitating negation. Just go down to Smith's hardware, buy a couple of canisters of pink spray-paint, then go to the yellow pages and call the Bronx Zoo." And the crazy thing was that he meant it. She still had the "Negation Is Debilitating" T-shirt all the apprentices wore that summer. But the experience had taught her one thing. There was always some kind of solution. "There are ways to lift heavy objects without a mechanical hoist," she said.

"Look at the pyramids," Walt agreed.

"This may sound like I'm going a long way around to get back to where I started from," Annie continued, "but Walt, you'll remember this. At school we did that original play 'God's Peculiar Care' about a thirties movie actress named Frances Farmer."

"Yes, I remember," Walt said.

"She went to Broadway and starred in a Group Theatre show, and when she came back to Hollywood, a producer felt she'd gone all hoity-toity and needed putting in her place. The picture was called 'Flowing Gold', about oil wells, and in the scene her father's car is stuck in the mud. The director wanted her to push the car. Her father would rev the motor and spin the wheels and she'd be covered with mud. The story goes that Farmer said to the director, 'Instead of getting covered in mud, why don't I just put a plank under the bumper and pull up: Resistance, fulcrum, leverage. The character would certainly know that, wouldn't she?'"

"I see what you mean," Billy said. "We could lift six hundred pounds if we had some kind of leverage." They were approaching Terre Haute and he asked her to drive into town where they looked for a hardware store to buy two crowbars and three five-foot pry-bars.

Back on highway 70 there was a sign, "Welcome to Illinois."

"Signed by the governor," Annie pointed out.

"I'd rather be welcomed by the people." Walt used his revolutionist's tone.

Adult books were advertised at a trucker's stop; the Embarras River; small, pumping oil wells about eighty miles east of the Missouri line.

"Carlyle." Walt pointed to the sign.

"Pocahontas," Billy pointed, some miles later.

"Every state has a Pocahontas," Walt said.

The rest was silence as Billy's mind raced with thoughts about vault openings. Now that he realized their plans had not taken into account several major factors, now that they understood that what they hoped to do was not only complicated but dangerous and there was a chance that they might get caught, each contemplated the problems.

"Hell," Billy finally exclaimed, "we don't even know how big Calvary Cemetery is."

～

Calvary Cemetery was very big. Three hundred and fifty thousand graves bordered by busy Florissant Avenue on the west, the Wabash railroad tracks and Broadway on the east, Riverview Boulevard on the north, and Calvary Avenue which separated Calvary Cemetery from yet another cemetery of almost equal size to the south. In addition to being sixteen blocks long and two thirds as wide, it was surrounded by a six foot iron fence.

It was nine o'clock Tuesday evening and their worst case scenario was realized. They had to collect themselves and think the thing through. Maybe the plan, what there was of it, just wasn't possible. "What do you think we ought to do?" Billy asked Annie.

"I think we ought to go back and check in to one of those motels we saw coming in. Forget this business of sleeping in the back of the van. As Noel Coward once said, 'small economy seldom if ever pays.' Get us a good hot shower and a decent night's rest in air-conditioned rooms. Get up about eight. Have a good breakfast—eggs, bacon, home fries or grits, orange juice, coffee—and then call the sexton or whoever the hell is in charge and go out there and see what we got, then figure out the solutions to the problems."

"All right," Billy exclaimed, relieved that Annie's plan would give them more time to think the thing through.

Annie found a Best Western—she paid in cash to avoid leaving a paper trail—getting two rooms, a double with twins for Walt and Billy and a single with a queen sized bed for herself so if things worked out....

After showers, the three were to meet briefly in her room to plan strategy for the big day. She was fluff-drying her hair after a long bubble bath and thinking about jack hammers when she heard the rap at the door.

Billy explained that an exhausted Walt, after a couple of drinks of Cutty Sark "in honor of Hart Crane," had gone to bed, and was fast asleep when he got out of the shower. "But maybe we can talk."

"Sure," she said, aware that his smile was gone and his tone of voice was very serious. She would explain what she had in mind to ease his worries, "About the jackhammer..."

"Let's try to figure that out tomorrow," he said gently, sitting in the chair. "I need to...talk...about us."

"So what about us?" she asked softly.

"I knew this summer that I wasn't being what you wanted me to be, but it wasn't because I didn't want to be what you wanted me to be, or, that my feelings weren't the same as yours because they were, exactly, and they have been since we met that night at Tennessee's place. I'm crazy about you and whatever happens tomorrow if, for some reason, we figure we can't do it or if something bad happens, I don't want you mixed up in this."

"Hey, wait a second," she interrupted. "I *am* mixed up in this. This is the three of us, together, and that's the way it's going to be."

"But if something happened..."

"What?"

"...if we should get caught."

She knelt beside him and took his face in her hands. "Look at me," she said. "What's wrong?"

"If we got in trouble, I don't want you..."

And now that he was facing her, to tell her what he had come to tell her, he was unable to do so. He'd tell her when it was all over. He would sit down with her and talk because he had never wanted anything more in his life than he wanted, needed, her, and being so close to her, seeing her beautiful eyes, he could not—not right now.

Seeing him so anguished, tears sprang to her eyes. She did not know what troubled him but she knew that he felt the same way about her as she did about him and whatever it was that had kept him from her for so long could no longer stand in their way. She reached out and drew him to her, and as the tip of his tongue touched her lips and went into her mouth, she drew a sharp breath as a shudder passed through her body. Then suddenly he rose. "See you tomorrow," he said and went to the door, opened it, and without turning back, closed it.

Chapter III
Wednesday, 14 September, 1983

Early Wednesday morning, June listened from her home phone to the saccharine-voiced recorded message, "...the residence of Julie Laurel. I'm sorry, but I can't come to the phone..." and slammed down the receiver in the same way she had the day before.

Naked, she was about to step into the shower when the phone rang. Who the hell would be calling her at home at this hour? It was David Lesco, reading Cindy Adams' column in the *Post*. "'Ann Laurel, TV actress, was a no-show for filming at NBC yesterday. The network is frantically trying to find Laurel because she figures prominently in the future story lines of 'One Woman's Family' and without her they're going to have to scrap a lot of footage.'"

"Where could Adams have gotten that story?" she asked. Then playing on his well-known insecurity she added, "This sounds like an inside leak. Who wants your job?" she purred suggestively, waiting for his sputtering to end. "Tell you what I'd do. I'd take the bull by the balls and capitalize on a bad situation. Why not make a brief appearance after today's episode and announce Annie's disappearance? You're worried as hell, like a father's feelings. After all you have a daughter of your own and you're out of your mind fearing what might..."

"You know I'm not married," he said.

"...and you're worried sick that something may have happened to her." She paused to listen to his reservations. "Of course not, no police or FBI; infer temporary amnesia." She paused. "Loss of memory you think was brought on by trauma." She paused again. The son-of-a-bitch was dumber than she thought. "We can decide on what kind of trauma later. Say you know she has good friends in the St. Louis area, because I know she has. And, here's the gimmick..."

In her bathroom she gazed at the shiny new shower nozzle she had screwed in place all by her lonesome a week ago. Screw the ecological assholes in her building that ruled only water saving nozzles giving a prissy little stream could be installed. She loved her early morning cold shower and figured that she wouldn't be around when the big water shortage hit and the nation's water supply was "privatized." The hell with them!

If there was one thing she had learned in her business it was that, whether a plug or a pan, publicity couldn't hurt a showbiz career. She had a hunch that this mess could end up a win-win situation. It might even generate national media attention. And if, as Doug said, she got back in a week so the studio would not lose any already shot footage, things could work out just fine.

Of course, Annie would lie about where she's been. June expected that and she would raise hell. But in the meantime, the publicity about her disappearance and the mystery and uncertainty could only enhance her marketability. There wasn't a star June could remember who didn't show some independence; it came with the spirit and fire that made stars. The only person who was going to be hurt in this situation was Lesco and all she could say was, screw him, and damned if she didn't know the right sleuth for the job of getting Annie back.

Under the noise of the stinging spray hitting her ample flesh full force, she sang: "I'm a little debil, red and mean, I got me a plan and it's so keen."

ᵔᴥᵔ

When Annie knocked on their door at nine, Walt was showered and ready and Billy was just coming back from packing the van. After a big breakfast at a nearby Shoney's of exactly what Annie had said they would order, they went back to her room. Having talked about some of the problems they anticipated, Annie found the number in the yellow pages. "You call," she said, smiling at her Billy.

"You have reached the gate house at Calvary Cemetery..."

Billy started to speak but realized he was talking over a recorded message.

"...we are open from eight-thirty to four-thirty weekdays and Saturdays until twelve- thirty. We have information about securing your own family lot..."

He replaced the receiver. "It's getting so you never talk to people anymore."

She patted the inside of his thigh comfortingly. "We'll just have to go to the cemetery and inquire."

The great iron gates of the cemetery's main entrance at Union Street were open. At their center was what Walt called an Egyptian obelisk inscribed with "Calvary ICH" and "He Hath Promised Us Life Eternal." To the left was a stone building.

"That must be an office of some kind." Annie was about to get out of the van.

"Maybe Billy should go in alone," Walt suggested, putting a restraining hand on her shoulder.

"Why?"

"I'm getting a little worried," he confessed. "If anything goes wrong—not that I think it's going to—but if it does, the three of us together, two young kids and a black man, are pretty identifiable. I wish I hadn't gone in to Willis' Funeral Home yesterday."

"Well, if you hadn't, we'd never have gotten the crank to open the coffin," Billy said through a laugh.

The office manager reminded him of a young Lena Horne, whose picture he'd seen on the cover of one of Annie's record albums. She was light brown, about thirty and beautiful. "Hi, I'm Miss Peterson. May I help you?"

Billy had learned from the Willis interview that he shouldn't be so unsure of himself. "I'm doing some research on Tennessee Williams," he smiled. "I was wondering if I could find out where he's buried."

"No problem." As she went into the inner office, he could not help but notice the natural swaying of her beautifully shaped behind. When she returned, she charted a route on the map with a magic marker. "Tennessee's grave." She made an X to mark it and leaned over, retracing the line so that he would know exactly how to get there. She was not wearing a bra and his eyes strayed from the map to the warm brown cleavage and the well formed outline of her breasts. She smelled of a flowered perfume. In the middle of tracing the route she suddenly looked up at him to see if he was following.

He felt the color rising in his cheeks. "Many people visit him?" he asked awkwardly.

"No, not really," She gave him a half amused, but warm, smile. "We get a lot more requests for Sherman than we get for Tennessee."

"Sherman?"

"William Tecumseh Sherman," she laughed slightly.

She had a nice laugh.

"You know, the guy who burned Atlanta during the Civil War? You probably saw the movie."

Billy had to think a moment before he remembered, "Oh, sure." He could tell from her smile that she knew what he was thinking and that she was attracted to him and flirting. "Why would anyone want to visit Sherman?" he asked. "We're in the South, aren't we?"

"Well, yes and no." She frowned slightly. "St. Louis isn't exactly the South. I think Missouri was a border state in the Civil War."

She had pearl-white teeth and a really inviting mouth. What the hell was happening to him? He was there on business. He had to focus on getting the information he needed but it was hard to come out of a blush when he knew she was accurately reading him.

"Where are you from?" she asked.

"New York. Didn't get in till about seven and I drove over here thinking I could find a night watchman while it was still light."

"We have night watchmen, but to tell you the truth they're often sleeping in their office here in the gatehouse."

"They don't patrol?"

"That's what they're hired to do, but help is hard to find these days. And Calvary's a very big cemetery."

"So," he added, trying to avoid looking at her, "I just stayed over at the motel so I could get a look at the grave this morning and then be on my way."

"Where are you headed?"

"Flor...California," he corrected himself.

She laughed slightly, "I always get those two mixed up, too; must be all that sunshine."

She had a really inviting smile.

"Too bad you can't stick round for a day or so. You're not going to find Calvary very lively. St. Louis can be fun. It's swinging downtown by the old train station." She smiled again, eyes meeting his directly.

"What time do you close?"

"Four-thirty. Actually, we close the gates at five but we say four-thirty so people won't get trapped in the cemetery overnight. All of us are off at five, except, of course, the night watchmen. That's when they come on."

"Two of 'em?"

"Uh huh. Why? Were you planning on staying overnight?"

"Oh, no," he said quickly, too quickly. "I was just wondering. I've got a friend who might want to visit the Williams' gravesite sometime and I've got to remember to tell him to be here before four-thirty."

"If you change your mind about staying over, let me know," she said in a playful voice, the invitation not lost on him.

She handed him a two-page fold-over. "Here's information on the historic tour with thirty-eight places to visit in case you're interested and decide to stay till quittin' time. Sherman is number twenty-six and Tennessee is number thirty-eight. It's all here."

"Well," he said, taking the map somewhat awkwardly, "thanks a lot." But that was not enough so he added in a low voice, "You've been really...swell."

She held out her hand and he took it. She had a firm grip.

He turned and walked toward the door but once there, turned back. "When I get to the grave, how do I get back?"

"You come out the same way you go in." Her tone was ironic as though to cover disappointment. "Otherwise you might get lost, Blue Eyes."

They did get lost. Walt had assigned the planning phase of the trip to Billy and he had begun to feel that he was pretty darn good with maps, but there wasn't a straight line on this Calvary Cemetery map.

Annie drove slowly, trying to follow Billy's uncertain directions. When she saw a red pickup truck and above it, on an aluminum ladder, a husky, bare-chested young man trimming tree limbs with an electric saw, she stopped the van, backed up, and waved.

The young man took his time climbing down and ambling over.

"Is this where we are?" She held the map and pointed.

Instead of taking it outside, the guy leaned his head into the van's open window and propped it against the steering wheel. When he turned, only a few inches from her face, he asked, "You lookin' for William Tecumseh Sherman?"

"No, we're just driving around looking at various monuments." She was good at feigning casual, but what she was feeling at very close quarters was the chemistry between this tree trimmer with a handsome face and gorgeous body and herself.

He pointed to the map. "You're at this intersection." He turned to her again and smiled, then turned back. "Right here is W. T. Sherman, number twenty-six. If you're going up this way there's J. Clemens, Jr., number eleven." As he continued, with occasional looks in her direction, she knew he was mentally undressing her. "Clemens was a cousin to Mark Twain. Over here in section fifteen, on the First Dolor, is a fairly new one, the writer T. Williams, who came in last March." He smiled as his tongue slowly slid from one side of his lower lip to the other. "I see," he said, withdrawing from the window, "by your plates, you're from New York so I s'pose you came to see William Tecumseh Sherman. He's the hot ticket in St. Louis except for the Cards."

"Think they'll have a season?" She was fascinated by the beautiful curves of the muscle of his upper arms and the curly hairs protruding from beneath them. Armpits, she decided, have had a bad rap; they were terribly underrated.

"I'm with 'em all the way."

She arched her brows questioningly, "Even if they're not having a very great season?"

"I'm no fair-weather fan."

"Jack Clark is some power hitter."

"You can say that again." A grin told her he was glad she was not against the Cards. After a pause, she said reluctantly, "Well, thanks."

"Not a problem." He turned with never a look in the direction of Billy or Walt and ambled—she couldn't help but notice his muscular butt—back toward the aluminum ladder.

As she drove on, Billy observed with some humor, "You and Joe six-pack were sure snapping jocks. I knew you knew football. Where'd you learn baseball?"

"When I first moved into the city, I worked at a bar on Third Avenue. It was a hangout for baseball players. I dated a couple of the guys."

"Oh, yeah?"

"Yeah. There was a pre-Billy Lamb Ann Laurel. Was there a pre-Ann Laurel Billy Lamb?"

Billy looked quickly at the map. "What's a dolor?"

"Dolor means to suffer," Walt answered.

Billy thumped the map, "Looks like there are a whole mess of 'em."

"Seven," Annie said. "The seven sorrows of Mary."

"What's that?" Walt asked.

"I suppose...the prophecy of Simeon which forecasts Mary's suffering, the flight into Egypt, the loss of the child Jesus in the Temple, Mary meets Jesus wearing a crown of thorns and carrying the cross, the crucifixion, Mary removes Jesus from the cross and Mary's journey to the grave for the burial of Jesus. The Catholics have a rosary of these sorrows for those who are themselves suffering, probably to remind them of what Mary had suffered."

"Where did you learn all that?" Walt asked, impressed.

"In scene study. I played Mary in 'Family Portrait.'"

"Is everything you know from shows?" Billy asked.

"Yes," she said after a moment, "Almost everything."

Tennessee's grave, on the First Dolor, was on the underside of a hill on which stood majestic live oak trees beginning to hold autumn in their leaves. The trio stood facing the marker, a simple pattée cross etched into the white stone with:

TENNESSEE WILLIAMS

1911 – 1983

The leaves of grass just in front of the marker were high and needed cutting but the rest was clipped short. To the right, facing Tennessee's tombstone, was an unmarked stone.

"Probably for his sister Rose, who is still alive," Walt guessed.

To the left, about eight yards away, and facing Tennessee's stone, was the mother, Edwina Daken Williams, August 9th 1884 - June 1st 1980. "Thy Servants Sleep, O Lord, Grant Them Eternal Rest."

"Fat chance," Walt said. "In real life, she almost drove Tennessee as crazy as she was toward the end of her life when she started calling herself Edwin. Now that I see their proximity, I can guarantee you that he's not getting any rest, which renews my faith in what we're doing."

"I wish," Annie said, "that they had put 'poet' on the marker, and maybe carved a rose."

"Yes," Walt agreed, "and had the sensibility to add something from one of his plays, like, 'The violets in the mountains have broken the rocks.'"

Billy, who had been thinking about what Miss Peterson said in her half-kidding way about staying overnight in the graveyard, had headed across the road to a barely noticeable dirt lane that cut through a clump of trees. Following it, he came to a gully that sloped downward to a small flowing stream bordered by wide dry banks.

He returned to the grave and said, "We ought to hide the van behind that clump of trees tonight so we have plenty of time to do our work and drive out in the morning."

Annie was alarmed. "With night watchmen patrolling, wouldn't it be better to do as we planned and park outside the cemetery?"

"What I got from the woman in the office was that the night watchmen may not be doing their job so very good. When Walt hatched this scheme, I had no idea how big the place was." Pulling the cemetery map out of his pocket, he pointed to it with a twig fallen from the dead limb directly over the grave. "We're dead center in the graveyard. If we park outside we're gonna have to carry the tools, along with the body about half a mile and when we get to the iron fence we're gonna have to hoist it, and the tools, up and over. The point is, we don't know how long the operation will take, and we still don't yet know how difficult it's going to be to break open the vault. Being on the spot gives us more time if we need it."

Billy was beginning to take hold of the operation, Walt thought, as he watched him move the twig-pointer across the map and listened to his explanation.

When he was finished, Annie turned to him. "What do you think, Walt?"

"I think Billy's got it right," Walt said simply.

Back at the gate, Billy asked Annie to stop so he could go into the gatehouse. There were people waiting at the desk, but when Miss Peterson saw him she came out into the lobby.

"How'd you make out?"

"Fine, but I have one more question."

"What?"

"That's a big lot. Is Tennessee buried in front of the stone or to one side of it?"

"Hold on." She disappeared and then returned. "This is a Xerox of the official record from the ledger. Tennessee has lot number sixty. It's one hundred square feet. As you can see he's buried in front of the stone, smack dab in the middle."

"I sure hope they guard this place well," he said folding the Xerox and putting it in his shirt pocket.

"Why?"

"Someone is sure to steal that marker eventually and make a coffee table of it; lot of crazies in this world. You got electronic surveillance?" He tried to make the question sound spontaneous. But as soon as he said it he knew it was a little too on-the-money.

She frowned. "You sound serious."

"Nah," he laughed. "Security's my business."

"No, we don't have any electronic surveillance. Maybe we should."

"Well, thanks again."

"You're welcome." She held out her hand.

He took it. But this time they did not shake. Rather, he held her hand and told her silently that she was beautiful.

As they were driving out the gate, Walt said, "I just thought of something else. What about the 'clean white sack' Tennessee wanted to be buried in?"

☙

Jake had helped June out before. Jake was a no-chaser kinda guy, the only private dick in the business who had an in with John Gotti. The Boss had been enormously helpful on a couple of high profile cases in which reluctant or missing TV actors had to be traced. Jake had also sleuthed his way into some about-to-happen drug busts and by doing so saved the asses of some high-rollers, all on the QT for, of course, ready cash.

At his seedy office on 39th and Eighth Ave, his "girl Friday," ("or any other day of the week he wants me" she declared in her best vibrato) a voluptuous Brooklynite brunette who had been an actress in June's stable until she found "something a hell of a lot better than acting," ushered June into Jake's small office. Jake, a throw-back to the hat-wearing, cigarette smoking, monosyllabic private eye of yesteryear; a show business votary, a regular late-night diner at Elaine's, and an All-American boffer, was the kind of guy who preferred his pants held up by suspenders.

June plopped down in the cruddy leather chair at the side of Jake's desk and lit a Parliament, exhaling smoke from her nostrils. "Got a job that can only be done by a straight-eight guy like you," she said.

"Maybe a little exaggerated," Jake said laconically. "What's up?"

June told him of her interview on Friday when Annie had said she needed to take a week off and she'd said no. When June found out Annie had actually not showed up at the studio on Monday she had gone to her apartment which the super had "kindly" opened for her. Handing him the road map she found on the coffee table under the New York Times, she looked him directly in the eye. "Jake, you got to find her and make sure she gets her ass back here before Monday because she's got a big future on the soap if she doesn't blow it. And no one's to know anything. You need to work fast before David Lesco does something stupid, like calling the cops. You can see that the town she's circled on the map is Fort Lauderdale, but there is also a circle around St. Louis. I'll leak the news that she may be in St. Louis. Today is Wednesday. If she left on Sunday she is sure to be in Florida by now, so let's get the crazies on the St Louis scent so you can get yourself down to Lauderdale, find her and bring her back."

"Nobody can force her back, June, not even the studio. They can sue for breach of contract but they can't force her to work."

"I know that. That's why I'm talking to you. I definitely do not want the cops involved."

"Got any ideas who might know where she is in Lauderdale?" Jake asked.

"Start with her building super. Find out about the boyfriend, where he works."

Jake looked at the map. "Why would she circle St. Louis?"

"I haven't a clue. When can you leave?"

Jake looked at the desk calendar. "Depending on what I find out here, hopefully, we can leave tomorrow."

"We?" June asked.

"I need my assistant," Jake indicated the reception room.

June thought for only a moment before she said, "Whatever it takes."

❧

Back in the motel room, Billy worked at the desk. The Xerox from the ledger was proving to be invaluable. "Okay," he said as Annie drew up a chair, "I think we can now plan definitely how we're going to get down to the vault's lid." He had drawn a nine-by-six rectangle, divided into fifty-four one-foot squares. "After we cut through the sod, saving it to re-cover the grave when we finish, we dig down just a little under three feet."

"Not any further?" Annie asked.

"No, just to the lid."

"But the vault is only–what did Willis say?–seven by three, so why are we digging out an area nine by six?"

"So we have room around the vault's edge just in case there's a possibility of prying off the lid with the tools we got in Terre Haute. This is something we don't know. A jackhammer is going to make a lot of noise and take a lot of room to operate, so if we're able to remove the lid that way, fine, but that's a very big if. We just got to wait and see. One good thing. Once we get the lid off you can see from the Xerox that the coffin is six-sided."

"Shaped like a mummy case."

"Exactly, which means I'll be able to fit the crank in the hole to open the casket without us having to lift it out of the vault."

Walt joined them. They wanted to spend the next half hour resting but the tension only mounted. Along with his worry about the vault, Billy began to think about how much actual work could be expected from Walt or Annie. Before they talked to Willis, he had thought they would be digging six feet down, but that was only because of the misconception caused by the saying, "six feet under." He now knew that there would be less digging—which was good—but there was still the matter of the jackhammer. Where were they going to get it? And once they got it, could he operate it? And what about the noise and the fact that the grave was right on the First Dolor? That's where it was and there wasn't a damn thing they could do about it. It was clear that he hadn't thought everything through, and it all had to be accomplished tonight.

Annie broke the silence. "We want the sack to be nice."

Billy propped himself up on an elbow. "What kind of a sack do you suppose Tennessee had in mind?"

"In Melville," Walt said, stretched out in the easy chair, "Billy Budd is buried at sea in his hammock."

"I don't know how we'd get Tennessee's hammock," said Annie.

"If he had one," Billy added dryly.

"The hammock was Billy Budd's 'canvas coffin'," Walt intoned. "They ballasted it with shot."

"Why?" Annie asked.

"So it'd sink quickly to avoid sharks when the plank tilted and the body slid into the sea."

"The shotted hammock slips into the sea," Billy pounded out the rhythm on his thighs.

"Canvas then?" Annie asked.

"Sail makers made Billy Budd's coffin," Walt told her.

"Good idea. We could get sailcloth," she concurred.

"Sailcloth and canvas could be awfully scratchy," Billy said, "How about cotton, like in my undershorts?"

"Cotton might be too flimsy," Annie cautioned. "What about unbleached muslin like we use for covering stage flats?"

"Who's going to do the sewing?" Walt asked.

"I can," Billy said.

"Where did you learn to do that?" Annie asked.

"I'm not very good but I can sew," he said, avoiding an answer.

"So can I," Annie added.

"Did you learn that in a show?" Billy gently kidded her.

"You think you can go to one-a-week summer stock and depend on the costumer to get you out there on opening night? I had to learn to sew. Where'd you learn?"

Billy deflected the question by asking, "Where are we going to get the cloth?"

"What would we do without this?" Annie said, turning to the yellow pages in the phone book. "Here's a fabric store that seems to have everything, and I've an idea about the jackhammer. You go ahead and take our bags to the van. I'll call from the phone in the lobby."

"What'd they say?" Billy asked when she came back to the van which was now packed and ready to go.

She consulted a slip of paper. "They have a light canvas sailcloth called 'bronco' and an unbleached muslin."

As they talked, the cleaning maid pulled her cart along the walk outside the room. "Are you folks checked out" she called.

"Yup," Billy answered.

She disappeared into the room.

"I think you're right," Annie said to Billy. "A good grade of cotton would be best. We shouldn't get material that's too coarse. We've got a lot of driving to do and the floor of the van is hard and if the..." She was about to say body, but didn't. "If he's bounced around that might not be too good."

The maid appeared from the room and dumped the sheets into the laundry bag attached to the cart's metal frame.

"Excuse me, miss," Billy said as she was about to reenter the room.

She paused and turned. "Are you talkin' to me?"

"I got a question. How big is this laundry bag?"

"It's big! You had to lift it you'd know how big."

"This has got to be..." Billy examined the bag. "It's got to be at least four feet deep and..." He checked the rectangular frame holding it. "And plenty wide enough. Is it strong material?"

"It's strong. Got to be strong for the beatin' those laundry truck drivers give it."

"I noticed it's got a good drawstring."

"It has. That string draws real good."

He felt the material between his thumb and index finger, "Cotton?"

"Yes, sir! One hundred percent."

He turned to Walt and Annie. "The material is heavy but it's real soft."

"It's soft 'cause it's been washed so much. New bags are not nearly so soft."

Billy smiled at her. "You wouldn't happen to have a couple extra of these bags, would you?"

Her laugh was good-natured. "That's one thing I sure got extras of—laundry bags. See, we just fill 'em up with laundry and leave 'em here on the sidewalk to be picked up. I gotta have extras or I'd be runnin' back to the linen room all day."

Annie had opened one of the bags. "This is perfect. All we'd need to do is take the stitching out of the bottom of one and sew two of them together. And we could sew the shot, or whatever you get to weight it down, in the bottom of the second bag."

The maid looked suspicious. Billy quickly drew her aside and lowering his voice, asked confidentially, "Do you suppose we could buy a couple of these bags?"

"They ain't my bags to sell."

"And you don't suppose the management would want to sell 'em?"

"I suppose not. But," she added quickly, "they don't know what they got in the laundry room. You know, tourists steal a lot of thing, like towels and wash cloths. Some even take the sheets and mattress covers right off the beds. And we had one who stole the mattress."

"Really?"

"Yes, sir. I think management kinda expects it. That kind of pilferin' just seems to come with the motel business."

"How much do you think one of those laundry bags is worth?"

"Oh, they can't be worth much more than a dollar. Maybe two," she added after a moment, looking into his eyes.

Billy took a ten from his wallet, placed the bill in her palm and doubled her hand into a fist. He spoke softly. "I can't tell you why I need 'em. I can't tell you what they're for. But I know if

I could tell you, you'd know that what they're for is something good, something honest and decent and right. I wish I could tell you, but I can't."

"You got the bluest eyes I ever did see," she smiled, putting the hand that held the money into her pocket. "But I can't spend all day talkin' to pretty blue-eyed boys. I got me some work to do."

∽

Jake buzzed the super at the brownstone on 76th Street. When Juan finally appeared and was asked whether he'd seen Annie with a boyfriend, he was reluctant to talk. When Jake greased his palm with a twenty dollar bill, both his memory and English improved rapidly. No, he had no idea where Annie went. No, he didn't know if she had any friends in Florida. Yes, there was a boyfriend. Yes, he knew where the guy worked, at a restaurant on Columbus; in fact it was called the Columbian. Yes, he did notice some unusual activity last weekend. Annie had showed up with a sixty-eight Volkswagen bus, whether rented or her own Juan could not say for sure, but it was parked on the south side of the street. On Friday morning she had gotten him to save a spot that had just been vacated in front of the building while she moved the bus, and yes, she and her boyfriend had done some packing of the bus late Sunday but it was not there Monday morning when Juan got up. The guy's name? Billy.

At the Columbian, the manager, Tony, was close-mouthed until Jake told him he and Billy were old army buddies, that he was in town for only a short time and wanted to visit. After that, Tony lightened up. Yes, Billy had said he needed a week off. Yes, he had a girlfriend named Annie who was getting to be well-known on a TV soap.

"Maybe they're getting married?" Jake suggested.

"I asked the same question," Tony answered. "I figured the girl was knocked up. I mean, what the hell other reason would make them take such a drastic step?"

"Do you know the names of any friends they might have in… say, Ft. Lauderdale, Florida?"

"No."

"Do you know if they had any close friends who might know where they went?"

"Well, there was an old black guy they both knew. He actually came into the restaurant a couple of times."

"What'd he look like?"

"Big guy, like he might have played football at one time. With the beard he looked like he was auditioning for Santa Claus at Macy's. One night a couple of weeks ago, the two of 'em got real worried about the old guy cause they hadn't seen him for a couple of days. I took it they must've found him because they never said anything about it after that."

৶৹

"You guys can run the last two errands: get needles and strong white thread and buy nuts and bolts at a hardware store to weigh the 'clean white sack' while I check out a jackhammer, which Annie envisioned as being like the pneumatic hammers used to rip up the streets of New York with drills so big it took an entire truck to supply the energy. If what the Rent-All had would not work, they would have to think of something else but no use worrying Billy about that at the moment.

The Rent-All she had called was about a mile from the shopping center where she let Walt and Billy off. As she approached the desk a young Mexican-American clerk came toward her.

"Are you Jose?"

"Yes ma'am."

"I'm the one who called about the jackhammer?"

"Oh, yeah?"

"I'm a grad student in the Cinema section of the Theatre Department at St. Louis University and I'm doing my thesis film. One of the scenes takes place in a graveyard?"

"Yeah?"

"The leading character in the film has to open a vault. You know, to extract the coffin?"

"Yeah."

"Well, I've found out that vaults are sealed with either asphalt or a kind of epoxy, and this character needs to pry off the lid. So what kind of jackhammer would he need for the job?"

"Okay, what we carry is called The Wacker. It's a thirty-five pound electric hammer."

"But where would he get an electrical outlet? See, the character's in the middle of a graveyard at night."

Jose thought a moment. "Okay. What we got is a generator to run a hydraulic breaker. It's a ninety pound breaker and it runs off gas. It's a portable unit. It's got an eighty pound hammer, and twenty foot of lead hose. The force system we make is done by hydraulics. It's a mobile unit."

"Could you get it into the back of a sixty-eight VW van?"

"Yes, you can put a hydraulic breaker in the back of a van."

"How heavy is it?"

Jose called to the other clerk who was on the phone, "Yo, Dan! Rough estimate weight on the hydraulic breaker?"

"One second," Dan said and continued his phone conversation.

"Can you back up close to the operation point?" Jose asked, "'cause if you can get within twenty feet you can use this machine with the main frame of it sittin' in the back of the van. Just start her right up, take out your hammer and do what you gotta do."

Dan was now off the phone. "Dan, hydraulic breaker, how much does it weigh?"

"Dead weight? I'd say one hundred and twenty-five pounds." Dan said, approaching.

"If I wanted to film that specific scene today, could I rent it right now?"

"Sure."

Dan was curious. "What do you need it for?"

Jose repeated what she had told him.

It was as if a light lit up the darkness. "You can't use a breaker," Dan announced. "The objective here is to remove the vault's lid, not to break it up, right?"

"The character has got to remove the lid so he can get into the coffin. It's a grave robbing scene," Annie said.

"Sounds like some movie," Dan enthused. "They should do something of a neat job if they're robbin' the grave. What I'd suggest is drilling a series of holes."

"But there isn't any electricity," Annie told him. "And a hand drill would take all night."

Dan snapped his fingers. "A saw, saw right around the lid where it's sealed. How deep do you have to go?"

"Just so they can pry off the lid," she answered.

"Okay. I've got a hand-held cut-off saw that's gas operated, light weight, a masonry cut-off saw that can be used on any sealer. It's like a chain saw, only with a twelve inch wheel and it can give you a four and a quarter inch cut. A kid can run it."

She was relieved, "Sounds great!"

"It rents for forty bucks a day or twenty-seven bucks for four hours. My name's Dan. I'm the articulate one here."

"She's takin' it overnight," Jose explained.

Dan ignored him. "The blades are ten bucks. You'll probably need only one to go through the grout but I'll throw in an extra just in case, which you can return and I won't charge you for."

"Is it dangerous to operate?" she asked.

"We'll rent you some eye guards. Get this little lady the equipment," Dan ordered Jose.

When Jose went to the back, Dan inquired while he was writing out the order, "Is this machine in the movie?

"Yes."

"You need an operator?"

"The character does the work himself."

"Maybe he could have someone helping him?" Dan was wired. "Because I'm not braggin' or nothin', but everyone tells me I should be in the movies. I've been told that since I was a kid. I guess its cause I'm always clowning around, you know? And I've been told I'm okay in the looks department, so I figure that maybe I oughta be in the movies."

Annie acted as if she was assessing his face to see how photogenic he was. "It's possible."

"About a year ago I was gonna hitch out to Hollywood, ya know? I figure why am I wastin' my life here humpin' jack hammers when I could be makin' somethin' of myself in the movies. So if you need somebody, even if it's only a small part, just ask for Dan, that's D A N. Dan the man."

"Well, thanks for the offer, but the character has to do the work all by himself," Annie said, and then flashing back to all the auditions she had gone through and didn't get a call back, she added, "but I'll keep you in mind."

ᖆᓚ

June watched the small screen as a man appeared. "Ladies and Gentlemen, the Procter and Gamble Company has graciously allowed us to shorten their commercial time today in order for producer David Lesco to make a very special announcement."

Lesco was dressed all in black. "As New York Post's Cindy Adams reported this morning, Ann Laurel is..." He fought for emotional control. "She's missing and I'm pleading with you to help us find Annie, the young actress who plays Lily. We are not certain but it is possible she is the victim of amnesia." His voice broke and he was unable to continue.

Another man appeared and assisted Lesco off the set while still another man explained, "David is a father to all of us. Let me say, for him, that we have some reason to believe Annie might be in the St. Louis area, although it is possible that she could be anywhere in this vast country. So as director of 'One Woman's Family,' David and I, along with the entire cast and crew, ask you, her loyal fans who love her as much as we do, to help us find Ann Laurel."

The man was quickly followed by an announcer-type who delivered the pitch: "What do you get if you find her? Win the Proctor and Gamble Award. A 'walk-on' part on a forthcoming episode of 'One Woman's Family.' Snap a picture of Annie and yourself, fax it to us, and you'll hear 'You're a winner!'"

"Damn good!" June said to herself as she zapped the TV.

◌

"A valuable lesson learned from Dan-the-Man at the tool rental place," Annie said as she drove through the gate into Calvary Cemetery. "Something actors should know: stay open to all possibilities. It was because of what Mr. Willis said, that we were all so fixated on a jackhammer we hadn't thought there could be any other way to open the vault."

Both Billy and Walt were elated that she had found a better way, and Billy knew from examining the saw that he could work it. But he wondered if the sound of the saw wouldn't be as bad as a jackhammer.

Pulling up just short of Tennessee's grave, Billy spoke calmly and assuredly, "Annie, you go back to Magi, and Walt you go up the hill overlooking The Way of the Angels. If you see any cars coming, make a noise I can hear."

Before either reached their sentry posts, he had backed into the dead-end road and down the gully's incline to the creek. Grabbing the machete from the back of the van, he cut branches and propped them against its chassis. He was just placing the last one when he heard a piercing whistle, which sparked a vision of Annie, little fingers in her mouth, whistling down a New York City cab. But the image was out of sync with reality; they were not on Eighth Avenue in New York City, they were in St. Louis, and the sound spelled danger.

On the hill overlooking Mt. Olive and The Way of the Angels, Walt heard Annie's whistle. His first thought was to hide behind the trunk of one of the giant oaks but since they were at some distance, he threw himself on the ground instead. He looked down the hill and saw a large black beetle-like hearse followed by a procession of cars. Pressing his face into the grass resulted in a sense of ostrich-like, head-in-the-sand, security. While he waited, the sun beat down and he felt ants crawling up his legs inside his trousers toward his thighs, and worse. He began to sweat but he could not, dared not, move.

When he could no longer hear the cars of the funeral procession he raised quickly, lowered his trousers and frantically brushed away dozens of red ants.

As soon as the last car turned out of the First Dolor, Annie ran up to Billy. "That was a close one," she panted as he moved out onto the road from the thicket, "but I don't think anyone even looked in your direction."

Billy indicated the earthen road behind him. "If they had, they wouldn't have seen a thing," he said. And then looking up the hill, they saw Walt, pants lowered, flaying his thighs.

At exactly five p.m. the door of the watchman's gate house office opened and Tom Goodman entered, placed his lunch bucket and thermos on the shelf, yawned, sat down and opened the St. Louis Post *Dispatch*. Tom felt tired all the time and his mouth was a continual yawn. Maude, his wife, pointed out that he only worked three days a week. "Three nights," he reminded her. So why should he be tired all the time?

The hours, five p.m. till eight a.m., seemed generous when he first took the job, but he could never seem to adjust to the night schedule. He stayed awake during the day because sleep didn't come naturally like it did at night.

Maude always packed him a good—he didn't know what else to call it; *lunch* just didn't sound right—and filled his thermos with steaming hot, strong black coffee. But as soon as he got to the office he started yawning. As a result he usually took a nap at his desk before he and Clo made their first rounds.

The cemetery was so big it was impossible to know exactly how to guard it, let alone know what he was guarding it against. There had been only one grave vandalized in his twelve years on the job and even that—some young antiwar activist had tried to deface William Tecumseh Sherman's monument with spray paint—had not been what you'd call a major crime. The six foot iron fence and the iron entrance gate tended to discourage vandals. Oh, yes, it was possible to climb over the fence, it wasn't razor wired or anything, but what for? Few professional criminals specialized in grave robbing. Not only was it not lucrative—people didn't bury corpses covered with jewels—but there were strong taboos (social conventions, religious customs and superstitions) not to mention a kind of stigma about robbing the dead. If a young person decided to become a career criminal, Tom thought, grave robbing would have to be at the bottom of the list of possible choices, that is, if the guy had any brains.

As he was dozing off, he thought to hell with it. The energy he had to have at this kind of work wasn't exactly the same as if he was guarding a Brinks truck.

꙳

At the far side of the van, Annie sat on one of the tarps turning the laundry bags into Tennessee's clean white sack. Billy had wanted to help, but she insisted he get some rest. So while Walt sat in the front seat of the van reading, Billy stretched out on the blanket next to Annie and once again read the directions on how to use the saw.

Five o'clock came. The trio listened for a patrol car checking to see that everyone was out of the graveyard, but no car came. Five o'clock passed without incident. In fact, in the entire afternoon after the funeral procession departed, there had been no cars on the First Dolor.

Annie looked at Billy lovingly. "You should try to sleep," she whispered.

"I'm too wired," he answered.

❦

It was almost five-thirty when Clo entered the watchman's office, waking Tom from his snooze. Stashing his lunch pail on the shelf next to Tom's, he asked, "Did I wake you?"

"No," Tom yawned, "I was just reading the Post Dispatch. Did you read about this orphan boy? Played hooky from school. Walked by the train track and found a bag of diamonds and gold bracelets. Under Missouri law, found property is turned over to the finder if not claimed in six months. The stuff was worth a million. Damn near three hundred people called. Like it was probable that all those folks lost a bag of jewels? I don't think so. Then the police pushed back the date the kid could claim the loot because—wouldn't you know?—the lawyers couldn't agree on the claiming procedure. I wonder how much of the profit from the sale is going to those lawyer sons-of-bitches."

"I don't know," Clo yawned, slumping in his chair. "I only read the funnies."

❦

It was a dusky seven o'clock and the sun had set when Billy stretched, sat up, and started pulling on his work shoes. "We might as well get started."

Annie checked the sky. "You think it's safe?"

"If anyone gets within seeing distance they'll see us," he answered. "But we're in the center of the graveyard. There hasn't been a patrol car. We're in a hollow so no one can see from beyond the hill in back of the grave or from the other side of that clump of trees across the road. The only possibility of getting caught is if a car comes along the First Dolor."

When the equipment was unloaded, Billy reached for the edger, spades and pickax.

"Let me carry some of that heavy stuff." Walt took the pickax.

"No, Walt, save yourself."

"Hell, what for?" But as soon as he slung the ax over his shoulder he felt a sudden sharp pain.

"You okay?" Billy asked.

"Sure."

Annie and Walt held the ends of the chalk-line as Billy snapped the strings. They spread a tarp on which to lay the sod squares in the order they were removed. Billy cut the first square in the lower right-hand corner with the edger, lifted it out and gave it to Annie to place on the tarp.

Slowly and methodically they stripped the grave's surface. While they worked, Annie kept watch in either direction for a patrol car. But as evening twilight turned to murky dusk and dusk into a protective velvety night with just a sliver of a moon, she stopped looking for headlights, stopped thinking about a patrol car and simply did her work, work which was more demanding than she ever could have imagined.

〇〜〇

It was almost eleven when Tom yawned, stretched and woke Clo who was snoring, the funnies spread out on his lap, "Time for us to go on our appointed rounds."

"In today's Dispatch," he said as he drove, "there's a story about how the schools are going to need five hundred million dollars over the next five years to desegregate."

Clo bugged his eyes and whistled. "That's a lot of mazoomy."

Where did the dumb cluck pick up that word? Tom wondered. "I keep reading the word million in the paper. Never thought about how much a million is, have you?"

"I think about it all the time."

Talking to Clo was like talking to yourself, only slightly more respectable since Clo was human with ears on his head. Everything that Tom said to the damn fool seemed to pass through one big ear and out the other. Still, having him there was better than nothing.

Everything was secure at William Tecumseh Sherman's grave. Turning east on the Way of Bethany toward Magdalene, Tom figured they'd check out The Graves of the Archbishops.

"I got to thinking about the word million," he said, "because there's talk of starting a state lotto like they got in New York. Did you know that if you won a million dollars and it's distributed over twenty years you'd be getting a check for fifty thousand dollars a year?"

Clo bugged his eyes and whistled. "That's better than I'm doin' now."

"Do you know how much a million dollars is?"

"Nope," Clo confessed.

"You know what a thousand is?"

"Yup."

"So you know what a hundred thousand is."

"I guess."

"Well a million is ten hundred thousand."

Clo bugged out his eyes again and whistled. "That's a lot of mazoomy."

Just hearing him say that word pissed Tom off but he let it pass. "What intrigued me about the school desegregation story was figuring out the cost, per student." He had gotten out Maude's nineteen thirty-nine Webster's Collegiate Dictionary and looked up the numeration table. "A million is ten zeros, one hundred thousand is six zeros, a billion is one thousand million, that's nine zeros and a trillion which Reagan's talking about as the national debt, is twelve zeros."

"That's a pot full of zeros," Clo commented, philosophically.

"And I was amazed to find that beyond a trillion there's a quadrillion and then a quintillion and finally, a sextillion."

Clo laughed, actually brayed like a jackass, saliva dripping down his chin, "I sure like sex."

Tom turned southwest down St. Rita and headed back toward the gatehouse. The only point of interest in the northwest section was the Graves of the Religious Orders, which nobody ever bothered with, and there was nothing of interest in the southwest section.

"The upshot of this new tax?" Tom asked rhetorically. "We're now paying three dollars and sixty-five cents for each one hundred dollars of assessed value on our property. The proposed eighty-six cent increase will hike that to four dollars and fifty-one cents and generate thirteen and one-half million which will be matched by the state under terms of the desegregating plan."

He was approaching Mt. Olive when he remembered he had not visited the Lawn Crypts in some time. "Maybe we ought to drive over to section fourteen."

"Do we have to?" Clo whined.

"Won't take a minute," he said, turning east.

"Dead as a doornail," Clo yawned looking at the Crypts.

Hanging a U-turn at the Seventh Dolor, Tom drove back down the Way of the Angels. "We haven't been by the Williams' grave in a blue moon, might as well swing into the First Dolor on our way back."

❦

Annie saw the headlights. The three stood frozen, unable to move as they watched the car slow down. But instead of turning onto the First Dolor it suddenly speeded up and headed down the Way of the Annunciation.

They waited in breathless silence until the car's motor was no longer heard. "Now that we know they do patrol," Billy whispered, "we're gonna have to keep a sharp lookout both ways for however long it takes to finish the job. What time is it?"

"Midnight."

Chapter IV: The Fourth Day
Thursday, 15 September, 1983

Walt and Annie had spread out tarps on both sides of the opening right up to the cut. All dirt removed from the hole was to go on the tarps so that none of it was in the grass when the grave was closed. The work was slow and methodical. Foot the spade, push it into the earth, lift, and throw the dirt. Repeat. Once they were through the thin layer of topsoil, they were dealing with clay.

"Take a break," Billy called.

Annie looked at the thinness of his body, drenched with sweat as he swung the pickax over and over loosening the clay. She could hardly watch the back-breaking work but it was not long before they heard the metallic sound of the axe striking cement. Billy had come in contact with the vault's lid. They worked together with renewed energy, and the concrete lid finally appeared. It was only a matter of scooping up what was left of the dirt after which Annie swept the lid clean. Then they dug several inches below the lid's seal line on all sides; enough space to maneuver the saw.

"Where'd you learn to work so hard?" Billy asked, trying to sound jovial and make his breathing appear normal.

"Movement class at school wasn't exactly grave digging," she said, throwing a shovel full of dirt on the tarp, "but the teacher sure as hell knew how to get you in shape for just about anything. First day of class I thought I was going to die right there on the studio floor. We used to call her class, 'movement with strain, yoga with pain.' But I got used to it, so used to it in fact that I took classes from her in the city after graduation."

They kept digging along the edge of the lid.

They had to rest.

Keep working, goddamn it! Walt thought.

But they had to rest.

It was two-thirty when Billy called for a break while he dug deeper on the vault's right side. Fearing a cave-in, he warned Walt and Annie to take it easy when they got out of the pit. Walt sat on the edge, spread out, quickly rolled away from the grave and lay on the ground.

He felt cold on his forehead. Annie had wet a handkerchief from the water jug and was bathing his face and neck. Then, like an angel of mercy, she fanned him with a piece of cardboard. He closed his eyes. The breeze felt so cool but he kept thinking over and over and over, I must not go to sleep. I must not go to sleep. I must not...

"Hey, sleepyhead." The voice seemed to come from a long way off.

Walt opened his eyes. "Have I been out long?"

"About fifteen minutes," Annie answered.

He started to rise. He would not let the moan escape his throat. He lay back.

"Take a couple of deep breaths before you get up," she advised.

He breathed deeply.

"Feel better?"

"Yes."

Annie, strong, clear-eyed, firm of purpose and resolve, bent down and kissed him on the forehead and smiled reassuringly. He smiled back. "I'll be okay," he said.

"Hey, you two lovebirds," Billy called, "time to get your asses in gear and get back to work."

"Slave driver," Annie hissed.

"Okay, now we get the noise factor. Annie, you take a flashlight, go to the top of the hill and keep watch. If you see a car's headlights, give us a quick signal. If it turns on to the Dolor and we get caught, you split to the other side of the creek and in the morning, walk out."

"I couldn't do that," she said.

"You're gonna have to." Billy's voice was level and hard. "It'd be damn foolishness for more than two of us to get caught. Now go. Quick!"

Head down, she turned and hurried up the hill. Billy said to Walt, "Your job is to take that flashlight and shine it on the seal line. Keep it close so the light doesn't spill all over the place, but also keep it out of my way so it doesn't interfere with the saw. And keep looking up the hill to see if Annie gives us any signal." Walt turned on the light while Billy fitted the goggles over his eyes and picked up the saw.

The cut was difficult because he had to lie on the vault's lid and look over the side in order to hold the saw's blade to the seal line. There was precious little space for maneuverability, and the noise the blade made as it cut through the epoxy, was a screaming, shrieking, wailing sound. Sure, the cemetery was big and they were in between a hill and some trees, but how could that sound not be heard from Florissant, Broadway, or the Gate House? The night watchmen would have to be deaf, or asleep.

Hopeful as ever, he counted on their being asleep.

ᕯᕮ

It was near three fifteen a.m. and Tom couldn't keep awake. He'd eaten, which only made him sleepier, and reading the obituaries in the *Dispatch* was not exactly edge-of-your-seat news. But now he was yawning and his eyes were closing. If Clo, the damn fool, hadn't said he had to pee, Tom would have checked the First Dolor when they were out and that would have been the end of it. But something told him it probably wouldn't be smart to risk only one check, no telling when the powers-that-be checked on the night watchmen. "I think we'd better get going."

Angry that the news media called social security "a handout," intimating that it should be privatized, Tom had found his rant for the drive. Getting mad always helped him stay awake. "Damn politicians! Pretending they're going to 'shore up' social security. If the government paid seven percent interest on all they borrowed from the fund..." He stopped talking suddenly, cocked his head and slowing down, listening intently. He could hear the sound as clear as a bell, like someone cutting down a tree.

He stopped the car and turned off the ignition.

∽

The work Billy was doing was time-consuming, meticulous, and dangerous, and cutting into the epoxy seemed to take forever. The greatest danger was cutting himself with the whirling blade or being burned by the sparks when the blade hit the vault's cement, above or below the seal line.

He had finished cutting around the right side, the top and the bottom when he turned off the saw. He was wringing wet with sweat; the eye guards had fogged up and his view was obstructed.

∽

What are you doing?" Clo asked sleepily.

"Listening,"

"What for?"

"Did you hear a sound?"

"Just you talking."

Tom knew the dumb-bell hadn't heard a word he'd said. "I'm not talking about human sound. I'm talking about some kind of... screaming sound."

"Sounds scary," Clo feigned a shiver. "Screaming sound at night in a graveyard; suppose it's a ghost?"

Now that Tom had stopped and turned off the motor, the sound could no longer be heard. He didn't appreciate Clo's snotty remark but it could have been just his imagination. He turned the key in the ignition and drove on. "Now stay awake," he warned, "because I'm trying to explain something to you."

"I'm listening."

"If your average worker earns the maximum taxable income and retires at the age of sixty-five, he and his employer will have put in eighty-five thousand dollars after a lifetime of work and that amount would be used up in seven years. So if he lives beyond seven years they say he's getting a handout from the government. Bullshit! What about the time value?

"Time value?" Clo echoed.

"Interest the money's earned."

∽

Billy wiped the eye shields with his soggy headband and put them on again, but they were streaked with dirt.

"Better take a break," Walt said.

"Ah, to hell with it," he said throwing the shields up on the pile of dirt, "We don't have time to mess around with 'em."

Walt turned on the flashlight and Billy inserted the blade into the seal line, causing a shower of sparks.

∽

Suddenly there it was again. Tom stopped talking and listened. "Now do you hear it?"

Clo cocked his head.

"Goddamn it! You mean to tell me you can't hear that, you deaf and dumb son-of-a-bitch?" Pulling up in the middle of the Way of Mount Zion, he turned off the ignition and got out. The high whining sound was clear as a bell but he couldn't exactly tell which direction it was coming from. "You hear that?" he asked Clo, who had gotten out of the car.

"I hear it," Clo admitted.

"What do you make of it?"

Clo listened for a moment before a gaped-tooth grin appeared on his moon face. "Sounds to me like a couple of cats ruttin'."

The sound stopped. Tom waited for it to start again. "I think you're right," he finally conceded, "couple of rutting cats." He checked his watch. It was almost four. He drove on toward the First Dolor.

❧

Annie did not know how long the sawing actually took but it seemed an eternity before the whine of the saw stopped and she heard Billy's voice calling her back to the grave. At the site, Walt looked as if he was about to cry and Billy's head rested on the vault's lid. When he rose and turned, it was as if she was looking at a ghost. His face was covered with white dust, his clothes soaking wet and his hair matted.

"The eye guards, didn't you use the...?"

"They fogged up and he couldn't see," Walt said, near tears.

"My God, your eyes, your precious eyes," she said running for the water. Using a handkerchief she wiped around them.

❧

Inside the patrol car, Tom, still angry from Clo's sarcasm and further aggravated by attempting to explain to the dumb cluck why the government wasn't giving any goddamn "handout" to those on social security, yelled, "Time value means interest. If the government had paid compound interest over thirty-five years on the accumulated savings at the same rate as long-term treasury bonds—seven percent—by the time the worker retired he would have eighty-five thousand in his account plus two hundred thousand in interest."

The patrol car was now on the First Dolor within a few feet of the open grave and going very slow. Tom was angry and hollered his indignation. "And assuming the two hundred and eighty-five thousand dollars, less the retirees' monthly benefit, also continues to make interest, the average worker wouldn't draw out all his—do you hear me?—*His* money if he lived to be a hundred. So, do you see? We ain't getting no goddamn 'handout' from the government."

"Then you think," Clo hollered back, "the government's givin' it to us up the ass?"

❧

Waiting until the sound of the car's engine diminished, Walt said, "Did I hear that right? The government's giving it to us up the ass?'"

"That's what I heard," Annie said.

"What the hell was he talking about?" Walt asked.

Turning to Billy, who was shaking his head in wonderment, Annie said, "Surely they saw the open grave."

"I don't think so," Walt said. "I was peeking from behind the headstone and the driver was turned in the opposite direction and yelling at the guy on the passenger seat."

"But he must have seen the piles of dirt."

Walt shrugged. "I don't know."

"How could he miss them unless he's an absolute numbskull?"

"But if he had seen them," Walt reasoned, "why wouldn't they have stopped?"

If the watchmen had seen the open grave and were going to notify the police, there was only one response. "We gotta work fast," Billy said.

He and Annie fitted the beveled ends of the crowbars into the newly sawed seal of the lid and on a count of three, pushed down. They could hear the cracking of the small amount of epoxy that remained as the lid of the vault lifted and Walt inserted stones into the open space. The crowbars removed, Billy thrust the pry bar over the lid of the coffin—the fulcrum—straightened it out so they could get a purchase on the end, then did the same with a second pry bar. On a count of three he and Annie easily raised the six hundred pound concrete lid. Almost immediately it was dislodged from the lip of the vault and settled perpendicularly into the other side of the grave. Walt held one of the pry bars so that there was no chance of the lid falling back onto the vault.

"Ah, shit!" Billy said.

"What?" Annie asked.

"I forgot the crank."

"Where is it?"

"It's in the glove compartment."

"I'll get it," Walt volunteered.

"No, you hold the pry bar so the lid doesn't fall," Annie said and she was off.

Seeing her go, Billy rested his head on the grave's edge.

"What a gal," Walt said.

"Oh yeah," Billy smiled.

"You got a really great woman, there."

"I know."

"The first time she came to my office at school, she had on men's high-tops and she put her foot on my desk and tied her shoelace." Walt had tears in his eyes. "Such audacity!"

"What time is it?"

Walt checked his watch, "Four-twenty-three."

Annie, rib cage heaving, returned and handed Billy the crank

"I love you," he said evenly.

"You're just saying that 'cause you want to get more work out of me," she gasped in her best Mae West imitation.

Billy nodded. He put the crank into the hole, turned it, and lifted the coffin's lid. Annie snapped on the flashlight to reveal the body, wearing a dark blue blazer and surrounded by ruffles of white satin.

Breaking the sorrowful mood, Walt said, "Doesn't appear to me there's even a speck of mold on the necktie."

Billy looked closely. "He's not wearin' a necktie."

"No mildew, no shrinkage, no drooping eyelid, no corner of the mouth turned down," Annie added.

"And," Walt said triumphantly, "he didn't turn green."

They stood for another moment of silence before Billy glanced at the sky. "We gotta get humping," he ordered.

It was surprising how light Tennessee was, and it felt strange holding him so close. Annie opened the white sack while Billy slid the corpse inside and tied the drawstring.

Billy jumped back into the grave and closed the coffin's lid. He jumped out went to the other side where Walt still held the pry bar. When Billy removed it, the lid remained perpendicular. Then without much effort, with Annie and Walt standing well back, Billy knelt and pushed and the six hundred pound slab settled back in the grave. Using the coffin as the fulcrum for the pry bars, he and Annie quickly started to fit the lid over the vault's opening.

"Do you have to do that? Couldn't you just cover the lid with dirt?" Walt asked.

"Maybe," Billy answered, "but not putting the lid back would mean more space to be filled and we might not have enough dirt." When he finished the job, he said, "Now, while I'm gone, you two work as fast as you can and shovel the dirt back into the grave. Remember we don't want any dirt in the grass. Work well away from the edge so there are no cave-ins."

Billy walked slowly to avoid stumbling as he carried Tennessee to the van. The sun was now just below the horizon, its warm rays reflecting upward against the clouds in the west, making them yellow and pink.

When the dirt was leveled about an inch and a half from the top, they quickly, but carefully, fitted the grass squares back, exactly as they had been removed. When half of them were in place, and knowing that it would take several trips, Billy told Annie and Walt to start returning the tools to the van. "Put 'em on the right side.

Tennessee's on the left," he said as he continued carrying the sod to cover the grave.

Finally, with the equipment removed, all that remained was for Billy and Walt to drag the tarps to the side road, shake them out on the bank of the creek, fold them and put them in the van. That done, Billy went back to the grave for a last-minute inspection.

"What?" Annie asked at the look on his face which was still covered in the white dust of epoxy.

"We started at seven o'clock last night." His voice was low. "We removed fifty-four one-foot squares of sod, dug three feet down, sawed through the seal of a six hundred pound vault's lid, leveraged it open, raised the lid of the coffin, removed a body, closed the lid, put the six hundred pound lid back over the vault, filled the grave, leveled the ground and replaced the fifty four one-foot squares of..." He looked at the sky and then his legs buckled. He tried to rise but couldn't. He just laid there, body quivering like a stunned animal.

Annie knelt by his side. "What is it?"

He tried to get up again but muscle spasms shook his body.

Throwing herself on him with a ferocity that astonished Walt, she covered and held him. It was as if, having gone beyond the limits of physical endurance, his body needed recharging and she was the jump cable. She soothed and comforted him and as he grew warm, she could feel his muscles relaxing. When she was sure that he was all right, and using her Mae West voice, she whispered into his ear, "How's it hangin'?"

He started laughing and the deep gasps of air needed for the laughter took away the cramped muscles. He stopped twitching and between gasps of laughter, moaned, "Oh, God, I may never be able to get it up again."

"If I had thought that," she said with fierce sincerity, "I'd have never agreed to this gig. I'd have said, 'to hell with it, let Tennessee stay here with his mother.' Now let's get the hell out of here."

Back at the van, she told him to get some sleep.

"You're gonna drive?" he asked

"Sure."

"Then you get the sleep."

When her breathing was regular he made his way, somewhat shakily, to the stream, stripped, and using his headband for a washcloth cleansed himself in the cold water. Dressed in clean clothes, he told Walt, "You're next." And as the old man left, somewhat reluctantly, Billy sat by Annie, watching her breathe, protecting her. Touch, take care of, make love to, and work hard for, grow old with...He woke her with a kiss. While she washed in the creek, Walt and he removed the shrubs camouflaging the van, their leaves already starting to wither, and placed them in a pile on the rocky embankment well out of sight of the road.

At a quarter to nine, Annie drove the van up the steep incline into the lane. After Billy had scuffed up the tire and foot tracks, she drove back onto the First Dolor. The grass near the grave was matted from the weight of the dirt on the tarpaulins, but the replaced sod was fresh with morning dew, and unless one looked closely, there was no telltale sign that the grave had been entered.

As they were congratulating themselves on a job well done, behind them on Magi they heard a sound. It was the red pickup truck traveling north headed for the First Dolor. In a breath-holding moment, Annie, knowing there was no possibility of not being observed, was planning what she was going to say when, instead of turning, the truck continued northeast. It was the tree trimmer, probably off to his work in another part of the cemetery. The van would certainly be identifiable if he had seen it. Once the truck had disappeared, she drove quickly to the main gate.

❧

After returning the saw to Dan-the-Man with Annie's thanks, Billy exited the rental facility all smiles. "The guy wants to be an actor," he told Annie.

"Poor bastard," Annie exclaimed. "Well, that's the end of our work in Saint Louis."

"Thank God," Walt said. "Now all we have is a leisurely drive to Florida."

Ahead, over the squalor of the industrial nightmare of bridges and roadways and cement over-and-under-passes and tracks and electrical wires and the filth of downtown St. Louis, rose the fantastic silver arc in the shape of a rainbow, ascending heavenward out of the rubble. There was something so incredibly hopeful about seeing it at that moment. Its luminescence was perfect for the elation they felt, perfect for the giant doorway to the unknown.

"Why is it so wonderful?" Annie wondered.

"Because an arc travels forward to its end which is its beginning," Walt answered.

She could not but think of the wonder and rightness of it. Follow your arches to whatever corners of the sky they pull you.

⁀

It was early afternoon when the muscular tree trimmer, shirtless, having finished his work on the Seventh Dolor, drove south toward section fifteen. As he drove, there was stirring in his groin as he fantasized about the good-looking redhead he'd given directions to the day before. Once there he methodically erected the aluminum ladder against the tree with the dead limb, extended its center section, secured it, and picking up his electric saw begin to climb.

He had reached the offending limb and was about to turn on the saw when something below caught his eye. The grass was curiously matted. Puzzled, he climbed down and examined the plot. A piece of sod by the headstone seemed to be sunken into the ground. Squatting, he put his hand into what appeared to be a cut and easily lifted the sod square.

Further examination revealed that other squares of sod could be removed.

A moment later he was speeding along Magi headed to the gatehouse.

～

South of St. Louis the van traveled across the Meramec River and into the hill and bluff country of the Ozarks, with signs reading, "Herculaneum," "The Trail of Tears State Park," and "Fruitland," followed by a used car lot and a Southern First Reform Fundamentalist Church of Christ with a big red neon sign, "Jesus Saves."

"The southern poor seem always between a used car salesman and Jesus," Walt commented. "Car payments for rust-outs and ten percent tithe to the church to pay for salvation for their humanness. Powerful stuff."

A bumper sticker read, "All the way Jesus."

Finally, there was a lifesaving invitation: "Catfish and Throwed Biscuits, Lambert's Café, Sikeston, Missouri."

"Let's eat. I'm starved," Billy said, realizing he had had nothing for over twenty-four hours.

Walt spoke from the back of the van, "Me too."

"Why not?" Annie asked. "Sikeston is a little off the highway, but what the hell? I'm gonna have the specialty of the house."

Walt added gleefully, "And I'll have a double Old Grand-Dad on the rocks."

When they got out, there was the sudden realization. "Do you think one of us should stay and guard the van?" Annie asked.

Neither Billy nor Walt had thought of the corpse. Billy volunteered to stay, but Walt suggested that all they need do was throw a sleeping bag over the white sack and be certain the doors were locked. "Who would want to steal a sixty-eight VW van?" Annie still had some doubts but as hungry as she was, and as eager to wash up, she decided not to voice her fears.

～

Billy couldn't help but drum his fingers against the table when a full-throttled two-four time "Dixie" played on the juke box. The walls of Lambert's were covered with pictures of Missouri mules. A waitress came to the table. "Y'all want biscuits?"

"Sure," Annie answered.

He threw her a hot one. Annie caught it, but Billy fumbled his.

"How about some fried okra?"

Walt tasted okra for the first time.

"Want more?"

He shook his head.

"Sorghum?" Yes! Thick, dark, pungent syrup to spread on the hot buttered biscuit.

They ordered catfish, hush puppies, slaw, and fries. "What will y'all have to drink?" the waitress asked.

"I'll have a double Old Grand-Dad on the rocks."

"We got lemonade, root beer, ice tea, coffee, regular and cherry Coke," she answered, pursing her lips to indicate her feelings about alcoholic beverages.

The noise level was high. There were tables of senior citizens, black couples, and families. "They're having more fun than Wall Street yuppies at a two martini luncheon," Annie observed.

"I wouldn't go so far as to say that," Walt said, his little finger extended, disdainfully sipping cherry Coke through a straw.

The bill was twenty-one dollars and sixty one cents. Annie left a twenty and a ten.

"It's more than you need to leave for a tip," Billy advised.

"I know."

"I say that as a waiter," he said.

"I leave it as an ex-waitress."

They were just about to get up when an elderly woman, with pen and paper, came to the table. "Excuse me."

"Yes?" Annie replied.

"Are you...oh, what's-her-name? You know, the new character, Lily, the one who says 'trust me' on 'One Woman's Family'?"

"You must be confusing me with someone else," Annie said.

"I'd swear..."

"Sorry."

"Well, you're a dead-ringer for her." The woman shook her head and rejoined the senior citizen group.

"I just can't believe she recognized me," Annie whispered as they were leaving.

"You're famous," Billy smiled.

"I certainly hope not, at least not for the rest of the week."

While waiting for Walt to go to the men's room, they looked at the enlarged photograph of a uniformed young man. A caption told them it was the owner's son, who was nineteen when he was killed in Vietnam. There was a framed poem at the side of the picture. It was not a very good poem but Annie read it beautifully and with emotion. As she did, a burst of laughter came from the dining room.

Walt reappeared.

"I'll drive, you catch some sleep," Billy said, noticing her eyes were watering.

"Nah," she said, putting on her sun glasses. "I'm fine."

"You sure?"

"Sure, I'm sure!" It came out angry, but he knew that her anger was not directed at him. It was only to cover the deep feelings, which were the same as his own, about the death of the nineteen year old son of the owners of Lambert's Café in Sikeston, Missouri.

❧

They traveled a straight road through the flat land of the Mississippi basin. The sign, "Braggadocia, Missouri," made chameleon Walt a braggart warrior.

"Cotton Bowl Vocational Tech."

"Welcome to Arkansas."

"Memphis seventy miles."

Bumper stickers: "Jesus, #1", "Born Again!" and "All the Way, Jesus."

And almost before they were out of Memphis there was a "Welcome to Mississippi" followed by pine trees and magnolias.

༄

Late afternoon, in Calvary Cemetery's section fifteen, workers operated the mechanical grave-digging equipment. When the vault was uncovered, the tree trimmer swept it clean. Two St. Louis policemen helped him lift the vault's lid. The coffin was opened by one of the policemen.

"Miss Peterson," the policemen asked, "will you notify the relatives?"

"I'll call the New York law firm that handles the Williams' estate," she replied.

༄

They were just north of Winona when Billy saw flashing lights. "Cop," he whispered, covering the digging equipment with a tarp.

"Don't say anything," Annie cautioned Walt.

"Why?"

"This is a southern cop, we have New York plates, and..."

". . . and I'm a black man," he finished the thought for her.

Pulling off onto the shoulder, she watched the cop's approach in the side mirror.

"Officer," she said, in her best southern accent when he was alongside, "I'll just bet I was doin' somethin' wrong and that's why you turned on your flashers."

"Ma'am?"

She turned to Walt. "Thank goodness to be talkin' again to a southern gentleman." She turned back to the cop. "Law enforcement officers up north are so rude." She turned again to Walt, "Don't y'all think they're rude?"

Walt started to answer but Annie hurried on. "No one in the north seems to understand civility; they're all in such a rush. Don't you think that's why manners are disappearin'?"

The officer seemed unsure, "Could be ma'am."

"I'm livin' in New York but I'm from Laurel. You know Laurel?"

"No, ma'am."

"You don't know Laurel, Mississippi?"

"No, ma'am."

"Well, I declare, I thought everybody knew Laurel. Our family home, Belle Reve, is there."

"Yes, ma'am."

"All our family is buried there; father, mother, Margaret, old cousin Jessie...but I seem to be doin' all the talkin' and I'll just bet you stopped me for some reason, didn't you, now? You stopped me for some reason, bless your heart."

"Yes ma'am."

"What could that reason be, I wonder?" She started rummaging through her purse. "I seem to be all thumbs. You want to see my driver's license?"

"No ma'am."

She paused. "You don't want to see my driver's license?"

"No ma'am."

"Then why did you stop me? What have I done?"

"Ma'am, your license plate seems to be hangin' by one bolt."

"Well, for goodness sakes!"

"If you'll permit me, ma'am, I carry tools for just such an emergency."

Her voice was still southern but there was a slight, and real, choke in it when she said, "Why, aren't you...precious."

They listened in absolute silence to the sound of his fixing the hanging license plate.

Finished, he came back alongside the van, smiling. "We got her, ma'am."

"Thank you so very much, officer," she said simply.

"Not at all, ma'am."

"Thanks," Billy added.

"Any time."

"Much obliged," Walt said.

"My pleasure, sir. You folks have a nice evening, ya' hear?" He tipped his hat and strolled back to his car.

"I was never so wrong about anything in my life," Annie whispered as she pulled off the shoulder. "Where do I get these wrong ideas about people?"

The patrolman passed. They waved and he returned it.

A few minutes later, another Mississippi State Highway Patrol car passed.

Billy examined the atlas. "I wonder if we'd do better to get on a less traveled road."

"What's your thinking?" Annie asked.

"A side road," he said, putting his finger on the map just east of Winona, "might not be patrolled. Highway Eighty-Two may not be as fast but on the other hand we can make time by going on an angle cross-country." He traced the route. "Through Alabama, down to Tuscaloosa, Montgomery, Dothan, across the southwest tip of Georgia, and on down to Tallahassee."

Annie turned off highway Fifty-Five and onto highway Eighty-Two.

⁂

At the funeral home that evening, the electric organ was still playing "Nearer My God to Thee," as Mr. Willis ushered the last of the mourners to the front door.

Emily Mistringer, an unmarried lady of uncertain-age, put her hand on Mr. Willis's arm and shook her head. "What are we going to do without our Jock Warren at the Kroger store?"

"You'll just have to carry on." Willis tried to keep his voice well modulated. "And keep in mind, he went fast and didn't suffer. That's the beauty of a heart attack."

"Goodnight, Herman," the woman sighed. "It was a wonderful service."

Willis closed the door, turned off the organ and turned on the eight o'clock news, once again searching the shag rug below the new coffin for the missing crank. The TV Newsman droned in the background. "James Draude, a Justice Department official announced today that the Reagan Administration has agreed to stop spraying marijuana with the weed killer, paraquat, for the rest of the growing season. And now news about a grave robbing last night in Calvary, St. Louis' famous Catholic Cemetery and the offer of a ten thousand dollar reward for information leading to the recovery of the body."

Willis turned toward the TV screen. "And we're pleased to have with us the man who discovered this crime, Mr. Stanley Butler." The camera closed in on Stan Butler dressed uncomfortably in a suit. "We understand, Mr. Butler, you were the person to discover that the grave had been robbed."

"Yes sir. See, I'm Calvary's tree trimmer and I was tree trimmin' trees over in section fifteen when I noticed how the grass was sunken in one place and when I examined it, I could see that someone had cut the sod into squares and then laid them back to conceal the fact that the grave had been entered. And the day before, while I was tree trimmin' trees, three people driving a sixty-eight VW van with a New York license plate..."

Mr. Willis ran to the office where he picked up the phone to call the police.

࿇

The night and day caught up with Billy and he closed his eyes. The next thing he heard was Annie saying, "I think I've had it."

He had no idea how long he'd slept. "If you think we should go further, I can drive," he told her.

"Nah! Enough already! I'm exhausted," she said, turning into a Best Western. "What we all need is a good shower." She could not help but notice that Walt had grown rather ripe. "Who was it who said that 'the American bathroom has a greater civilizing effect than all the cathedrals of Europe'?"

"Edmund Wilson," Walt answered. "But he lied."

Billy brought in the bags for his and Walt's room, showered and told Walt, "I've gotta see Annie. I'll be back in a minute."

Annie was about to take a shower and asked him to get a bag she had forgotten to bring in from the van. When he returned she was still in the bathroom and he sat on the bed, listening to the shower and thinking. He'd leaned down to remove a shoe when there was a rap on the door.

"It's open," Billy called.

Walt stuck his head in. "What about Tennessee?"

"He'll be okay in the van." Billy removed the second shoe.

Walt waited for a moment as Billy leaned back and rested on the pillow. "I wonder."

"No one's gonna break in the van," Billy argued. "You said so yourself this afternoon when we went into that place to eat. If they were gonna heist a vehicle they'd pick a hell of a lot later model than the van."

"It's been hot all day and it doesn't seem to cool off at nigh," Walt said. "Willis said it was about sixty degrees year-round three feet under."

Walt, Billy knew, could be persistent and persuasive. "You think maybe Tennessee'd do better in air conditioning?"

"Yes, just to be on the safe side."

"Okay," Billy said.

"You can stash him in our room." Walt said.

As he moved across the parking lot, he could see the desk clerk in the office. He went to the back of the van where he slipped the white sack into a sleeping bag, zipped it up, got out and looked toward the office. The woman was no longer there.

He was about a dozen feet away when the door next to Walt and his room opened and a man about Billy's age appeared.

"Evenin'."

"Evenin'," Billy answered.

"You know where the ice machine is?"

"Sorry. We just checked in."

"My friend's gotta have her some ice."

Billy eased toward the door.

"Where y'all headed?" the stranger asked.

"Florida," Billy answered.

"Taking highway Seventy-Five?"

"Yeah, we'll cross over to Lauderdale on Alligator Alley. You have a good one."

"I will if I can only find me some ice."

The man watched as Billy entered the room in which the door seemed to open and close mysteriously by an unseen hand.

Inside, Walt asked Billy in a whisper if he thought the man had looked suspiciously at the sleeping bag. "Nah," Billy told him as he placed the bag on the floor in front of the air conditioner. "I'll be back in a minute. You go on and get some sleep."

As Billy left, the man on the walkway turned in his direction. He was about to disappear into Annie's room when a voice called, "Zekie-Bob, did you get the ice?"

Turning, Billy saw a young blonde woman in scanty attire step out from the next room. She gave him a quick smile and called to the man, "I told you, I gotta have me some ice for my Coke."

Billy entered Annie's room. She was already in bed. He stood for a moment before turning out the lights. He quickly undressed and crawled in next to her. But she was sound asleep. He held her close, smelling her freshness, and in another moment he was asleep, spooned up beside her.

Chapter V
Friday, 16 September, 1983

E zekiel rose from the bed, naked. The Blonde, as he called her, stirred, yawned and asked, "What time is it?"

"Mornin'," he drawled as he opened the door for a weather check. Closing it to about an inch, he observed the parking lot where he saw the hippy-looking guy carry a sleeping bag across the tarmac, followed by an old black man toting two bags.

"Zekie Bob," The Blonde complained, "it's too early to get up."

Ezekiel enjoyed watching others unobserved. Sometimes at night when he was bored—and Old Houlka was as boring as any small town could be—he'd walk along the sidewalk, listening to the katydids, until he saw a light in a window. He'd sneak up, look in, and if the person was lying on the sofa watching TV, he'd just watch from his secret place. There was not only power but also glee in watching unfettered human behavior without being seen. It aroused him.

As the guy placed the sleeping bag in back of the van he seemed to handle it with a lot of care. After he and his friend loaded the luggage and closed and locked the van's back door, Ezekiel noticed the New York license plate. The two men started toward the dining room and were joined by a young woman wearing a kerchief that covered her hair, and dark glasses.

Closing the door, Ezekiel turned toward the bed.

The Blonde shook her head, offended at the sight of his erection. "You should put something on."

He stretched and yawned. "What time is check-out?"

"Noon, why?" she pouted.

"I figured I might as well get one more bang for my buck." And with that he bounded across the room.

∽

As they moved toward the breakfast room, Walt saw a white shuttered Victorian house across the highway with a lacy iron crown. There was something vaguely familiar about it, not this specific building, but its type. He could not place where he had seen one like it, if indeed he ever had.

In the breakfast room, the waitress poured coffee. "You folks got breakfast chits from the motel?"

"Yes," Annie said.

"You get pancakes, eggs, homemade biscuits and gravy, grits or home fries, and either bacon, ham or sausage."

As they ordered Walt kept looking through the window at the white house.

"You folks traveling?" the waitress asked.

"Yes. We're sightseeing around the area," Annie answered.

"What town is this?" Walt asked suddenly.

"Columbus, Mississippi."

"Columbus?"

"Yes. That's where you're at."

Walt turned to Annie and Billy. "Columbus is where Tennessee was born. I thought there was something familiar about that place across the highway."

The waitress knitted her brows.

Seeing the look on her face, Walt added, attempting to jog her memory, "the playwright?"

"Oh, him," she said dismissively. "I suppose you've already been up to Tupelo?"

"Tupelo? What's in Tupelo?" Walt asked.

"Where Elvis was born," she said.

"Who?"

"Elvis Presley."

"Oh, him."

Billy cringed. Walt liked Elvis's singing. Walt knew "Blue Suede Shoes." Hell, he could even hum it. But Walt had a mean streak and Billy knew this was Walt's way of saying, "The hell with you, Lady! You 'oh, him' my man, I 'oh, him' yours."

With a thin-lipped and scarcely concealed disgust at the ignorance, the waitress asked, "How'd you folks like your eggs?"

Walt gave her a conciliatory smile. "And I'll start with some orange juice."

She smiled back. "Juice don't come on the breakfast ticket, juice is extra."

∽

Outside again, Annie told Walt, "We'll check out the house if you like."

As they drove slowly pass the big antebellum home, Walt suddenly pointed down the block, "There it is!"

"What?"

"Where Tennessee was born."

"How do you know?" Annie asked.

"I know because the house is in the very shadow of the Church."

In the middle of the block, surrounded by a well manicured lawn, stood a yellow and gray Victorian, its fretwork trimmed in white. A sign in front, between the sidewalk and the curb, had a logo depicting a fully opened seed of cotton:

THE FIRST HOME OF
ONE OF AMERICA'S LEADING PLAYWRIGHTS.
TENNESSEE WILLIAMS
WAS BORN HERE MARCH 26, 1911.

HE RECEIVED THE PULITZER PRIZE
FOR "STREETCAR NAMED DESIRE"
AND "CAT ON A HOT TIN ROOF"
BOTH STORIES SET IN THE SOUTH.

The lack of anything special about the house reminded them of the Crane home in Garrettsville. Oh, it was nice enough, but as Walt commented, it was the church and the shadow it cast that was more telling of Tennessee. Made of red brick, its Architectural style was pseudo-Tudor with converging weights and stresses, counterbalancing buttresses and arches, parapets, and pinnacles.

When they had observed to their satisfaction, Annie said, "We got a late start but we needed that rest. As long as we're here, we might as well take a tour of the town, one last look where the poet of the place was born."

She drove slowly following the historic district markers. Columbus had been spared destruction during the Civil War. Many antebellum homes were essentially unchanged. House-high magnolias stood in the yards of Riverview, White Oak and White Hall. It was Tennessee's mother's South, a world of gracious living.

Before one of the most beautiful homes, she pulled up to the curb. A very thin woman of medium age sat on the front porch, rocking rapidly, her long black hair set against white transparent skin. Realizing she was being observed, she attempted to counter the sudden flush of her face by fanning rapidly. On the face of the fan was a picture of the beautiful long-haired Jesus.

Annie noticed the street ahead was treeless, not a branch, not a leaf to give protection from the sun's merciless glare. But here, near the house where the woman sat, life-giving elm trees shaded the walk.

༃

They crossed from Mississippi into Alabama; about five miles out of Columbus, a sign read "The Heart of Dixie." Swamps, rolling country, timber production, Pentecostal churches, automobile graveyards, First, Second, Third Reformed Churches of Christ, red, red earth, and trees along the highway completely covered with vines, making grotesquely beautiful forms.

At a small country station, Annie asked the young girl pumping gas, "Are those grape vines covering the trees along the road?"

"No ma'am. That's kudzu."

"How's that?"

"Kudzu."

Walt leaned out the window "How do you spell it?"

"I don't know how to spell it, sir. All's I know is that it's kudzu."

⁊⁌

"President Reagan's budget for military music for the Army, Navy, Marine Corps and Air Force bands call for $102.1 million, up from $99.7 million last year."

The TV droned in the background under the grunts and groans of their fornication. Ezekiel was nothing if not a news junkie. But for the fear that he might go soft if he pulled out, he would have gotten up and bounced up the volume a few decibels.

"The House of Representatives sent to President Reagan a military bill that would end United States moratorium on production of chemical arms by authorizing a new form of nerve gas weapons."

Thrusting as deep as he could into the tight wet flesh, he shot his load with a groan. His weight resting solidly on The Blonde in an almost blacked-out state, and with a fly buzzing his flop-sweat butt, he struggled to hear the announcer, and at the same time thought of the times, as a boy, he had caught flies and ripped off their wings just to see their amazed reaction when they couldn't fly.

"Advocates of the nerve gas program argued in debate that voting for the measure would send a message to the Soviet Union in response to the fatal downing of a Korean Air Lines passenger jet."

The Blonde didn't have any illusions about Ezekiel's loving her. He just used her to get off like all the guys she had been with since she was twelve. He had no more feeling for her than he had for a tight banana skin. So what was the attraction? And she had to admit there was an attraction. He was different than the boys at high school. And yes, she did get some sexual kicks with him, not because of his feelings for her, but simply because he sustained longer than any of the boys she'd been with.

Having wriggled out from beneath his hairy chest, covered with post-coital perspiration, she modestly pulled the sheet up around her neck, lit a cigarette, inhaled deeply and popped the cap on a can of Coke. Taking a swallow she made a face. "Y'all know, Zekie-Bob, how I hate a Coke without ice. Drinkin' a Coke without ice is like..." She tried to come up with a metaphor rather than a simile although her teacher had never been able to clearly explain their difference. But she sensed that "in the evening of life" was a metaphor while "red as a spanked baby's bottom" was a simile and the difference was that the former was more elegant.

"The body of Tennessee Williams has been robbed from Calvary Cemetery in St. Louis and an undertaker, Mr. Herman Willis, from Richmond, Indiana, thinks he may know something about the suspects."

Ezekiel sat upright in bed watching the wimpy man on TV.

"Well, I don't know what drinking a Coke without ice is like, but..."

"Shut up!" he commanded.

"It was Tuesday afternoon that these people stopped at my funeral parlor and the young man—there were three people, an old Negro with a beard, this young hippie boy with blond hair and the girl was red-headed—anyway, they stopped at my parlor and the boy said he was writing a mystery novel and needed information about what a body looked like after it had been buried six months. I granted him the interview, because I myself am a writer, and then, lo and behold, last evening, I saw on the TV news that Tennessee Williams had been grave robbed from Calvary Cemetery and I put two and two, or maybe I should say three and three, together because when they left, they were driving a VW van and I noticed it had a New York license plate."

"I understand," the announcer said, "there's a ten thousand dollar reward offered by the estate."

Ezekiel sprang from the bed wiping his groin, chest and armpits with the sheet he had yanked from The Blonde and went quickly to the door. "Oh Shit!" he said, seeing the van was gone.

∽

It was just a little over a half-hour later that he crossed the parking lot, ahead of The Blonde who trailed after him. "What's your hurry?" she whined, trying to shove her diaphragm case into her clutch bag. "I didn't even have time for a good hot soak in the tub."

As they approached the black Ford, a soulful-eyed cocker spaniel puppy looked up and lifting a leg, peed on the Ford's whitewall tire.

"Oh, look. Isn't him a thweeth-pie," The Blonde baby-talked.

With one swing of Ezekiel's right foot the dog was lifted off the tarmac and flung into the grass where it looked up with great moist cocker spaniel eyes, whimpering as it limped away.

The Blonde stamped her high-heeled foot. "What'd you do that for?"

"That's for me to know and you to find out." Ezekiel laughed as he got into the car and slammed the door. He turned the key but the car wouldn't start. She got in as he cursed and switched the key on and off. When the engine finally caught, he burned rubber out of the parking lot.

As they headed home, she thought how mean he was. She considered herself an animal-rights activist; one of the few in Old Houlka, and the response of her four-legged friends—dogs, cats, horses—to her tender mercies and ministrations was the only thing that gave her any sense of self worth. Not being able to trace her ancestors back beyond an unwed mother who drove into town in an Edsel, pregnant and from up North—talk about your three-time losers!—to get a job as a maid in one of the town's old plantation houses, she was pond scum to the snotty little bitches in her school, most of whom claimed ancestors back to the Daughters of the Confederacy.

Of course most of the tiny bitches had teeth braces and sharp features. If an angry god had done nothing else for her, he had at least given her a perfect set of pearlies and a pretty face. And when, after seeing an old Jean Harlow movie, she had bleached her hair almost white to contrast with her black eyebrows and pubes, she had known she was a knockout. And if she was not accepted by the pillars of society in Old Houlka, at least she was very popular with the boys on the football, basketball, and baseball teams along with the elderly gentleman for whom her mother cleaned house and who was president of the bank. But of course, no one knew about that relationship, not even her mother.

☙

In the Sheriff's office of the Chickasaw County Court House in Old Houlka's town square, with its de rigueur statue "to our confederate dead," Ezekiel talked excitedly. "Sheriff, I heard the TV news interview with that undertaker up in Indiana. He said the grave robbers stopped at his funeral parlor and when he described them I put two and two together. That hippy-looking boy was carrying that body they robbed in a sleeping bag. That's why he was handling it so damn careful."

The Sheriff, chewing on a plug of Red Eye, took his time before speaking. "You may be right," he drawled, "and for your information, the Williams' estate is offering a ten thousand dollars reward for the body's recovery."

"I heard that on the TV and whoa! Did I figure I could use that money?"

"Before you go gettin' yourself all hot and bothered about collecting a reward, let me ask you a question. What the hell were you, a convicted felon out on parole, doing over there at that motel?"

Ezekiel hedged. "I'd rather not get into that."

"Well, Zeke, if you was to report this information, hoping to get the reward, which is, incidentally for the return of the body, not just having seen the robbers, you'd have to get into that, like you was probably gettin' into whoever it was you was getting into over there at that motel."

Ezekiel took a moment before he answered. "What if I was driving to Florida and heard the report and description of the suspects and just happened to come across 'em and figured it was my civic duty to see justice done and snatched the body from 'em?"

"Well, that'd be fine but how the hell would you know where they was headed?" The Sheriff wondered at the sudden smile that spread on Ezekiel's face. "And even if you did know, you think you got a snowball's chance in hell of findin' 'em? And maybe ten thousand dollars ain't enough money for the risk you'd be takin' for leavin' the state without permission." He shot a squirt of tobacco juice into the cuspidor next to the desk, wiping the residue from his lower lip on his shirt sleeve, "Now you git on home to yo mama, boy."

❧

"Senate Democrats moved tonight to force President Reagan to seek authorization under the War Powers Resolution to keep marines in Lebanon."

In the front room Ezekiel—legs spread, lounging on the ruptured sofa in his sleeveless torso-T shirt and shrunken Fruit of the Loom jockey shorts—sat watching the five o'clock news and finishing a bottle of Jax beer.

"Democrats, meeting in a party caucus, decided unanimously to take the issue to the Senate floor by introducing a resolution saying that the marines are involved in 'hostilities' and that the President therefore has to seek Congressional approval under the War Powers Resolution to keep the marines in Lebanon."

"Ma, fetch me another beer," Ezekiel yelled.

"French and Arab sources said today that France has decided to go forward with plans to supply Iraq with jet fighters. The United States, Britain and West Germany concede that their arguments against the sale have had no effect and that the transfer of the planes, five Super Étendard attack aircraft, is imminent.

"...and now for more late-breaking news on the grave robbing of Pulitzer Prize winning playwright Tennessee Williams. This afternoon, the co-executor of Williams' estate spoke from her London townhouse."

Ezekiel's mother, a heavy-breasted woman in a faded silk kimono and faux-fur pink mules, shuffled in, handed her baby a Jax, and left, "This is an unspeakable crime against the twentieth century's major playwright. Yesterday we offered a reward of ten thousand dollars leading to the recovery of the body. Today we have upped the ante to twenty-five thousand."

Ezekiel zapped the TV, chugged the Jax in three gulps, crushed the can in his fist, ran upstairs to his room, dressed quickly, got his revolver from the bureau, dialed and waited for a response. "Can you get your act together and leave town in half an hour?"

"Oh, Zekie-Bob," The Blonde whined, "I'm just getting up. Can you give me an hour?"

"Make it forty-five minutes," he whispered. "Baby, we are gonna make ourselves some real money in the next couple of days."

Hearing him coming down the stairs, his mother shuffled in from the kitchen wiping the sweat dripping down her cleavage with the dish towel, "Where ya goin,' Hon?"

"Out!"

"But I'm cookin' you your favorite, collard greens, Johnny cake and sowbelly."

Ezekiel gave her the finger and slammed the door behind him.

Wrapping the gun in a bandana handkerchief and locking it in the glove compartment, he swore loudly when the car wouldn't start. When it did, he roared out of the driveway.

His loving mother looked out the window. Ezekiel (from the Hebrew meaning, "God makes strong"), her only son, had always been a problem. A cute but mischievous little boy with an unusually inquisitive and active mind, he was forever pulling pranks and getting into trouble. College was never even a consideration, and, it seemed, he couldn't ever keep a job without getting into some kind of tomfoolery. And then the final straw, when he used a butter knife to threaten an old lady and highjack her car, and was caught joyriding in it by the sheriff. She had pleaded with the judge and her baby was given one year in the local correction facility, seven years probation and forever after, it would seem, have a felony rap attached to his record so that there was little point in filling out a job application or apartment rental form unless he wanted to perjure himself.

Where, she wondered, was reform, let alone redemption, in the penal system of this great country? It seemed to her that this one crazy mistake—and that was what it was, a piece of youthful mischief—now committed him to a life of crime since no jobs or a place to live were open to him.

◦◦

The van had passed through Tuscaloosa where a great rib joint was advertised, but since they had eaten breakfast so late, no one was hungry. It was ninety-two miles to Montgomery, then the Black

Warrior and the Alabama rivers, "New Mobile Homes, $7,999," and at length, "Montgomery, Capital of the Confederacy."

"And home of Zelda and Tallulah," Walt said.

Bumper stickers, "Hank Williams, 1923-1953," and "Praise the Lord, I saw the Light."

A sudden downpour.

Annie slowed the van. "Any leaks back there?"

"Sure are," Billy answered.

"Water," Walt declaimed, "'is a sore decayer of your whoreson dead body' if I may quote Shakespeare."

Billy re-arranged the corpse and the grave digging equipment.

Fifteen minutes later the sun was out. It was hot. He spotted a license plate marked 'Hart C' near Ozark, Alabama. Seeing hanging moss, Walt recited: "'I saw in Louisiana a live-oak growing, All alone stood it and the moss hung down from the branches...'"

"We got Spanish Moss on the road to Troy," Billy sang, beating out the rhythm on his thighs.

They crossed the Choctawhatchee River, through Dothan, the Chattahoochee River and into Georgia. "Welcome to Georgia, State of Adventure."

"I hope not," Annie said. "I've had enough adventure for one week."

It was early evening when she turned into the Day's Inn just east of Bainbridge. Having eaten an hour before and with Tennessee safely ensconced for the night in the next room, Billy showered as Annie waited for Mary Hart's "Entertainment Tonight." He was just rinsing off when he heard her yell. Cutting the water, he ran into the room.

"Listen," she told him.

". . . The actress, who plays the fiery Lily–'Trust me!'–on 'One Woman's Family' is still missing. 'Entertainment Tonight' has learned through a confidential source that the actress now receiving more fan mail than anyone else on the soap, may have been having problems with Producer David Lesco over her salary, which, regardless of her popularity and talent, is said to be the lowest of anyone in the cast."

"My God," Annie gasped. "Did I hear that correctly?"

"Yeah, you got it right."

He dripped as he went back into the bathroom. She followed and sat on the toilet lid. She'd never seen a man dry himself before and she was fascinated by how he did it, hurriedly throwing the towel over his back, roughly pulling it back and forth, armpits, chest, crotch and thighs, legs and then bending down, drying between each toe with the utmost care. "I haven't had any problems with David," she told him. "We've been getting along fine. The guy's a little insecure but I can handle that. I've never complained about the salary."

Hearing the clipped English accent on the TV she stopped talking.

"...unspeakable crime against the twentieth century's major playwright. Yesterday we offered a reward of ten thousand dollars leading to the recovery of the body. Today we upped the ante to twenty-five thousand."

They were out of the bathroom in an instant. Mary Hart was seated on her stool, legs crossed, calves pressing together from the side, making them slender and sexy. "In addition to that announcement from London by the Lady St Just, co-executor of Tennessee Williams' estate, it has now been confirmed that the suspects are traveling in a nineteen sixty-eight VW van with a New York license plate. The three are described as a young woman with red hair, a man of about twenty-five to thirty-five with long dirty-blond hair and an elderly African-American man with a beard."

"My God," Annie exclaimed.

Billy zapped the TV, and knotted the towel around his waist before crouching in front of her. "Look, maybe you need to split and get back to New York. Walt and me can..."

"No. I'm with this operation all the way. Nothing's going to bum me out. And damn it, now I'm famous, I'm going to take a leisurely bubble bath."

"But Walt and I can do the rest."

"No, it's the three of us."

"If we're caught, you..."

"Forget it," she said as she poured in the bath crystals. "We're gonna make it."

Billy thought for a moment. "Well, then, what we gotta do is take less traveled roads." He found the atlas in his backpack and opened it first to Georgia, then Florida. He sat on the bed examining it as he watched her undress. "We can leave early in the morning, staying on...Eighty-Four and then turn south on... Nineteen in order to avoid the big towns like Tallahassee. If there are cop cars on Nineteen, we could cut west to the Gulf coast on...Three Sixty-One." He pretended to be going over the route again but his eyes strayed from the map. "Yes, it's the route we should take all right. And let's not burden Walt with the news."

"Sounds good to me," Annie said, stepping into the tub and sinking into the bubbles.

He waited a moment. "I'll find us a baseball game."

"Leave the door open so I can hear," she called.

He surfed until he found the replay of the Mets and the Cards game. "I'll leave the door open so we can both hear," he laughed, throwing off his towel and getting into the tub with her.

Later, in bed, after making love again, he whispered, "Sorry I was a little rough."

"Sometimes I like it that way."

"Not much foreplay," he apologized.

"We met in February..." One by one she mumbled each of the succeeding months, "Half a year of foreplay. What the hell took you so long?"

They lay facing one another and he pressed into her and came alive, but her breathing was now easy and when he rose on one elbow and looked at her face, her eyes were closed. He stayed that way for some time before he lowered his body, checked the clock, saw that it was almost eleven, and drifted off in a sea of wet warmth.

Policeman Hurricane Jackson was patrolling his territory, Corkscrew Swamp Sanctuary and Big Cypress Swamp on Highway Forty-One, just south of Fort Myers. The state had just bought a whole bunch of brand new nineteen eighty-three patrol cars that were made in *De*troit where workers still took pride in their work, and Jackson had one of them.

Hurricane always had the radio set on the country and western station. Jimmy Rogers, Jerry Lee Lewis, Johnny Cash, Merle Haggard, Willie Nelson, Waylon Jennings. Tennessee Ernie Ford, Don and especially Hank Williams, who'd died of alcoholism before he was thirty. They were his favorites. Real singers with real voices; voices that sounded like the singer had some hair on his chest and a set of low hangers between his legs.

> "Very close, very close
> That's what life's about

When Don Williams sang those words, Hurricane's throat went tight.

That was a song with real feelings and words that the normal ear could understand. It wasn't that he hated music like his son Sammy, and Sammy's friend Calvin Coolidge Jones, enjoyed. Hell, no, he loved music. It was just that he hated their kind of music, although you really couldn't call what Sammy listened to as music. More like noise is what it was.

The country music station was followed by the ten o'clock news. "Three radicals who said they were fighting for black liberation were convicted today in upstate New York of murdering two policemen and a Brinks guard and stealing one point six million dollars from an armored car in Rockland County nearly two years go. The defendants were each found guilty of second-degree murder and first-degree armed robbery. And we have been watching a late-breaking story about a grave robbing last night in St. Louis' own Calvary Cemetery."

The oncoming headlights passed slowly enough so Hurricane could see that the car was driven by a long-haired young man. In the rear view mirror, he saw the familiar New York license plate on what appeared to be a light blue eighty-three Cadillac. He hung a fast U-turn and in the same instant the Caddy took off.

"A young woman with red hair, a man of about thirty-five with long hair and an elderly African American male with a beard allegedly robbed the grave of Tennessee..."

Hurricane did not hear the rest of what the announcer had to say because he hit the siren and gave pursuit. The Caddy rounded a curve at high speed and nearly went off the road. Hurricane called for backup. He was in close proximity when the young man fired the first shot. It would be, Hurricane reasoned, from a six bullet max, thirty-eight.

Turning on his flashers, he swerved from lane to lane to avoid being a too-easy target when another shot rang out. "Two," he counted aloud. A third shot hit the hood of his car, causing sparks. He shifted to the left lane only to see oncoming headlights from around a curve and pulled back into the right lane. A fourth and fifth shot rang out and the windshield took a hit on the passenger side. He was just short of being a car-length away from the Caddy when the sixth shot was fired. "That's it, you hippy son-of-a-bitch," he muttered. "You're gonna regret tangling ass with this cracker." Sparks flew when he bumped the side of the Caddy. The driver put on the brakes and Hurricane nudged the Caddy again, edging it toward the ditch where it skidded, turned over, rolled upright and came to a steaming stop, just short of the swamp. Hurricane jumped out on the run, gun drawn, and yelled, "Get out!"

The driver was too stunned to move.

"I said, get the hell out of there," Hurricane shouted. The hippy opened the door and did as he was told. "Hands on your head, hands on your goddamn head, up against the car." Hurricane frisked the thin young guy, pulling up his shirt to reveal a four-inch belt filled with heroin. In the report he would, of course, say, "white powder substance," but he sure as hell knew what heroin looked like at this point in his career.

The boy slowly turned to face him. He could not have been more than nineteen. What would happen to him in prison?

Hurricane felt sick to his stomach. He shook his head as if to clear it of the look of the boy.

A blaring siren announced the arrival of backup. The young officer ran forward drawing his gun. "You okay?" he asked Hurricane.

"Oh, yeah."

An older cop moseyed forward. "Hey, man, you get yourself another dope runner?"

Hurricane handed him the belt, "Appears so."

"That's seven so far this month and you got a couple of weeks to go. How the hell do you do it? "

"I got me an instinct," Hurricane said simply. "I spot one and I just know."

"I guess you must have had lots of experience with that boy of your'n."

Hurricane turned sharply and the older man's mouth snapped shut like a turtle.

Swapping cars with the two officers who would deliver the shackled prisoner back to the station, book him on possession and put the patrol car into the garage for repair, he told them he'd do all the paper work in the morning. In the meantime there might be some more drug runners south, coming from the same place as the hippy. Of course he knew that was unlikely. What he wanted to do—*needed* to do—was to see Grace at The Dixie Bar and Grill, a few miles south. He was tired, but he knew the road like the back of his hand. Hell, he had known the Corkscrew Swamp Sanctuary road all his life.

୧⁓ৎ

The neon sign was turned off as Hurricane drove into the parking lot of the Dixie Bar and Grill but he could see Grace sitting at the end of the bar looking up at the blue light coming from the TV. Harry, her husband, couldn't have picked a worse location if he'd tried, as anyone could of told him who looked at a map. There wasn't anything south of Ft. Myers, except the Golden Gate Toll Road, known as Alligator Alley, which ran across the swamp to Miami. They could damn well call it "The Everglades" but a swamp was a swamp was a swamp. The point was, no one stopped after Ft. Myers. If they was headed to Miami they gassed up in Ft. Myers and drove straight on through.

It was tough about Harry. A man works all his life, then bingo, dead of cancer. But Grace seemed to be taking it in stride. Hurricane wondered how Ruby would take it if he died. Probably throw a block party. No, not really. Ruby and he used to be fine, then...you know—if you're married you know—there's nothing like sleeping in the same bed with a woman you ain't sleeping with, which is why he slept on the Florida porch. And all those fights when Sammy was growing up about the goddamn drums.

Grace came to the door to meet him, "Hurricane!"

Grace was a looker. A real looker. Blonde, a little younger then he was, she was short and had a good figure, a real good figure, which she always showed off by wearing low cut blouses or tight fitting sweaters. And she was peppy, talked fast like New Yorkers talk. "I'm not keeping you up?" he asked, removing his hat and preparing to make himself at home. "I could drive on down to Naples for coffee if it's any trouble."

"I was just watching Johnny Carson and having a cup of decaf. Want some?"

"Regular, if you got it."

"It won't take a second."

He took off his gun belt and jacket and sat at the bar.

"A tough day?" Grace asked, fixing the coffee.

"Usual. Road patrol," he answered. However much he had wanted, needed, to see her, there was shyness in him now. He could talk but could not say what was most on his mind.

"So few people on the road, I closed early and let Pearl and Sherlee go home."

Grace brought him coffee. He liked sitting next to her and talking about things that happened in his past, liked her long fingernails combing the hairs of his forearm, liked her nearness and moments when her knee touched his or when she sometimes put her hand high on his thigh. And he liked the smell of her. He was aware that she was ready and open, especially after Harry died, and Hurricane wanted to, but he didn't know quite how to initiate the action. So he talked, looking into her blue eyes, not knowing how to go the extra step that would bring about what they both wanted. Truth was, it had been so long, he was out of practice.

"How come you know Corkscrew Swamp area so well?" Grace asked.

"Oh, I don't know..."

There was a rare moment of silence between them. Grace patted him on his thigh, got up and poured more coffee.

"You heard the news about Tennessee Ernie Ford?" Hurricane asked.

"No. What?"

"Grave robbers dug him up."

"I didn't know Tennessee Ernie Ford died. I'm sorry to hear it, I know you like his singing."

"Yes I do; heard the news on the radio this evening."

Hurricane talked on, never of course, about what was really on his mind, until at last, looking at the clock over the bar he said, "I'll be damned, almost midnight, I gotta be moving on."

"Oh, do you have to?" She put her hand on his arm.

"I'm on duty patrolling the roads."

"But there's nobody on the roads this time of night. There are few enough cars on this road at high noon," she said, laughing.

"They gotta be patrolled."

"Why?"

"There's lots of crazy people around nowadays." Then, in another awkward moment of silence, he checked his watch. "Thanks for the coffee."

"You're welcome."

He moved over to the pegs where he had hung his coat and hat.

"I know," she said suddenly, ringing up the cash register, taking out a coin, and going to the juke box. The song was a slow 1940s number; slow songs from another time were all Grace had on her juke box.

"Sometimes I wonder why I spend these lonely nights..."

"Dance with me," she said, her arms raised, moving toward him.

"Dance?"

"Yes, dance with me," she pleaded.

Grace stood in front of him, holding up her arms so he would put his arms around her waist. He hadn't heard that song since nineteen forty-three, hadn't put his arms around a woman in... seemed like a long time. Ruby didn't dance and so he hadn't danced in years.

"Dance, dance," she was saying, swaying to the music.

"I can't dance," he said strapping on his revolver. "I'm on duty."

As he backed out of the parking lot he could see her in there, moving, her hands up, like she was holding on to someone, which he couldn't help but wish was him.

Grace danced by herself.

Chapter VI
Saturday, 17 September 1983

I t was past midnight when Ezekiel pulled in at the rest stop. He sat in the stall reading the graffiti: *"No use standing on the seat, the crabs in here can jump ten feet."* Emerging from the building, he saw The Blonde talking to an elderly woman on the walkway.

"Come on," he called. "Get in."

The Blonde took another sip of her Coke. "Well it's been nice meeting you, ma'am."

"You, too, honey."

"Goddamn it," Ezekiel hissed when she was in her seat. "You'll talk to anybody, won't you?"

"I like talking to people."

"Well, I don't." He thrust the key in the ignition. The car would not start. After several attempts and growing more and more angry, he saw a man sidling toward him.

"Trouble getting her started?" the old gentleman smiled.

Christ! Ezekiel thought. *No, I can get her started any time I want. I just do this because I get off hearing the grinding sound of the engine, you fuckin' retard.* "Yeah," he answered, turning the key again with no success.

"Let me take a look."

Ezekiel punched the release latch for the hood.

The man limped to the front of the car. "Try startin' her again," he called.

Ezekiel turned the key.

When the man returned wiping the grease off his hands on a handkerchief, he offered his assessment. "It appears you got fuel pump troubles."

"Damn!" Ezekiel slammed the steering wheel.

"I worked in a garage all my life; retired a couple of years back because of this bum foot. Looks to me like you'll have to get a new fuel pump. The place where I worked is open all night. Me and Noodle—Noodle's my wife—wouldn't mind being good Samaritans and running you back up to Montgomery."

A certain Samaritan had compassion on me, Ezekiel remembered from Bible class. "How long you reckon it'll take to get the fuel pump and install her?"

"Hard to say. I'll work as fast as I can."

"Get out!" Ezekiel hissed at The Blonde.

"Well, cripes, don't get mad at me. It's not my fault."

The women were relegated to the back seat.

"Probably should introduce ourselves," the elderly gentleman said. "I'm Bo Springer and my wife's name is Noodle Springer."

Ezekiel closed his eyes for a moment as if in pain. *Oh, your wife's last name is Springer? I thought maybe it was Noodle Gimpfoot,* a thought he could not express, at least while Gimpy was doing him a favor. "I'm Ezekiel and back there's The Blonde."

"Oh, that's just what he calls me," she giggled in embarrassment. "My real name is Rosemary."

"Rosemary," Noodle repeated. "What a pretty name."

The engine of Bo's 'sixty-five Cadillac purred like a cat as they headed toward Montgomery.

"Where y'all from, Rosemary?" Noodle asked as a conventional pleasant entree to what she considered civilized conversation.

"I'm from Old Houlka."

"Old Houlka," Noodle pondered the name. "Just help me here a minute. Where is that?"

"Old Houlka is just east of Houlka."

Again Noodle thought for a moment. "I can't rightly place either of them towns."

"You know where Thorn is?"

"I can't say as I do."

"Let me see now." The Blonde took her time. "Do you know where Tombigbee's National Forest is?"

"A National Forest named Tom Big Bee?...I don't think so."

"Do you know where Houston is?"

"Texas!" Noodle answered brightly.

Ezekiel had heard enough. Turning, his eyes now a cold killer black, he smiled upon Noodle Springer. His voice was well modulated when he said, "Let's put it this way. Old Houlka's just south of Tombigbee's National Forest in Chickasaw County in the state of Mississippi in the United States of America, in the continent of North America, the planet earth which is part of the solar system....Ya got that?"

Up to a point in her young life Rosemary had always thought because of what she was taught in Sunday School that there was something redeemable about all...she was thinking "God's creatures," but she changed the thought to "humans." God had been just a myth to her ever since her mother was killed in a traffic accident. What kind of God would allow her mother to be killed in an automobile accident? Wasn't the accident more like a random happenstance? God was not up there controlling such matters. And if he was, if he had looked down and said, "Let's get Rosemary's mother in a traffic accident today," then what kind of a God was he?

The morning sun was just below the horizon when Ezekiel climbed back behind the wheel and turned the key in the ignition. The Ford's motor started right off and purred so smoothly it took a moment before he realized that it was running.

Bo closed the hood and wiped his hands on his handkerchief as he crippled back to the driver's side of the car. "If my danged foot hadn't been hurting so much I could of got her done faster," he offered, apologetically.

"You sure you finally got her fixed?" Ezekiel asked with barely concealed impatience.

"Absolutely," Bo replied as he reached into his shirt pocket for the receipt. "As I told you, Noodle and me are churchgoing people and as Good Samaritans you only have to pay the bill for the fuel pump which comes to, thanks to the discount as a former employee, only thirty-seven dollars."

Ezekiel put the Ford in reverse and backed out of the parking space.

Unsure of exactly what was going on, Bo smiled and limped toward the rolled down driver's window, holding out the bill. "I ain't charging a cent for the labor. As I say, Noodle and me are Christians, 'Do Unto others . . .'"

Ezekiel shifted into drive and with a squeal of rubber the Ford shot forward before Bo was able to move his lame foot out of the way. As the car's back wheel ran over it, he hollered in pain and jumped up and down on his good foot. Noodle sprang from the car and ran toward her Good Samaritan, steadying him in her arms. She looked up and saw the Ford's tail lights disappear around the curve of the rest stop, heading toward the highway.

"Well, I never!" she exclaimed.

༄

It was just north of Port Charlotte, on highway Forty-One, that they ran into heavy construction and detours. "There's only one way we can bypass this congestion and get past the Ft. Myers area and make any time," Annie said. "As risky as it will be, I've got to take highway Seventy-Five to exit twenty-one, then get back on the shore road."

Billy agreed.

She turned onto Seventy-Five at exit twenty-eight. Every muscle went tight when she saw a patrolman's car in the rear-view mirror. She waited, half expecting him to turn on his flashers, but he passed. A mile or so further south, another patrolman passed.

Because of the warmth and humidity in the back of the van, Billy removed his shirt, raised his arm and took a whiff. Opening his duffel bag he found the Old Spice stick and applied it.

The pleasant smell of spice was what made Annie look in the rear-view mirror. As Billy picked up the red-checked shirt she saw something fall from its pocket.

"What's that?" she asked.

Billy held up the remains of the nickel bag of marijuana. "Tony gave it to me, remember, the night before we left."

"And you brought it along?" she asked incredulously.

"Not intentionally. I was wearing this shirt."

"You packed a dirty shirt?"

"I only wore it the one day."

"Well, this trip is hardly the time to start smoking pot."

"Don't intend to start ever again," Billy told her. "I've aged out. Just forgot all about it being in my shirt pocket."

Smelling the shirt he had removed, he decided it was okay and carefully folded the shirt he had removed from the bag and placed it back in his duffel.

♘

It was the weather that made Grace apprehensive, one of those awfully humid days, the sky overcast and the barometer topping out, a sure sign of rain. She was strictly a sun person which was why Harry and she moved to Florida.

The day had been a disaster. The wind chimes on the bar's front porch had driven her crazy. At lunch she had only nine customers, a father, mother and young boy plus six blue-haired Florida widows, all dieters, who each drank two frozen margaritas and then three of them ordered another, along with extra frozen glasses, so they could split one for the road. They had Caesar salads with dressing on the side, presumably because of their diets, but kept calling for more of Pearl's specialty, hot buttered bread.

Grace stood on the porch as they slowly pulled out of the parking lot without a glance at the eighteen-wheeler approaching from the south. The truck, carrying pine logs to the paper mills, was going about seventy miles an hour. Grace thought for certain the blue-hairs' Mercedes Benz had had it, but the trucker braked, thank god, and the blue-hairs drove on, oblivious. A proposed law would make the drink server responsible for the accident, but how on earth was Florida going to legislate geriatric drinking?

The wind chimes were now louder than ever. She decided it would be a good idea to talk over the weather situation with Pearl, her wonderful cook, and Sherlee, the best waitress she had ever seen. In relations with your help it was best, Grace told herself, to be on a human, rather than a management/worker basis. All the books said the Japanese were asking for input from their workers and that's why their car companies were so productive.

Since she already had half a lime cut, she figured why not? She wouldn't put much tequila in, no use getting the help drunk. So with marguerites blending, she called Pearl in from the kitchen and told Sherlee to stop the dinner set-ups. "Just sit at the bar and relax while we watch the weather report," she said, snapping on TV with the remote.

"...One of the rarest large mammals, the giant panda, known as the Ailuropoda melanoleuca..."

"Public television. Gimme a break!" She clicked the remote.

Sounds of groans from a bikini clad woman with a sleek sweating body pumping away at a rowing machine. "Wishing doesn't make it happen. To build a great body takes work."

"That's Cher," Sherlee said.

Grace clicked the remote.

"President Reagan cut the budget for the National Endowment for the Arts so that its total investment in professional music, symphony, opera, chamber, everything, is now just under eleven million dollars."

"Why is it so impossible to get a little weather news?"

"Beats me, unless you're on the wrong channel," Pearl said, taking the remote and clicking on the weather channel.

". . . gale-force winds up to one hundred and twenty miles an hour tore through the heart of downtown Havana yesterday noon…"

"I sure hope it got ole Castro and took him up high over the rainbow," Pearl said, sucking up the slush of her margarita, the sound of which drowned out what the announcer was saying.

". . . Thermal instability, high humidity and the convergence of a low-level air mass with cool drier air has caused the storm to veer from the east coast out into the Gulf of Mexico…"

"Well, at least that's away from us." Sherlee sounded relieved.

"Hurricane Edwin, the fifth tropical storm of the season, began sometime in the early Thursday morning in the Caribbean, weather experts being at a loss to explain the cause."

Pearl zapped the T.V., sucked up the last drop of her margarita. "I think I gotta get myself home," she said.

"But the announcer just said the storm was headed out into the Gulf."

Pearl leveled a look at her employer. "How long you been down here?"

"Why, Pearl River," Grace said, "you know the answer to that question as well as I do."

"That's what I'm sayin'." Pearl leaned over the counter and shot her straw into the garbage can. "If there's one thing you got to know about Southwest Florida weather it's that those New York casters cannot predict it. I'm gettin' myself home."

"Me, too," Sherlee followed.

"What about the customers?" Grace called after them.

Pearl turned. "Honey, take a reality check. Do you see any customers?"

Grace looked over the dining room, wondering what her cook was getting at.

"There ain't gonna be no customers, not tonight, unless they're blown in by a high wind." Pearl disappeared into the kitchen, Sherlee following.

"It's Saturday night. I can't manage alone," Grace called.

Sherlee reappeared followed by Pearl, big white purse in hand. "Why don't you turn off the neon sign and lock the door. Folks'll get the idea."

Grace stood below the wind chimes on the porch and watched them drive away. She could see by the fronds rustling in the palm trees that the wind had picked up. There were heavy cumulus clouds. It was getting darker. Still, the announcer said the hurricane was headed out into the Gulf. But then again, maybe Pearl was right. Who could predict the path of a hurricane? She'd better get busy and tape the windows and get the storm windows up. This would be the first time since Harry passed she'd have to do it by herself.

෬෨

Speeding along highway Seventy-Five at eighty miles an hour, just north of Ft. Myers, a weary Ezekiel spotted, through half-closed lids, a VW van in the distance. At the same time, in his side mirror, he saw a highway patrolman's car. Slowing down to seventy, he shifted into the right lane. The plates on the van looked like they were from New York, with his luck this could just turn out to be another false alarm like everything else in his life. He had to check and see who was driving the van.

The cop car behind him was still in the middle lane. Traffic was heavy. He waited for an opening and then, just over the speed limit, edged into the middle lane and was almost abreast of the van when the cop turned on his siren and flashers. The moment the cop car shifted to the left lane, the van's right turn signals started blinking. Another car was tailgating the van. There was no way Ezekiel could make the exit. "Goddamn! Fuck! Shit!" He screamed.

The Blonde woke, terrified. "Honey," she said when she had oriented herself to her surroundings, "You know I just can't tolerate a rude remark anymore than I can a vulgar action."

She knew instinctively at the burial of her mother, that God was dead. And she identified with Zarathustra, alone in the forest, saying to his heart: "Could it be possible? This old saint hath not yet heard that God is dead?" She had discovered Nietzsche her senior year at Old Houlka High. And when she had taken her mother's place as cleaning maid at old Mr. Peck's house, where she was given a room—where else was she going to live?—she had looked long into the abyss and the abyss had returned her look.

∽

Annie had driven no more than a couple of miles on highway Forty One, the shore road that passed through the outskirts of Fort Myers, when she suddenly veered onto the soft shoulder to avoid a car.

"Damn it!" she yelled out the window. "Learn to drive!" It took some doing to maneuver the van back on the road. When it was righted, Billy moved forward between the shovels, pickax, and tarps. "You okay?" he asked.

"Six old women in a Mercedes. The driver was talking to the three in the back seat and heading straight across the yellow line at us."

Billy massaged her neck.

"All we need at this point is to get into an accident," she muttered.

"You're just tired," he said, thrusting his hand down the back of her shirt and massaging her spine. "When we get to Naples we'll head over to Lauderdale. It can't be more than a hundred and fifty miles, and then we'll rent us a boat and sometime early tomorrow we'll…"

"Yes," Annie smiled, loving his healing fingers.

A downdraft hit the side of the van and it was all she could do to keep it on the road.

"Getting windy," Walt observed.

"Gusting," she said. "I wish the car radio hadn't been stolen so we could tune into the weather station."

"Well, remember you got him down to four hundred bucks because of that."

Then, quite suddenly, the turbulence was gone. It was calm again and with the calm came heavy humidity.

As they drove in silence Walt edged up in his seat and looked intently down the two-lane highway.

"You want to lie down back here for awhile?" Billy asked him.

"No," Walt answered and turned to Annie. "Could we stop at the next gas station?"

"Sure."

The wind picked again and Annie concentrated on her driving as she passed a gas station.

"Could we stop at the *next* gas station?"

"Oh, sure, Sorry."

They passed another gas station.

"Oh, damn!"

From in back, Billy couldn't help but laugh. "Maybe you'd best just go by the side of the road."

"I think there's a place up ahead." Walt said, pointing to a sign.

❧

Jake and his girl "Friday" sat in a booth at Lauderdale's posh Royal Poinciana Palms Hotel right on the ocean. They had arrived early afternoon on Thursday, rented a car at the airport, and set up their office at the hotel. The next morning, and all day Saturday, they worked the phones. Those who refused to give out information were placed on a "check this personally" list and Jake, in contact with her by phone, made the rounds.

Jake had a detective's badge that worked wonders. He would go up to the desk, usually manned by a Cuban expatriate or someone from south of the border who had been hired on the cheap, introduce himself, pull out his badge, and simply ask them to look up the name of Ann Laurel, or any similar name, to see if she had checked in during the week, or had made a reservation. If that didn't work he asked them if anyone driving a sixty-eight VW van had registered. Without exception, he found both the badge and his big easygoing low-key manner was enough to enlist cooperation.

He and Friday had covered motels and hotels in and around Fort Lauderdale. There was not a single lead.

They went to the bar to relax.

"Before you got back, I turned on Mary Hart's Entertainment Tonight, and caught part of the story about the grave robbing of Tennessee Williams from a St. Louis cemetery. You heard about it?" she asked.

"No."

"The suspects were identified by some man in Indiana as a young hippy type guy, an old African-American man with a beard, and a young woman with red hair. I didn't hear the whole thing but as soon as they gave the description of the woman, I thought of Ann Laurel. But the rest of the story didn't figure."

"It figures perfectly."

"St. Louis and the two guys?"

Jake's smile was slight. "You just solved the case." He told her about the map June had found that had St. Louis and Lauderdale circled, and Juan and Tony giving a description of Billy, and Tony saying that they had a friend who looked like he was about to audition for Santa at Macys. "So there you have it, baby. It's a no-brainer."

"It's so Annie," Friday laughed. "You going to call June?"

Jake thought for a moment. "If Annie is involved in a grave robbing and gets caught she's in deep shit. Nothing a private dick can do about that. She's your friend, right?

"I was a year behind her at school and she helped me get June as an agent after I graduated. After I met you and said to hell with acting we kinda lost touch."

"But she's still a friend?"

"Sure."

"Well, there really isn't a hell of a lot we can do. The main thing June is interested in is that Annie report to work on Monday. We can't help her if she's in trouble with the law, so I see no point in giving June that information today."

"What's next?" she asked, sipping her Bombay gin martini with a single olive.

"We just hang loose," Jake said, "Since we're here in the tropics and June is picking up the tab, I think our next move is to order another round of drinks, go up to the room and screw our brains out, shower and dress, and come back down and have a good seafood dinner. Tomorrow we sleep late, catch a little sun, and take an evening flight back to the city. And on Monday we'll know how all of this has played out."

༄

When Annie pulled into the parking lot of the Dixie Bar and Grill, heavy dark clouds were low in the sky and it had already started to rain. She backed into a parking space and in answer to Billy's questioning look, explained, "So the license plate's not in everyone's face."

"Are we going in?" he asked.

"I'm worried. Maybe we can find out something about this weather," she answered.

As they entered, the woman behind the bar turned from lifting a bottle out of the bar rack and wrapping it in newspaper.

"Howdy," Walt greeted her. "I need to use the men's room."

"Sorry," she told him, "customers only."

"Delighted," Walt said. "I'll just have to buy a drink."

Walt had already disappeared into SEÑORS when the woman called, "Hey, wait."

Billy smiled. "His need is pressing, ma'am,"

"Could we get some coffee?" Annie asked.

The woman seemed as though she didn't seem sure how to handle the situation but didn't want to be rude. "Sorry, I'm closing up."

"You usually get this much wind down here?" Annie asked.

The woman looked up, more in wonder than irritation.

"Those palms in the parking lot are really showing the wind," Billy said.

"Is the storm going to be bad?" Annie asked.

Grace stopped packing and shook her head in disbelief. "Don't you have a radio in your car?"

Billy turned from the front door and answered, "No. What's up?"

"What's up? A hurricane, that's what's up."

"Can we drive further south and avoid it?" Annie questioned.

"Honey, I can't advise you what to do. Me? I gotta close up. I'm sorry but you folks have to move on." She said this firmly, although her feelings were conflicted, not wanting them there but at the same time not wanting to be alone.

"A double Old Grand-Dad, straight up, please," Walt ordered when he emerged from SEÑORS.

"Hold on, Walt," Annie said, turning to the woman. "Do you think it's safe to drive on?"

"I have no idea."

"Van doesn't weigh a lot," Billy said.

"No," Annie replied. Noticing the taped back windows of the restaurant and the plywood over them, she added, "I think we may have to stick it out here."

Grace stopped her packing. "Oh, no, you don't. I just told you, you can't stay here."

"Why not?" Annie asked.

"Cause...I've got no protection."

"Protection?"

"Insurance, like if you're injured on the premises you might sue."

"But if we drive on and the storm hits, we could be killed."

"I'm sorry, I truly am, but that's not my problem."

"What could happen here?"

"Like the roof could blow off? That's what could happen here."

"What's the nearest town south?" the boy asked.

"Naples."

"How far is it?"

"Fifteen, twenty miles."

Annie went to the front door and looked out. Grace saw that the wind had picked up and the fronds of the palms were now like a churning sea silhouetted against the sky.

"May I get the weather report?" Annie asked.

"Sure, go ahead," Grace said.

Annie picked up the remote.

"We interrupt this newscast for a special report on Hurricane Edwin. The fifth tropical storm of the season began shortly before dawn on Thursday in the Caribbean. Having erratically veered north and east, it is now scheduled to hit shore, with wind velocity up to one hundred and thirty miles an hour, near just south of Fort Myers. All residents in that area are warned not to evacuate. Best thing to do is get into your cellar..."

"We don't have a cellar," Grace cried.

"...or under heavy furniture, anything to protect yourself against falling timbers. And now we take you back to WGFK, Miami."

Grace shook her head. "Hit right here. Two hundred and eighty-five-thousand dollars worth of property, Harry's retirement, and all I've got in this world."

Annie spoke calmly. "I think we should introduce ourselves. My name is Annie, that's Walt and this is Billy."

"I'm Grace."

❧

The rain erupted as though the heavens had opened. The sound of the thudding deluge against the roof was terrifying. It was followed by a whining sound from the casement. Grace looked up at the roof as it groaned and swayed. Another gust and the beams in the ceiling might give and the roof blow off. "All right," she said during the lull that followed, "I guess we're in this together."

The sound of a slamming door upstairs startled her. "Excuse me," she said, "I'll be right back."

As soon as she was gone, Annie hissed, "We've got to get him out of there."

"Him?" Billy asked.

"Tennessee," Annie pointed toward the parking lot.

Billy looked around the room in search of a place to stash the body. "How about the SEÑORS?" he asked. "There won't be any customers tonight."

"Perfect!" Annie said, tossing him the car keys.

As Billy opened the front door the rain, driven by the wind, seemed to be coming sideways. "Be careful but, hurry!" she called after him. Closing the door she told Walt, "Get the mop behind the counter and wait for Billy to get back. I'll go upstairs and try to delay her.

Billy was halfway to the van when a nearby electrical pole snapped. Standing motionless, he watched the wires sparkle and hiss in the driving rain and begin to snake along the road. The sight galvanized him into action and he went to the van where he cut a hole in the tarp's center. Putting his head through it, he grabbed his duffel bag and secured it to himself with his belt. The wind increased and the van rocked as he carefully placed the sleeping bag beneath his homemade poncho and readied himself to open the door.

⤫

After closing the banging door upstairs that led into the apartment, Grace went to the bedroom and dialed Hurricane's number at the station. The line was busy.

She was re-dialing when she heard the voice call, "Hello?"

She immediately hung up. "I'm back here," she hollered.

"You okay?" Annie asked.

"Sure."

"I thought you might need some help."

"No."

"You closed all the windows?" Annie asked.

"Yes."

"If it's a hurricane, I've heard that it's advisable to leave a couple of windows open a little so the wind can blow through."

⤫

As Hurricane rounded a slow curve, he saw, dead ahead, the live oak split and start to fall in slow motion toward the road. That tree had stood there for years, even after being struck by lightning in a long-ago thunder storm. He stepped on the gas and the Plymouth jerked forward, the wind and rain beating against the windshield so hard that he couldn't see. He heard branches settle on the trunk but the car was still moving so he guessed he'd made it all right. *Well,* he thought, *that was another live oak that the preservationists had prevented from being cut. If the thunderbolts don't get 'em, the winds, or some other force in nature, will. Yessiree Bob! That sucker was gone for good.*

⤫

Once out of the van, Billy steadied himself before leaning into the wind and starting toward the porch. The wind plastered the tarp against his body and the back of it sailed outward. The strength of the wind, plus the added draw of the billowing tarp, forced him backward and for a moment he feared he might lose Tennessee. Finding himself backed against the trunk of a palm, he waited until the gale had diminished before continuing. He was halfway to the porch when a frond, catapulted by a gust of wind, hit him. He waited until his head had cleared, and with fear providing the strength to move, he again moved toward the porch but stopped when an electrical pole split like a toothpick, its felled wires sparkling like fireworks and hissing, as they moved along the edge of the parking lot.

❦

Upstairs, Grace had cracked the window in the opposite end of the hallway as Annie had suggested and was now heading for the door that led down to the kitchen when Annie called, "Oh, what a wonderful watercolor."

Grace turned. "That was painted by a snowbird from St Paul."

"Snowbird?"

"That's what they call people from up north who come down here every winter," Grace explained. She was about to say more about the painting when there was another blast of wind.

"We gotta get back downstairs," she said. "Safer down there."

Walt opened the front door for Billy who headed straight for the men's room. Running back, Walt mopped up the water that had blown in. When the floor was reasonably dry, he ran the mop back behind the bar, grabbed the bottle of Old Grand-Dad, held it high, and took a swig from the pouring spout.

"Right," Annie said loudly. "Let's get back downstairs."

Warned that they were returning, Walt ran to the other side of the bar and seated himself as Grace entered the bar from the kitchen. "How'd the floor get wet?" she asked.

"Door blew open," Walt answered. "Rain got Billy. He's changing his shirt and pants."

❦

In the SEÑORS, Billy propped the body against the far wall of the stall, locked the door from inside, crawled out from underneath, removed his wet clothing, dried himself with paper towels and hurriedly put on fresh underwear, dry trousers and the red-checked shirt. He wrapped the wet clothes in paper towels and deposited them at the bottom of the duffel bag along with the nineteen-thirty-two map. He took a deep breath and turned the knob of the door that opened into the bar.

∽

On highway Seventy-Five, just ahead of the Ford, downed electric wires whip-lashed the highway and grounded a car. The Blonde screamed as other downed wires snaked in various directions. When the pyrotechnics had subsided, people climbed out of their vehicles to help an injured driver, and the already snail-like traffic came to a standstill.

"Aren't you going to get out and help that poor man?" The Blonde asked.

"Fuck 'em! There's gotta be a whole posse of Samaritan A-holes already on the scene."

Samaritan A-holes! People trying to save a man's life? She couldn't stand it. Who in all of life and literature was this man like? No prototype of a sociopath that she knew. Even when she read "Mein Kampf," she had managed to find a few isolated places—his dropping out of high school, his mother's death, being rejected as a painter by the Academy of Arts, and being gassed and wounded in WWI—where she could feel pity for Adolph Hitler. But Ezekiel Rycheck was an anomaly.

They were just a few miles north of Golden Gate, the entrance to Alligator Alley that would take them over to Ft. Lauderdale. But it took a long time for the ambulance to thread its way through the snarl of traffic that was backed up almost to Bonita Springs. When it finally did pass, lights flashing and siren blaring, there was a further delay before the paramedics did what they had to do, loading the injured man into the ambulance and making their way through traffic that was by now backed up to the Fort Myers International Airport. But even after the ambulance was gone, the traffic didn't move.

"Goddamn! Fuck!" Ezekiel yelled.

The temper tantrums, The Blonde thought. There was something of an uncontrollable infantile rage in Ezekiel. It was just plain abnormal for a grown man to get so mad.

The traffic eventually began to inch forward.

"Lots of traffic headed north," The Blonde observed, noting that the cars were bumper to bumper in the three lanes across the meridian.

∾

"Thought maybe you'd fallen in," Grace said as Billy emerged from SEÑORS.

"Is everything OK?"

Billy smiled to reassure her.

Nodding in Walt's direction, Grace confided to Annie in a low voice, "I have a soft spot in my heart for poor old men. Why shouldn't they drink? Work all their lives, pay all that money into social security, then it's 'over the hill to the poorhouse trudging their weary way.' I just love Will Carleton's poems, don't you?"

When Walt made a gagging noise, Billy looked at him and shook his head.

"Would you like a glass of water?" Grace asked.

Walt shuddered. "No thanks, just another Old Grand-Dad, straight up."

From the sound of the wind Billy could tell the storm was getting worse. He knew, by the way Grace was chumming up to Annie that she was scared and was glad that they were there.

As she fixed Walt's drink, Grace said, "This place is not the tropical paradise we envisioned when we bought it, but it's not as bad as some of those other places in Florida; Clearwater for instance.

Clear water, that's a laugh. Sarasota, Palm Beach, even the Keys, all high rises, condos and blue-haired widows."

∽

As soon as Hurricane turned into the parking lot he saw the V.W. He turned off his headlights, parked on the van's far side, put on his yellow slicker, and went behind the vehicle to check the license plate. He attempted to open the doors but they were locked. He directed his flashlight through a window and saw digging equipment. That, and the license plate, was all he needed. He checked the chamber of his revolver, climbed up on to the porch, and entered.

Billy felt the wind on his back and thought the door had blown open. When he saw the uniformed policeman he instinctively sat back down.

"Hurricane! Boy, oh boy, are you a sight for sore eyes," Grace said. "I tried to call the station but the line was busy."

Billy could see by her outstretched arms that the cop was more than just another fuzzy dropping by for free java on a stormy night. But when she threw her arms around him, he stood stiff and unmoving; something about his stance made Billy shiver, some long ago scene instinctively known but not clearly remembered.

"Let me help you with your raincoat," Grace said.

"Blowing up pretty bad out there," Hurricane smiled. "They say she'll hit shore halfway between here and Naples."

"Then it's a darn good thing you folks didn't move on," Grace said. "What's the wind?"

"A hundred and thirty miles an hour near the eye." But while he addressed Grace, his eyes were on Billy.

"Your name's Hurricane?" Billy said, not coming up with anything better to say.

"That's right, my name's Hurricane."

"What'd they call you that for?" Annie asked.

"Because I was born during a hurricane. September eighteenth, nineteen-twenty-six."

Annie broke into a big smile; "Happy birthday, one day early."

"Happy birthday," Billy added.

The cop turned and locked eyes with Billy, sending an electric current through him.

"In the twenty-six one, Lake Okeechobee overflowed," Hurricane said absently. It sounded to Billy as though the big cop was disconnected from his thoughts, as though on automatic pilot.

"Over three hundred people drowned, damage estimated at one hundred and sixty-five million and that's when a dollar was a dollar."

"Officer, let me buy you a birthday drink," Walt said. Then to Grace, "And I'll have another."

"How about it?" Grace asked Hurricane.

"Thanks. Don't mind if I do. A Bud will do me fine."

When Hurricane snapped the can open and raised it in some sort of a salute, there was another loud gust of wind and Grace looked at the ceiling and shivered. Hurricane patted her arm. "It's okay," he said, He turned to Billy. "That your van out there?"

"Yes, sir."

"Noticed it when I drove up, don't see many of them VW vans on the road anymore. Let's see now, what year is it?"

Billy knew that the cop knew the year but answered anyway, "Nineteen-sixty-eight."

"Florida's just like New York only worse," Grace said to Annie, "Miami being the murder capital of the world."

"How many miles you got on her?" Hurricane asked.

"Over three hundred thousand."

"That's a lot of miles."

"I mean the kids don't even visit," Grace said. "No one wants to visit because when they want to visit, you know, like in January or February, it's too cold."

"Travel a lot?" the cop asked.

"Not too much," Billy answered.

"Last year it got down to twelve above," Grace said.

"You must have traveled some to get three hundred thousand miles on her," Hurricane observed.

"Bought her secondhand," Billy told him.

"We had to keep the toilet running all night so the pipes wouldn't freeze. Colder here than in New York."

"Previous owner must have traveled a lot," Hurricane commented.

"Yes sir, appears so."

"Most of the bums in Miami went up north. At least up there they could get on a warm air grate."

"You from New York?" the cop asked.

"I am," Annie said before Billy could answer.

"The orange crop down here was destroyed," Grace said.

"Where you from?" he asked.

"Washington."

"Up in New York they were selling oranges on the sidewalks."

"I was in Washington once. Saw..."

When he said it, something happened in Hurricane's throat, a kind of catch, so that he had to stop talking.

"What?" Billy asked.

"War Memorial, with all them names raised on panels." He again stopped talking.

"Oh," Annie said, "you're talking about D.C. Billy's from Washington State."

"Pretty country up that way, I hear," Hurricane said to Billy.

"Yes, sir."

"Oh!" Grace said, "I forgot to introduce everyone. This is Annie, Walt and Billy."

Billy extended his hand.

Hurricane shook it. "And you're from the state of Washington?"

"Yes, sir. Seattle."

"License plate is from New York." The cop added casually, "Just happened to notice when I drove up."

The hell you did, Billy thought, *not with the van backed into the parking space.*

"It's my van," Annie said, "I bought the license plate in New York. That's where I'm from. Oh, I'm not from there," she added quickly, "but that's where I settled."

"Why?" Hurricane asked.

"That's where the work was."

"I see."

"The vehicle registered in your name?"

"Yes," Annie answered.

"Visiting people down here?" Hurricane asked.

"No, sir," Billy replied. At the same moment Annie answered, "Yes."

"On vacation?"

Billy said, "Yes, sir," and Annie answered, "No."

Hurricane chuckled knowingly, "'Pears one of you is visiting and one vacationing. Pretty bad month to vacation in Florida," he told Billy.

"That's what we're finding out," Annie said before Billy could answer.

Hurricane didn't bother turning in her direction. He asked, his voice low but filled with menace, "Lady, why don't you let the boy answer for his self?"

During the silence that followed, Billy unconsciously started drumming on the table top.

Hurricane watched him for a moment. "Grace?"

"Yes?"

"You ever hear of a grave robbing?"

"Why, what do you mean?"

"I mean, someone digging up a dead body."

Billy stopped drumming.

"I been in law enforcement for a number of years and this is the first time I ever run across such a crime."

"Well, there was that case you told me about last night," Grace said.

Hurricane turned to Walt and Annie. "What do you folks think about some low-life scum who would kidnap a body that's in a grave?"

"Give me a refill?" Walt asked Grace.

"Sure."

"Kidnap means to carry someone away against his will by unlawful force, doesn't it?" Walt asked.

"You could say that," Hurricane answered.

"What if the carrying away was not against the person's will?" Walt continued.

Hurricane smiled and turned back to Billy, "Your friend here a lawyer?"

"What if a body didn't want to be buried where it was buried, what would you call that; to unlawfully bury a person someplace against his will?"

Hurricane thought a moment. "I don't know what you would call that."

"Buried next to the last person on earth he wanted to be buried next to," Walt was angry.

"Who'd that be?" Hurricane asked casually.

Walt's answer, "His mother," was covered by a sudden increase of the howling of the wind from a crack in one of the casements.

The cop watched as Billy's fingers beat out a rhythm on the table top. "You nervous, boy?"

"No, sir, why?"

"All that drumming with your fingers."

"Does it make you nervous?" Billy asked, looking the cop in the eyes. "I'll stop."

"I heard that an undertaker up in Richmond, Indiana, told the police in St. Louie that three people stopped in, couple, three days back, inquiring…"

"What about?" Annie asked casually.

"About how to exhume a body," Hurricane replied, keeping his eyes on Billy. "In what condition they could expect to find the body, how was a vault sealed, things like that."

"Why would anyone want to know *that*?" Annie asked.

"This undertaker said there was a girl," Hurricane said, now looking directly at her. "Had red hair." He turned to Walt. "An old man with a beard…."

"Did you know," Walt said over the crying sound of the wind, "that you have a prominence in your left eye?"

"How's that?" Hurricane asked.

"The right eye of a man looks forward into eternity; the left, backward. The prominence in your left eye means that you're looking backward into time. Not until your left eye is brought into focus with your right eye will you ever achieve any…unity of vision."

Walt held the cop's gaze for a moment before he turned to Grace. "I'll have another."

While Walt had been talking, Billy saw Grace looking from Walt to Annie and then at him. "Oh, my God!" she gasped. "Hurricane, are you saying…?"

"Interesting thing to me," Hurricane interrupted, "is that if they took the body out of the van where'd they put it?" He moved behind the bar. "Back of a VW bus would be a good place to stash a body but if there's no body on the bus…a body ain't an easy thing to hide." Bending over to check under the counter, Hurricane was, for the moment, hidden behind the bar. That's when Billy made the mistake of looking in the direction of the men's room.

"Uh-huh," Hurricane said, having risen faster than Billy had expected, heading for the SEÑORS.

"Hurricane," Billy said, his voice low but urgent.

Hurricane stopped.

"Let me lay something on ya," Billy said, trying to keep his voice steady.

"What is it?"

"Something that might explain..."

Hurricane hesitated before he moved back and perched on the edge of a table. "Okay, shoot," he said.

"Sometimes, things are hard to understand if you go at 'em direct." Billy paused a moment to come up with a sideways approach. "Once I looked out this window and I saw a canary. It was late March and I saw a whole flock of canaries flying over a field. Canaries don't fly as fast as humming birds, tiny bird that zips around like crazy. You know humming birds? Beat their wings so fast it makes a humming sound...can't even see 'em they go so fast, only a blur. Of course, canaries don't fly as fast as humming-birds. Anyway, I'm looking out this window and I think what are canaries doing the last week of March flying over this field?"

"Maybe you were just seeing things." Hurricane smiled a smile that was not a smile in the ordinary sense. It had sorrow behind it.

"No, no, no, no, man. No! I wasn't mistaken."

"It was a flock of canaries?" the cop asked.

"Yeah. What I'm trying to do is to make you see one thing for another like Walt sometimes does. See, Walt's a poet. He might have seen the canaries as a metaphor."

"For...?"

"Freedom! See, like these crazy, little darting canaries, in winter, in the middle of a field are doing what they need to do."

"I don't see."

"Like regardless of what happens to them, they're free. That's like a poet being buried where he wants to be buried."

Hurricane's face flushed with anger, "All right, goddamn it! Let's cut the re-bop!" Breathing hard, he headed for SEÑORS. He paused at the door and looked back at Billy, shook his head as if to clear his sight, and entered the bathroom.

Billy hardly dared to breathe. Then he heard a sound that could only be made by the cop putting his shoulder against the steel door of the toilet stall, breaking the metal lock and it hitting the tile floor. There was no sound now except his heartbeat over the outside sounds of wind and rain.

༄

At the entrance of the toll road called Alligator Alley, two patrol cars with whirling red lights blocked the highway. "The Alley's flooded. You'll have to go back up to Ft. Myers and cross on Eighty to South Bay and then take Twenty-Seven down to Lauderdale," a patrolman instructed Ezekiel.

"You haven't seen a sixty-eight VW van pass, have you?" Ezekiel inquired, casually.

The patrolman laughed. "Twenty-five big ones for the return of the body, you think we'd let that pass?"

"Are there places to stay on coastal road Forty-One?"

"Yeah, several towns if you're not in a hurry to get to Lauderdale. Seems they weren't hit too bad over that-a-way."

Ezekiel seemed calm as he swung the Ford at a leisurely pace into the cross-over road that led to Forty-One. The Blonde would have predicted he would have blown up at the cop as though it was the cop's fault that Alligator Alley, built over a swamp, was flooded and closed. But as soon as they were out of sight of the officers, Ezekiel screamed, "Fuck!" and floored the gas pedal, sending the car upwards of eighty miles an hour on the wet two-lane road.

"You're drivin' crazy," The Blonde told him. "Slow down!"

She ducked in time to avoid the back of his hand full force on her jaw.

༄

Hurricane returned to the dining room and gave Billy a look that was hard as steel, contrasting the disappointment in his sagging shoulders. Everything was the same as when he'd left the room. Only nothing was the same. Nothing, Billy sensed, would ever be the same again.

Hurricane pointed to a table. "Sit down," he said without emotion.

In the silence that followed, the storm's velocity increased. Billy heard objects, he imagined coconuts, hit with the speed of a fast-pitched baseball against the side of the building.

"Grace," Hurricane said when the three were seated at the table, "maybe you'd be more comfortable upstairs in the apartment."

"No," Grace said, "I'm more comfortable right here." She sat at one of the bar stools facing them.

Billy was glad Grace was staying. He sensed an ally in her and figured he would need all the help he could get.

"You know your rights, anything you say can be used against you," Hurricane told him.

"Yeah, I know all about that."

"Well then, go ahead, start."

"The plan was fairly simple," Annie said.

"Let the boy tell it."

Billy quickly told Hurricane the facts of their journey. When he was finished Hurricane seemed perplexed. "Didn't it pass through your mind that asking questions of an undertaker might be incriminating?"

"The reason we stopped to see Mr. Willis was that we were unsure about what condition the body'd be in," Billy explained. "All any of us knew was what Walt said, a tanner's body would last nine years."

Hurricane looked at Walt. "Tanner? Tennessee was a singer."

"A poet," Walt corrected.

Hurricane thought a moment. "Well, if...if your people wanna call him that," he said and turned back to Billy. "I'm surprised they didn't catch you in St. Louie. I can't think of a worse crime than grave robbing." Hurricane shook his head. "Now, you told what you done but you didn't tell me why you done it. What's the motive for doing such a damn fool thing?"

"We did it because..."

"No, let me," Walt interrupted. "It was my idea. You see..."

"It was mine," Billy and Annie said in unison.

"Well, I see you two finally agree on something." Hurricane turned back to Walt. "All right, so if it was your idea, why would you?"

Walt knew that explaining the why for doing such "a damn fool thing" was not going to be easy, nor could he very well say, "Just trust me." Instead, he said, his voice low, "No one ever made the connection."

"What connection you talking about?" Hurricane asked.

"I'm talking about the connection between the two poets."

∽

It was the fall of nineteen-sixty-nine. Students in tie-dyed tee shirts protested the Vietnam War outside on the mall, but inside the lecture hall the professional theater students ("Be there, on time, and prepared – or else!") from the School of the Arts listened to Walt's lecture.

"Thirty-eight years ago," he said in his deep, sonorous voice, the American poet Hart Crane, returning from a Guggenheim fellowship in Mexico, walked to the fantail of the cruise ship, the Orizaba, on which he was returning to New York and an illustrator's job that he hated, looked into the blue-green water, and purportedly said, 'this is not a time for poets.' He folded the coat he was wearing, draped it over the railing, and leaped to his death. Hart Crane most certainly may have influenced Tennessee Williams in his play, 'The Night of the Iguana,' today's assigned play."

He picked up a book—"Hart Crane, The Life of An American Poet" by Philip Horton—and read: "'During a visit to Taxco, in nineteen-thirty-two, Hart Crane met the Mexican painter David Siqueiros, and sat for him for his portrait. That the painting represented him with lowered lids was owing to the fact that Siqueiros, despite repeated efforts, could not paint Crane's eyes, so startling were they, so desperately expressive of the fate that was poised within him, ripe for fulfillment.'"

Looking up from the reading, he asked, "Do you connect this with any lines in 'Iguana'?"

Smart and beautiful eighteen-year-old freshman Ann Laurel, raised her hand.

"Yes, Annie," Walt said.

"In 'Iguana', Hannah says to the defrocked minister, Shannon…" She took time to find the place in the text. "'When the Mexican painter, Siqueiros, did his portrait of the American poet Hart Crane, he had to paint him with closed eyes because he couldn't paint his eyes open. There was too much suffering in them and he couldn't paint it.'"

The poet's death, the tragedy foreseen by the painter, brought sudden sadness to Walt's eyes. "Do you think that Tennessee may have read Horton's book before writing his play?"

"Absolutely," Annie replied.

"So do I."

Ann Laurel graduated *summa cum laude* in the spring of 1973 and gave a brilliant commencement speech. After the ceremony, she introduced Walt to her mother and told him some good news. As part of the professional training program, senior actors in the Theatre Arts and Film Division appeared in scenes before New York City theatrical agents. From these auditions, Annie had received several call-backs including one from the powerful June Saffron Agency. She promised to call Walt and leave her number just as soon as she got her phone installed. They hugged and she disappeared into the commencement crowd.

Perhaps it was the realization of the life-cycle of arrivals and departures, as though Walt were in a play by Chekhov that accounted for the fact that he decided he wanted to spend some time on researching the influence of Hart Crane on Tennessee Williams.

His retirement was "roses, roses all the way and tears and cheers and goodbye Mr. Chips"—albeit retirement of the school's one black professor poster-boy caused some stir in Albany but not enough to counter the financial gain by the considerable savings in salary.

Then, years later, in 1982, Walt had his first face-to-face meeting with Tennessee. The two old men walked slowly, protected from an early afternoon sun by the canopy of leafy August branches hanging from the gnarled limbs of giant trees. The walkway, known as the Poets' Walk, in New York's Central Park, led toward Bethesda Fountain.

"The proposed writing," Walt replied in answer to Tennessee's question (he took a moment wanting to get it right) "is about connections. People don't understand one another unless they connect on some personal level and on a subject of mutual interest. Since you and Hart Crane never met, I'm attempting to find in his poetry what would have appealed to you when you were young 'Tom' Williams."

Tennessee's high giggle was piercing. "It doesn't take a rocket scientist to understand that, Professor. I heard he was hung like a horse."

Ah yes, the bawdy smart-ass answer, Walt thought, *and not exactly right but so refreshingly un-academic.*

"If you do eventually write a book what would be its title?" Tennessee asked.

"I'm thinking of calling it 'Taking Tennessee to Hart.'"

Three months later he was again on the Poets' Walk with Tennessee. Leafless gnarled branches overhung the walkway and there was, in the air, a touch of wintery frost. Walt had been pontificating in a desperate attempt to convince himself of Whitman's 1885 prophecy.

"What exactly was this prophecy that you keep harping on?" Tennessee asked cordially.

"Whitman predicted that 'the soul of the largest and wealthiest and proudest nation on earth might well go halfway to meet that of its poets, and the proof of a poet is that the poet's country absorbs him as affectionately as he has absorbed it'."

Gales of Tennessee's high pitched giggles echoed down the empty walkway. "God knows that in the past few years, the critics have not absorbed me with any affection. 'Mistuh Williams, he dead,' one said; 'His new play is more deserving of a coroner's report than a review,' said another. 'A play by a man at the end of, not his talent (that was long ago), but his tether,' and the coup de grace: 'His talent is white dwarfish. Like a faint, very dense star whose light filters vainly back to earth.' And as far as absorbing *any* American poet affectionately, see for yourself. There!" He pointed to the walk's beginning. "The statue of Shakespeare. Was Shakespeare an American poet? And over there is one of Chris Columbus; in tight sailor trousers walking down forty-second street; 'fresh sea food' maybe, but never, never a poet."

Tennessee moved down the walkway. "Now there's a statue of Scottish novelist and poet, Sir Walter Scott and opposite, one of the Scottish poet Robert Burns. The Scots take care of their own, Mr. Andrew Carnegie perhaps? And further on—why who, who, sir, do we have here?—a statue of Fitz-Greene Halleck."

Walt was perplexed, "I'm afraid I don't have a clue as to what he wrote."

"I checked him out," Tennessee enthused with such a degree of maliciousness that even his southern drawl did not temper his remarks. "Mr. Halleck co-authored a humorous column for The New York Post early in the nineteenth century and he wrote an elegy on the death of Drake called 'Green Be the Turf above Thee.' You see money talks, baby, and for many years Mr. Halleck was personal secretary to Mr. John Jacob Astor."

Tennessee let these words sink in before adding. "If then, as Mr. Whitman predicted, poets are absorbed by their country, where are the statues of—and I'll undoubtedly leave someone out here— Henry Wadsworth Longfellow, Edgar Allan Poe, Walt Whitman, Emily Dickinson, Robert Frost, Carl Sandberg, T. S. Eliot, Hart Crane, Edna St. Vincent Millet, or Langston Hughes? Look around you, baby. Where, on the Poets' Walk, in this, the greatest and richest country on earth, where do you find 'affectionate absorption' of poets by their countrymen?"

It was some months after the death of Tennessee and his burial in St. Louis that Walt failed to return one night to his room at the Charles. Billy figured he might have gone to the park under the Brooklyn Bridge. It was there he and Annie found him in a mood of bitter despair.

"Oh, I have a plan of action to take Tennessee to Hart," he said mockingly. "How? Well, simply by recruiting a couple of former students to go on a road trip with me. We will take a side trip to Garrettsville, to visit the memorial for Hart Crane, then proceed on to Calvary Cemetery in St Louis, exhume Tennessee in the middle of the night, put his body in the clean white sack he requested in the codicil we witnessed and signed, and carry it to Jupiter Light, where we would go out ten miles, and drop him overboard at high noon, in a blaze of sunlight.

"Just think of the pages of print news and hours of media coverage such an act would receive. Oh, sure! And if you believe that," he said with a sweep of his hand, "I've got a bridge to sell you. How in hell could burying a dead poet where he wanted to be buried compete with the really important news stories of the day such as the relationship of Koo Star and Prince Andrew, the dating of Burt Reynolds and Loni Anderson, or crowning a New Zealander, Lorraine Downes, as Miss Universe, or accusing George Brett of using pine tar to juice his bat and beat the Yankees? In fact, if one were to rob a grave of any American poet, you'd play hell finding out a damn thing about it. Why? Because...'this is not a time for poets'."

Above and to the left of them the great swag of the bridge was outlined against a full moon and the smell of the sea from the river was in his nostrils.

He was quiet for some time after his rant; the kind of quiet filled with the sound of raw nerve endings and despair, broken finally when he murmured, "And to think his body was taken back to St. Pollution and buried next to his..." Suddenly, he looked up at the span of the bridge and the moon, and raised a clenched fist, "Goddamn it! Hart and Tennessee were meant to be together."

"Yes," Annie said, for she felt what he felt.

At the anger, urgency and pain of Walt's voice and Annie's sympathetic affirmation, Billy said in a voice strong and clear. "Well, if it means that much to you, if what Tennessee wanted is that important, why don't we just go ahead and do it?"

"What?" Walt asked.

"Take Tennessee to Hart."

"How?"

"I'm not one of your former students," Billy said, "but Annie is. And I'd be glad to go along. Hell, the three of us could do it."

There was silence.

"But how," Annie asked.

"Just dig him up and take him to where Hart's buried," Billy answered, "like Walt said."

"But..." Walt stammered, "I was only being cynically ironic when I said it. I didn't actually mean...literally..."

"I thought you meant it," Billy said, his disappointed indelible. "But, whether you meant it or not, we could still do it if that's what you want. It's just putting a shovel in the ground, pressing down, and digging."

What had attracted Walt when they first met was the boy's hope. Hope was like one clear light radiating outward from Billy's center. For Walt, the light of hope had grown dim, almost to extinction in the last few months since Tennessee died and the codicil had been ignored. But in Billy, hope seemed always present, and it had obviously surmounted private grief and loss to which all flesh is heir, including the indifference of a weary world. Billy was Emily Dickinson's "Hope is the thing with feathers that perches in the soul and sings the tune without the words, and never stops at all."

"Yes," Walt said at length, "You're right. We could do that."

"Yes we could," Annie repeated.

"Yes," Walt murmured, "and as I see it now, in the red light of the womb, it is an idea of youth and magic."

"All right!" Billy said, his heart filled with joy.

༄

Now, Billy's heart was in his throat. Hurricane had stood there with growing impatience for what seemed like an eternity while Seemed like an eternity while Walt grappled with what he was going to say next to explain their motive "for doing such a damn fool thing."

"Yes," Walt said at last, "in a nutshell that's probably the answer to why we did it. Up to this point no one had understood the importance of the connection between these two poets."

Hurricane waited a moment before he answered. "You call Tennessee a poet."

"He was a playwright and poet," Walt asserted.

"What he was—at least to every person I know who hasn't lost all his marbles—was one of the best damn country-western singers in the business."

Now, it was Walt who looked confused. "Tennessee?"

"You never heard him sing?"

"I didn't know he could sing."

Hurricane turned to Billy. "Well it's damn hard for me to understand how anyone who grave robbed his body wouldn't know that Tennessee Ernie Ford was one of the best..."

"Tennessee Ernie Ford?" Walt asked.

Hurricane turned. "Now you pretend like you don't know who he is?"

"But the body in there is Tennessee Williams."

"Now hold on a minute," Billy told Walt. "We got a little confusion going on here that I think I can straighten out."

"I know who Tennessee Williams is," Grace said to Hurricane, sounding annoyed, "and I told you the other night that I didn't think Tennessee Ernie Ford was dead."

"I don't think Tennessee Ernie Ford is dead, either," Billy said.

"Damn it, we're talking about a poet, a playwright," Walt said.

Billy leapt in to save the situation. Turning to Hurricane, he said, "Walt felt that Tennessee Williams should be buried next to Hart Crane because there's a connection between 'em. And, Tennessee wrote this request in a codicil to his will. We know this is true because Annie and I went along with Walt to sign as witnesses."

"Tennessee called me late one evening," Walt explained "and asked me to come to the Elysée Hotel and bring two people as witnesses to sign a codicil to his will."

"In the codicil," Billy cut in, "he wrote that he wanted his body to be put in a clean white sack and dumped overboard so he could rest next to Hart Crane. This was his wish, so all I'm saying is that this codicil should have been honored and that someone broke the law in *not* burying him where he wanted to be buried. That's illegal isn't it? At least it should be."

Billy guessed that it was because Hurricane didn't want Grace mad at him that made him pull in his horns. But for whatever reason, Hurricane simply shook his head and said, "Well, that's a horse of a different color. I ain't arguing that. After all legal is right and illegal is wrong, period. All I'm saying is that I *can* understand digging up Tennessee Ernie Ford for ransom but why anyone would dig up...?"

Billy interrupted. "Tennessee Williams was pretty famous, too. You may not remember what for right now but I know how you can place him."

"How?"

"You know Hank Williams?"

"Everybody's heard of Hank Williams for god's sake."

"You ever hear of a country-western singer named Don Williams?"

"Of course."

"You ever hear Don Williams sing Bob McDill's 'Good Ole Boys'?"

Hurricane tried to place it.

"'I can still hear the soft Southern wind in the live oak trees'," Billy sang. "'And those Williams boys, they still mean a lot to me, Hank *and Tennessee*, I guess we're all gonna be what we're gonna be. So what do you do—'"

"'...with good ole boys like me.'" Hurricane spoke the last line. "Yeah, I remember, that song.'"

"Well, Tennessee's the other Williams boy mentioned in that song."

Hurricane mumbled, "Next time I hear it I'll listen a little closer."

Realizing the story was getting to Hurricane, Billy felt a need to press the advantage. "And Walt said that Tennessee Williams was not exactly appreciated toward the end of his life."

"Appreciated," Walt exclaimed. "He was absolutely castigated by the critics."

Fearing that Walt would slide into a full rant and get Hurricane pissed off, Billy interrupted. "And since Tennessee wrote in his will, saying when he died, he wanted to be sewn up..."

"Yeah, you already told me," Hurricane cut him off. "But none of this explains why *you* would do a damn fool thing like getting involved in this hare-brained scheme."

This time Walt spoke before Billy could stop him. "Hart Crane once said: 'It's a poet's business to risk, not only criticism, but folly, in the conquest of consciousness, to make people aware of something within themselves, and this duty is so great that the poet is given license to try anything, no matter how it's judged.'"

"Well, I can tell you that," Hurricane shot back. "It's gonna send you to jail, that's how it's gonna be judged."

Billy knew as soon as Walt started that it was a miscalculation. Squatted on his hams before the cop. he said, "Remember in the song when Don Williams sings, 'I guess we're all gonna be what we're gonna be'? Well, what Bob McDill is writing is...you're gonna be what you're gonna be and you're gonna do what you're goin' do regardless. If a guy drinks himself to death, like Hank Williams did, that's what he's gonna do."

A blast of wind blew a heavy object against one of the plywood window coverings. The sound of it caused Billy to lose his balance. He reached his hand back to catch himself. Hurricane grabbed hold of his arms as if to steady him. As he did, he saw the cellophane in the pocket of Billy's red-checked shirt.

What happened next happened fast. The cop's hand tightened on Billy's upper arms as he jerked him to his feet, spun him around and shoved him against the bar.

"Raise your hands. High!"

"What the hell are you doing?" Annie yelled.

"Just stay right where you are," Hurricane yelled back.

"You can't shove people around like that."

Hurricane's breath was coming fast. So was Billy's. But the boy hung loose while Hurricane did a quick frisk down the sides of his trousers, inside the trouser legs, around his waist, and up his chest.

"No weapons, I'm clean, man," Billy said in a low voice.

"The hell you are!" Hurricane plucked the plastic bag from Billy's breast pocket.

Billy turned to face the cop. "Hey, man, it's just what's left of a lousy nickel bag."

An angry Hurricane smacked him.

The backhand stunned Billy. He was beginning to like Hurricane and to think that someplace deep down, Hurricane liked him. "Back off," he said, his voice low and intense. "Don't you ever hit me."

Grace's scream caused Billy to turn and to instinctively reach out and catch the back of the chair about to come crashing down on Hurricane's head. He held it in his hands for a moment before throwing it to the floor. "You shouldn't have done that, Walt," he said. Billy knew that Walt was not a violent man, had probably never been in a real fight in his life. And now he'd done this incredibly dumb thing.

"I'm sorry," Walt said his voice breaking as his body buckled and he sank onto a chair, covering his face with his hands.

The wind moaned.

Billy turned to Hurricane. "Walt didn't mean it, honest to god," he said.

"The hell he didn't," Hurricane growled.

"No, I know Walt. He just got pushed too far."

"If you hadn't…" Grace said touching his arm.

"Another dope head." Hurricane's voice was husky as he held the clear plastic bag up against the light. "And I almost fell for your line of bullshit. Shoulda known you'd be like all the rest."

"I never smoked any of that. It was given me by the guy I work for just before we left, just enough for a couple of jays, less than half an ounce, man."

"You know where this is gonna land you?" Hurricane said as he put the baggie in his pocket.

Billy took some time before he answered. "Yes, sir, I know,"

It was then that the wind stopped. It just stopped. There was an eerie silence.

"Listen, it's over," Grace whispered.

"No, the eye," Hurricane told her. "It's the eye of the storm."

"How long before it hits again?"

"Few minutes to an hour, depending," Hurricane answered.

At Vanderbilt Beach, Ezekiel drove slowly through the rain-drenched parking lot checking the cars. "Goddamn!" he said, "where the hell could they be? They exited onto Forty-One. They were headed to Lauderdale. The cop would sure as hell have seen them if they had made it to the Golden Gate while we were stalled because of that bastard who got himself electrocuted. So it stands to reason they must have found out the Alley was flooded and stopped someplace between here and Fort Myers."

The Blonde wanted to ask if he actually thought the man got on the wrong end of an electrical wire deliberately so as to thwart Ezekiel's mission, but she was too frightened. It was the first time he had swung at her and she could not stand the thought of being hit. Although she had received only a glancing blow, her head was still ringing. If he'd struck her jaw as he intended, he'd have broken it. She had no money. Her only course of action was to get along by babying the son-of-a-bitch until this nightmare journey was over.

"Shoot!" she pouted. "I thought we'd be sure to find the van here. I'm sure we cruised every parking lot in Naples, Jungle Larry's Caribbean Gardens, and North Naples. You don't suppose they went further south toward Naples Manor, do you, Hon?"

"Are you're fucking stupid?" he growled. "Why would they go down the road that goes to Miami?"

"I just thought maybe with the Alley closed, they might take that road across Florida further south and then drive from Miami *up* to Fort Lauderdale."

Ezekiel thought for a moment. "Goddamn! Why are you always so negative?"

"I just want to help, Zekie-Bob."

"Well making me think I made a mistake ain't gonna do nothing for my confidence," he said. "Now shape up or ship out."

"All right, Hon." She turned on the overhead light and opened the map. "Our next place to check parking lots is Naples Park and after that..."

"Naples! East Naples, North Naples, Naples Manor and now Naples Park. Why is every town down here called Naples?"

"Maybe the people came from Naples. Like, you know, in Italy?"

"Don't smart-ass me. Just concentrate on one fuckin' country at a time," he warned her.

"I think you're gonna do it, baby," she purred. "And when you do and you get that corpse away from those mean sons-of-bitches, we're...*you're* gonna be a rich man."

As Ezekiel drove north, the silence was unbearable. "Zekie-Bob," she said. "Can't I turn on the radio?"

"You know I can't stand listening to music," he complained.

"Please, pretty please with sugar on it?"

"Oh, all right. But play the fucker low."

∽

When Hurricane turned back to face Billy, he asked in a voice without inflection, "A while back, when I read you your rights, what'd you mean, you 'knew?' Have you been in trouble with the law before?"

Billy rubbed his jaw and looked at Annie. "Yes," he admitted. "Seven years in the British Columbia Federal Penitentiary."

"Billy!"

It was a cry from Annie's heart and it struck deep into his own.

"What were you doing up there?" Hurricane asked.

"Getting the hell out of the U.S. of A."

"What'd you wanna do that for?"

"To avoid the possibility of getting killed in a war I didn't believe in. No," he said looking at Annie, "that's not right. I did it to avoid the possibility of getting killed, period."

Hurricane asked, "What'd they get you on, as if I didn't know."

"It's a long story."

"Shorten it."

Billy told him how he had been caught with LSD at the Canadian border, spent seven years in prison, was released, how the amnesty law worked for him and how he crossed the border back into the country. "And like John Prine said, 'things were pretty good, not bad, can't complain, but actually everything was just about the same.'"

"I'm gonna have to turn you in." Hurricane's voice was regretful.

"Can't you cut me some slack?" Billy asked.

"Why were you so goddamn dumb?" the cop yelled.

"I already told you. You wanna hear more?"

"Suit yourself."

He had never told Annie. He would tell her now. Although he would be looking at Hurricane, he would be talking to Annie, hoping against hope that she would understand.

"Back in Seattle, I met Clara. We were married. She'd been married before and had two wonderful kids. She had a good job doing computer specs for the government, but I couldn't put white bread on the table. You see, red-blooded American, pull-yourself-up-by-your-boot-strap work isn't exactly plentiful if you haven't gone to college, or if you're a draft dodger and have a record. Every form you fill out, you have to say if you've got a record. Not many want-ads for guys with nice personalities." He waited a moment before he could go on. "Just before Christmas I split. I didn't even get the kids presents." Annie was crying. He had hurt her, hurt her bad, real bad. "See, I didn't have no, what you call connections."

"You don't need connections," Hurricane sneered.

"The hell you don't. You're on the street, you know. You can't even get a place to live without...you need connections. Oh, in Seattle I'm kinda a folk-hero in a few arcane circles." He looked at Annie and said as evenly as he could. "No, Clara was right. I'm nothing."

∽

She'd proclaimed her disdain for him at the end of a long, hectic day. The kids had been having fun, yelling and chasing the dog. The dog barked incessantly. Billy ignored him. He sat in the kitchen and drummed his fingers on the table to the rhythm of a song only he could hear.

"Stop that and get yourselves to bed," Clara snapped.

They had been married almost seven years and he knew it wasn't just the kids that made her yell. When she came back from putting them to bed, he dried as she washed. Without even knowing it he began to drum on a plate. Clara pulled her hands out of the suds and dried them on her apron. "Why do you drum your fingers all the time?"

"I'm a drummer."

"Billy," she said, trying to sound patient like she did with the kids when they got on her nerves. But her lips were thin and bloodless. She rolled her left hand into a fist and pointed to it with her right index finger. "You're thirty-four years old," she said. She pointed to her left index finger which suddenly unsnapped from the fist. "You've got a record." Left middle finger straight up in the air: "With a wife . . ." Left fourth and little finger. ". . . two kids, and..." "Right thumb up. "And you don't even own the drums. Those damn drums belong to Lucy."

Four fingers and two thumbs pointed in the air.

"What are you getting at?" he stammered.

"Don't you see, Hon? You're a six-time loser."

∽

"Clara got it right," Billy said. "I'm just a dying breed of hipster too hip for my own good, lookin' in the window of some bakery, eight cents short of a maple bar." He turned back to Hurricane. "See, when living fast and dying young didn't work out for me I figured I was destined to be an old, old man so I split to New York where I met Walt. I was on the back side of any possibilities, let alone luck. Walt took me in, and after I got a job, I met Annie, one of Walt's students. I met her the night we signed the codicil and walked her home. Walt and Annie were the first people I ever knew who were smart enough to be depressed about abstract things like..."

"Like?"

"Poets." He lowered his head. "Please, man, let us go."

Hurricane sat rigid for a moment before he shook his head.

"If I may say something," Walt said.

"Go ahead."

"First, I apologize for my attempt to harm you."

Hurricane shrugged.

"And I want to preface the rest by saying...what I say, I will probably say in a way that sounds...erudite, scholarly and maybe even unfamiliar, but I'm trying to connect, and these are the only words and ideas I know to do so. To answer your question of why we would do such a damn fool thing, being buried where you or your family want you to be buried is, and has always been, fundamentally important to people. Sophocles wrote in his play *Antigone* more than two thousand years ago about a young woman determined to bury her brother against the wishes of the king. Abraham Lincoln consecrated Gettysburg as hallowed ground for the soldiers from both sides in our Civil War. And in this century there is Flanders Field in France, and the grave of the unknown soldiers in Washington D.C. And every attempt possible was made by all involved to bring back the men lost in battle during both the First and Second World Wars and in Korea."

"And don't forget Vietnam," Billy added. "Solders risk their lives to carry out the bodies of their buddies who were killed in order to ship them home for burial in..."

The sound that escaped from Hurricane was unlike any Billy had ever heard. Not loud, maybe not even loud enough for the others to have heard. It was the sound of an animal having something torn from somewhere deep inside, in this case the guts of this man who had suddenly turned from him. He knew instantly that he and Hurricane had connected.

∽

It was sometime before Annie broke the silence. She said to Grace, "I think this cop of yours is all hat and no ranch."

"How's that?" Grace asked.

Annie turned to Hurricane, "You're all hat and no ranch."

"What the hell's that suppose to mean?" he asked, his voice low.

"You got Billy to spill his guts, but you're still trying to keep yours tucked safely inside."

Hurricane didn't reply. Annie moved in. "I think somewhere underneath that uniform you're not what you want us to think you are. You're playing the scene like you're a tough cop. You got Billy to come clean—things even I didn't know—but—" She looked at Billy. "Which makes no difference, absolutely no difference, in my love for him." She turned back to Hurricane. "But why do I feel that you don't have the guts to be as honest? What's your story? There's something eating on you, isn't there?"

"Leave him alone," Billy said.

"Why?"

"He's not the one responsible here."

"He is."

"No!"

"Yes!"

"No! No one's responsible. Shit happens. It just happens."

The storm hit again. Loose objects became missiles battering the walls of the bar. The roof groaned as though it might be swept away. Billy listened to the howling wind. Grace got off the bar stool and moved closer to Hurricane. "Sounds like the wind's coming from the other direction," she whispered.

"It is," Hurricane said, his voice almost inaudible. "It happens that way after the eye. The strongest gusts, sometimes better than a hundred knots an hour, come right after the passing of the eye. They blow in a different direction to the winds before 'em."

Grace reached out and touched Annie's arm, a gesture the men could not see. Although Grace did not shake her head or utter a word, she communicated her thought: this is not your affair. It's something we don't understand. It's a guy thing, something they have to settle between themselves.

Annie felt a deep respect for Grace's wisdom. Then Grace returned to the bar stool and Annie looked at Billy and smiled. "This is the first time we've yelled at one another. I'm sorry." She turned and went back to her seat where Grace took her hand and gave it a squeeze.

Billy squatted, "Hurricane?"

"Yeah?"

"This gig is me doing the best I can with a hand I was dealt a long time ago. Just once in my life, I need someone in my corner for about half an hour. How about it?"

When Hurricane finally did speak his voice was low, as though he didn't want anyone else but Billy to hear. "I'm sorry I hit you."

"It's okay."

"But you made me so goddamn mad."

"I know."

"Screwing around with that shit."

"I swear I didn't smoke any of it. I'm aged out, man, believe me."

"Well, I believe you and, and I'm sorry I hit you."

"It's not the first knuckle sandwich I ever ate."

Hurricane gave a half smile, "And I'm ashamed to say, it ain't the first I ever gave."

While Walt had been recovering from his attempted act of violence and the humiliation of breaking down and crying, he had listened to the conversations and had come to the conclusion that what had happened during the storm was good. From the time of their first meeting Billy had been searching for acceptance and Walt had accepted him instantly. But that wasn't what the boy needed. What Billy needed was to achieve something for a taskmaster father-figure and Hurricane fit that iconic image. "It's the centrifugal force," he mumbled, "makes the wind blow in the opposite direction; centrifugal, pertaining to impulses transmitted away from a nerve center."

It took a moment for him to understand, but then Hurricane half smiled and blew his nose. "Pollen count's bad."

"It's the humidity," Grace murmured.

"How strong is a hundred knots?" Billy asked.

"Well," Hurricane explained, "a knot is a nautical measure. One nautical mile is six thousand and eighty, point twenty, which is different from your land mile that's figured five thousand, two hundred and eighty, a difference of eight hundred and twenty feet per mile."

Billy had asked the question to get the conversation going in a different direction but it suddenly hit him. "Damn!"

"Don't get all riled up," Hurricane reassured him. "If she didn't take the roof off the first time around she ain't going to now. A hurricane's velocity's on the downside just as soon as she hits land."

"That's not what I mean," Billy said. "You see, when I figured where we was gonna drop Tennessee off, Walt said it was two hundred and seventy-five miles north of Havana. I figured it in land miles."

Hurricane's expression mirrored his interest. "Well, if you did, you got it wrong."

"I wonder how far off we are," Billy said.

"You'll be two hundred and seventy-five times eight hundred, decimal, twenty feet off. That would be..."

Billy noticed that there was absolutely no hesitation before Hurricane started multiplying in his head. "Damn! If you hadn't mentioned knots we would've dumped Tennessee off in the wrong place."

"How'd you know it was two hundred and seventy-five miles north of Havana?" Hurricane asked.

"That's what the book said," Walt answered. "The passenger traffic manager from the Orizaba was quoted as saying that 'Crane jumped overboard two minutes before noon on Wednesday, April twenty-six, nineteen-thirty-two when the vessel was two hundred and seventy- five miles out of Havana.'"

Billy got the map from his duffel as Hurricane cleaned his glasses. "So, Walt got this nineteen-thirties map that shows the sea lanes." Billy pointed. "Those red lines, from Havana to New York. So what'd you get?"

"Son, why don't you pull those tables together," Hurricane suggested. "Make yourself a work bench and figure it out for yourself."

∽

The storm had eventually subsided and a deathly silence pervaded the room. Walt, sitting at one end of their makeshift work bench, sipped an Old Grand-Dad, while Annie, seated at the other end and Grace on a bar stool, watched as Billy crumpled yet another sheet of paper torn from the Blue Jay notebook Grace had provided for his "figuring." Hurricane stood looking over his shoulder as Billy once again wet the tip of the pencil on his tongue and started multiplying.

"Well, what'd you get this time?" Hurricane asked.

"It's about..."

"Goddamn it! There's no 'about' in figures. Figures are exact."

"Don't be so hard on the boy," Grace said gently.

"Well, the answer can't be 'about,' not if he wants to drop the body within hollering distance of where this other...this other 'poet' jumped overboard."

Billy checked his figures. "It's...forty-one, six hundred and seventy-seven, and, eighty-three tenths of a mile."

Hurricane gave a thumbs up. "All right. There, you see, you did it." He slapped Billy on the back.

"How about me rounding her off to forty-one and two-thirds of a mile?"

"What the hell?" Hurricane said expansively. "Body may have shifted some since…"

"Nineteen-thirty-two," Walt prompted.

"Now just figure from Fort Lauderdale where you thought the...'poet' fellow jumped, on up the coast," Hurricane said.

It would have been easy if all Billy had to do was measure a straight line but the sea lane curved slightly so the task took him some time. "Forty-one and two-thirds of a mile would bring us right up to...Jupiter."

"Jupiter!" Walt was excited. "That's it! In his biography, Horton said the ship was sailing ten miles off Jupiter Light."

"It figures out exactly," Billy agreed.

"And all this time I thought Jupiter Light was a lighthouse."

Hurricane looked at the old man. "Jupiter Light *is* a lighthouse."

"I knew the lighthouse was called Jupiter Light, but when Billy first figured the two hundred and seventy-five miles north of Havana it came out to the southern perimeter of Fort Lauderdale. That's why I thought Jupiter Light was off Ft. Lauderdale."

"No," Hurricane said, "it's called Jupiter Light because the light's off Jupiter." Hurricane and Grace exchanged a glance.

"Could you guys use something to drink, a Bud or coffee?" Grace offered.

"Coffee's fine. We'd better keep our heads screwed on straight here if we're gonna get this thing right," Hurricane cautioned.

"And may I have another Old Grand-Dad, doubled?"

Grace looked at Hurricane.

"Oh, go ahead. I doubt he'll have any input on this figuring." Hurricane pulled up a chair and sat across from Billy. "Now, how'd you expect to get ten miles out?"

"We calculated we'd rent us a boat," Billy answered.

Hurricane shook his head. "Risky, forms to fill out, identification, license plate number of your vehicle."

"I never thought of that," Billy admitted.

"You gotta learn to look before you leap, boy."

Billy smiled in remembrance. "It was what my dad used to say before he split."

"A stitch in time saves nine," Grace said, winking at Annie as she served Walt's drink.

"Whoa. Let me think here a second..." Hurricane's brows furrowed. "My Aunt Emily lives just up stream from Jupiter on the Loxahatchee River." He spent another moment thinking the thing through. "I'll just bet you Aunt Emily'd be glad to rent you her boat for little o'nothin', or maybe she'd just let you use it for free."

"Maybe we could call her and find out," Billy suggested.

"Aunt Emily," Hurricane said affectionately, "don't have a phone. She's kinda what you'd call a *re*cluse, peculiar; came down to Florida from Massachusetts; talks a tight-assed Up- East kind of talk. I'll just write her a note." Tearing a sheet from the Blue Jay notebook, he wet the tip of a pencil on his tongue as a prelude to the task of writing.

"How do we get there?" Billy pointed to the map. "Golden Gate toll road?"

Hurricane looked up from his writing, "No, Alligator Alley's clear outta your way. What you're gonna have to do is go back up to Ft. Myers and take highway Eighty over to Clewiston and Belle Glade and then Eight-Eighty to Eighty and on to highway number One where you turn north and go up to Jupiter. When Eighty ends you're just eleven and one-half miles from Jupiter Light. You can't miss it cause there's a big old white house there with one of them widow walks on it."

"Do you think we'll be at risk now that the van's description has been so well publicized?" Annie asked.

"Oh, we gotta get rid of the van. That's prima-facie evidence sitting out there. That van alone is enough evidence to raise a 'presumption of fact' that it was you three robbed the grave."

"Well, how are we going to get over to the east coast of Florida?" Annie asked.

"You can drive my Plymouth," Hurricane said. "I got one burnt-out front light but I don't think anyone's gonna stop you for that. But if they do and you get in trouble, I'll just say you stole it."

Grace frowned. "They can take my car."

Hurricane looked at her and shook his head.

"They can. It's mine and I said they could take it."

"Sure, good idea," Hurricane agreed quickly.

"Better anyway. It's older than your Plymouth, but..." She turned to Annie. "But it drives good and it's very comfortable."

When Billy and Hurricane went outside, there was a moon far up somewhere. Billy couldn't see it clearly because below the moon, layers upon layers of black skimpy clouds drifted quickly in opposite directions. "Awesome," he said.

"I never seen a storm with that much velocity peter out so fast," Hurricane added.

Billy was listening. "Kinda spooky," he said, "No airplane sounds, no cars."

Hurricane drove Grace's Buick while Billy followed in the van. While rounding a curve going south on Forty-One, Hurricane saw oncoming headlights. He instinctively cut his lights and held his arm out the window indicating a left turn.

⁓

Ezekiel had completed the search at Bonita Shore Beach and contemplated taking the beach drive, but decided if the trio had shacked up anyplace for the night it would be at a motel on highway Forty-One, and that was the road he took north.

It was The Blonde who saw the sign, Dixie Bar and Grill, "Only three miles. If it's open maybe I can get a Coke?"

"You and your Coke habit," Ezekiel groused.

It looked ahead that two cars had rounded a curve. "Kill that fucking music," he yelled.

In the car's sudden silence, he turned back to the road but the oncoming headlights had disappeared. "Goddamn! Where'd those suckers go?"

"Who?" The Blonde asked.

"Didn't you see those cars coming this way?"

"No."

"Are you fuckin' blind or somethin'?"

Are you using the F word here as an adjective, she wanted to ask but did not dare. Instead, she soothed, "You're tired and you've had so much Benzedrine. Maybe...maybe you were seeing things."

This was not what Ezekiel wanted to hear and he would have slapped some sense into her silly head if he hadn't had to concentrate on the road.

༄

Within a dozen yards after Hurricane had turned onto a road filled-with-muddy-water he got out.

"What's happening?" Billy asked, as he ran up.

"Turn off the engine," Hurricane told him.

Billy did and waited a minute in the silence before whispering, "Where are we?"

"Corkscrew Swamp Sanctuary." Hurricane's voice was low. "That car headed our way? Maybe it's one of our guys patrolling the area and there's no point in anyone, local or otherwise, seeing the VW or knowing where we're headed."

It was less than a minute before they heard the oncoming car pass the turn off and Billy had no sooner given a sigh of relief when he heard the car brake and back up.

⁓

The Blonde rolled down her window and looked at the side road. "Oh, Zekie-Bob, I don't think anyone in his right mind would use this...it can hardly even be called a road."

"What makes you think they wouldn't have turned in here?"

"Well, look at it. If you turn in here, you're apt to get yourself stuck up to your axle and then where'd we be? I think those cars you saw must be further up the road."

"Lot you know," Ezekiel sneered, getting out. "I'll judge for myself."

As he stood peering down the side road she heard a splash, and then another followed by a terrified moan. Ezekiel stood frozen in his tracks, his back to her, unable to move. "Oh, My God!" he whispered, "They're dropping from the trees." It was then that she saw the two snakes slithering through the muddy water toward him.

She got out of the car. "Water moccasins are good climbers and often hang out on limbs. Notice when their heads are up, like they are now, you can see the white inside their mouths? That's why they're called cotton mouths."

"Kill the fucking reptile lecture," he hissed, "and get me outta here."

"If you hiss like that, they may come after you," she said calmly with a wonderful sense of inner satisfaction. "They're highly venomous and have a heat sensitizer allowing them to detect warm-blooded prey." She hadn't enjoyed herself as much since the trip started. "You seem pretty hot under the collar right now." She could literally smell the fear seeping out of him. "But they're probably more scared of you than you are of them. Just turn around and get back in the car."

She heard the car start. She looked at the two big snakes, heads erect. "Now you guys just go back where you came from," she baby-talked to them.

Before she could snap her seat belt, Ezekiel had floored the accelerator and left tire marks on the road. "They always come out after a storm," she informed him. "Especially a storm with high winds. That's when they just slither inland."

A shiver went through Ezekiel's body. "Don't talk like that," he yelled. "You know I hate snakes."

"Oh, honey," she purred, "Don't tar 'em all with the same brush. Most snakes wouldn't hurt a flea."

❦

As soon as they heard the squeal of the car's tires, Hurricane got back in Grace's Buick and led Billy for about a mile on the rutted dirt road toward the interior of Corkscrew Swamp. They stopped and Hurricane replaced Billy in the driver's seat. Turning the van around, he pulled the choke, revved the motor, let out the clutch and leapt out only seconds before the van plunged into the black muck of the swamp.

The two men watched as the devouring quicksand upended and greedily sucked down the van, its headlights shooting up into the Spanish moss. Even after it submerged, the lights continued to filter through the ooze until darkness covered the swamp's surface.

"That van is G.O.N.E., gone," Hurricane said, and then added, "Quicksand's a powerful thing."

Chapter VII
Sunday, 18 September 1983.

It was past midnight when Billy, Annie and Walt headed north on coast road Forty-One. Above them was a clear narrow strip of sky and further above a bluish moon shone, illuminating a path almost as bright as day. "'The moon, a ghostly galleon tossed upon cloudy seas,'" Walt recited Alfred Noyes' "The Highwaymen." "'The road a ribbon of moonlight…'"

Passing over the bridge that spanned the Caloosahatchee River into Fort Myers, Billy headed east across Florida on two-lane highway Eighty, toward La Belle. As Annie sat beside him, with Walt to her right, her hand placed comfortingly on Billy's thigh, she thought the night the strangest she had ever seen. Low-lying fog shrouded the ground, which was strange considering the velocity of the wind at the height of the storm. The Buick's yellow headlights pierced the fog and the contrast was eerie, as though something in nature was out of sync.

By a sea of saw grass, a great white bird stood on one spindly leg, its neck forming an S and its long tapering bill stretching upward at the startling sky. A pair of herons flew over the road, their whiteness making them seem ghostly in the light of the moon. Other herons stood in drainage ditches, one foot in the water. Spanish moss dripped from overhanging limbs of cypress trees and the car's headlights revealed a dead tree grotesquely covered with kudzu.

On the other side of the road, at a distance, was an island of palms above acres of swamp grass. Once, when the moon was not hidden behind the lacy black swirling clouds, an eagle appeared in silhouette and, dipping its wings for the descent, soared low. On the road a marsh hare, hit by the yellow headlights scurried into the grass. Swooping, the eagle gathered the hare in its talons and soared skyward.

Later, in the yellow beam, Billy saw..."a dead animal?"

"They can play a death scene any actor would envy," Annie said.

"I don't understand."

"It's not dead. It's an opossum. When caught in the headlights they feign death."

"Not a bad defense mechanism," Walt commented.

༄

Ezekiel and The Blonde had spent more than two hours snooping around the various parking lots of Estero, Carlos Park, and Ft. Myers Villas, on highway Forty-One north without success and it was now well past midnight.

"It seems to me that all the traffic is headed out highway Eighty," The Blonde observed. "Why don't we try that? That's how the policeman said you should get over to Fort Lauderdale." She consulted the map. "At South Bay, near Lake Okeechobee, we can turn south on Twenty-Seven and go to Lauderdale."

He did as she suggested, she noted, without a thanks, go to hell or kiss my ass. Under all the meanness, she kept searching for some goodness. Or, maybe evil itself was attractive, and if that was so, she should kill the myth about there being some good in everyone just as she had killed the myth of an omnipotent God.

༄

When a car came from behind without dimming its brights, traveling at a high rate of speed, Billy slowed down to let it overtake the Buick and speed past.

"Guy must be in a hurry." Annie shuddered as the black Ford barely avoided a crash with an oncoming car.

There were fields of sugar cane as they passed Clewiston, "America's sweetest town"; orange groves and citrus processing plants followed.

On the one hundred and thirty mile highway they had not encountered a single patrol car. Things looked good, Billy thought, as he anticipated this last, and most important, part of their journey.

At an all-night gas station-diner, just outside of South Bay, the Ford that had passed them was standing empty at one of the gas pumps. They spotted it immediately, and while Annie was tanking up and Billy squeegeeing the windshield, Walt went to the men's room.

ᕙᕗ

Inside the diner, the TV blaring, a couple of weary truckers were having coffee at the counter in a back booth, The Blonde sat dumbfounded, mouth agape, staring in horror. She had ordered a Coke and Ezekiel a coffee and while waiting, he had caught a big green-backed—"shit house fly" as he called it—caught it with a fast swipe of his hairy paw when the fly landed in some spilt sugar. Instantly cupping his hand into a fist he imprisoned the fly. Uncurling his little finger to make a slight opening, the dazed fly made its way toward freedom. But freedom was not to be. Plucking it up, he tore off both wings and then, releasing it on the table top, leaned back to enjoy the insect's consternation.

"Now try to fly, fucker!" he whispered, a big grin spreading over his face.

The frantic insect attempted to take wing but it could not lift its body from the white chrome tabletop which formed the perfect background on which to observe the result of the amputation. Moving in a tight circle and buzzing frantically, the fly made attempt after attempt to soar as Ezekiel watched in delight. When the waitress brought their order, he gulped his coffee down quickly and told The Blonde, "I gotta take a piss."

The Blonde watched the hideously crippled insect as it moved nearer and nearer to the table's edge. There was no point in attempting to find any good in Ezekiel, she decided. If she ever found an opportunity, without a chance of getting caught, she should kill the son-of-a-bitch.

෬

Just as Walt rounded the corner, Ezekiel exited the men's room. Lowering his eyes immediately, he let the old man pass. Hurrying back to the dining room he looked out the window. Sure enough, there was the hippy, pumping gas and cleaning the windshield of a Buick. Goddamn! The grave robbers had changed vehicles on him. They had abandoned the van and were now driving a big-assed old Park Avenue Buick. Hurrying to the booth, he whispered excitedly, "That's them," and pointed to the man at the gas pump.

෬

Walt went outside, waved to Billy, and pantomimed drinking coffee.

"Walt wants to get a cup of coffee," Billy told Annie who was just returning from a fast moving stretch-out. "After coffee break, you wanna drive?"

"Sure."

"I'll park the car. You go on in and order me a cup of black."

While Annie headed for the diner, Billy drove the Buick to the parking area in front where, conscious of the corpse on the back seat, he parked on the far side of a truck to take advantage of the shadow it cast from the diner's lights.

෬

Inside, the waitress called, "Excuse me, is that black Ford parked in front of pump number one yours?"

"Yeah."

"Would you mind moving it?"

"No problem," Ezekiel answered. He whispered to The Blonde, "Just sit tight."

∽

While Annie was at the cash register paying for the gas she noticed the man leaving the booth and heading toward the Ford. He looked like the actor, Jack Nicholson in "Five Easy Pieces," she decided.

After settling the bill, she sat next to Walt at the counter.

∽

Using the master control in front of the left arm rest, Billy locked the Buick's doors and hurried to join Annie and Walt. As he entered, he saw the Ford moving away from the gas pump and thought how good it was that the maniac driver would be ahead of them on the road.

∽

Making a wide arc to the back of the station, Ezekiel drove the Ford to the far side of the Buick. Establishing the fact that the corpse was on the back seat, he tried opening all four doors. Finding them locked he removed the tire iron from the trunk of his car.

∽

Annie and Walt's orders had been taken at the counter and the waitress was about to pour coffee when Billy arrived. "To go," he said. Bewildered by the sudden change of plans, Annie looked up and followed his intense gaze to the back booth where a young platinum blond sat smiling at him as though they were friends. "I'll wait for you guys outside," he told them in an ominously low voice and hurried out.

∽

If the tire iron did not work, Ezekiel decided that he'd break open one of the back window, pop open the door from inside, snatch the corpse, and leave The Blonde in the diner. How would she get home? Let the bitch hitch. He would collect the twenty-five thousand dollars reward for himself.

He was just about to insert the tire iron into the side of the door when he saw Billy hurrying in his direction. Crouching, he moved quickly, intending to remove his gun from the glove compartment. But when he opened the Ford's door, the overhead light snapped on.

6~9

Billy saw the light. Taking his time unlocking the Buick, he walked slowly around the back as if he needed to unlock the door on the passenger side.

Snatching the opportunity while Billy's back was to the Ford, Ezekiel reached to release the glove compartment's latch. Goddamn! He forgot the fucker was locked.

Billy turned. "Morning," he said, looking Ezekiel full in the face.

"Morning," Ezekiel muttered pretending not to recognize him.

Annie and Walt were now coming from the diner with the take-out coffees. Billy tossed the car keys to Annie, and as they pulled out of the station, he told her, "That guy parked next to us in the black Ford? He's the same guy who stopped me when I was carrying the sleeping bag back to Walt's room at the Best Western in Columbus."

"You sure?" Walt asked.

"Absolutely. And the girl inside with the blond hair was with him."

"Did he recognize you?"

"He pretended not to, which makes me really suspicious."

6~9

Inside the diner, The Blonde watched with horror as the crippled fly edged in desperate circles closer and closer to the table's edge. Ezekiel suddenly reappeared. "Get your ass in the car while I pay the check," he said, swiping the fly off the table top onto the floor and crushing it with a stomp of his foot.

He started the car, but before taking off he decided that he needed the gun. He reached over to unlatch the glove compartment when he remembered it was locked. "Damn!" Turning off the engine resulted in more lost time. He unlocked the compartment, unwrapped the gun from the bandana, checked to see that it was loaded, and placed it on the floor under the seat of his now petrified companion, warning, "Watch where you move them high heels, this baby is loaded."

Traveling fast, he soon was able to see the Buick's tail lights. He slowed down. But at South Bay, where he expected the car to turn right and take highway Twenty-Seven south to Lauderdale, it kept straight ahead.

"Goddamn!" Ezekiel cried, "The sons-of-bitches ain't going to Ft. Lauderdale after all, they're headed toward the coast." As he predicted, the Buick went straight at Belle Glade on back-road Eight-Eighty, due east. "Look on the map," he ordered, "and see where they're headed."

"Palm Beach," she answered in a quavering voice.

The trick now, Ezekiel knew, was to let them keep far enough ahead so that the driver would not suspect he was being followed, and at the same time stay close enough so as not to lose them if they made a turnoff.

∽

It was not long before Annie began to notice the regularity of the Ford's headlights. When she speeded up, the other car speeded up. When she slowed down, it did the same. Finally, she had no doubts about it; they were being followed. The Buick was heavy and loaded with power. She pressed down on the gas pedal.

"Are you going kinda fast?" Billy cautioned. "I know it's early, but this is a congested zone."

"We're being followed," she answered.

"Are you sure?"

"Yes."

She flicked on the turn signals indicating that she intended to exit on Ninety-Five south. The car behind did the same. However, instead of turning at the ramp she sped ahead.

They both saw the car behind do the same.

Now there could be no doubt.

"It's that guy from the gas station," Billy told her.

Turning left on costal highway number One at a high rate of speed, they saw the white three-story house with a widow's walk and the sign that Walt had told them about. Eleven and one-half miles to Jupiter.

☙

The Ford was gaining on the Buick. "Get that gun," Ezekiel told The Blonde.

"Zekie-Bob please don't do anything foolish," she pleaded.

"Get me the fuckin' gun."

She handed it to him; he was fast approaching the Buick. "What are you going to do?" she whined.

"Shoot the fucker's tires out from under him."

"There's a sharp curve ahead and you're going too fast," she yelled.

"Shut up!"

☙

Annie saw the dilapidated sign, "Emily's Boat Rental," with an arrow pointing left. An oncoming car with blinding bright headlights had barely passed when she turned off the Buick's lights, braked, and made a sharp turn into a one-lane dirt road.

☙

Ezekiel, gun in hand, rounded the curve at full speed. He was blinded by the brights of the oncoming car and it was all he could do to keep the Ford on the road. Shaking his head and blinking his eyes to clear his vision, he cursed the son-of-a-bitchin' driver and continued full speed toward Jupiter.

☙

The road to Aunt Emily's was hardly a road at all. It was two dirt ruts paralleling the Loxahatchee for about a mile where it suddenly turned south and wound snake-like through marshy swampland. The Buick's headlights caught a gray-white, weather-beaten shack in its beams. The house, perched crazily on wooden stilts, on a rare spot of high ground, was at the very edge of the river. To the right of the path leading up to the door was the sign, "Emily's Boat Rental."

"I'm in awe of the way you shook that crazy bastard," Billy said, hugging Annie.

"Yes," Walt chimed in, "I thought for a moment I was riding with Mario Andretti at the Indy Five Hundred."

"'I never realized any mere physical experience could be so stimulating,'" Annie said, acknowledging their flattery with an imitation of Katharine Hepburn in "The African Queen."

"You two go ahead. I'll wait out here with Tennessee," Walt said, unscrewing the bottle cap.

৵

Billy had to keep looking down in order to avoid tripping on exposed cypress roots that rutted the path. They were almost to the shack door when they heard a deep, threatening growl.

There was a flicker of light in the shack.

"Who is it?" The woman spoke in a strong voice and as she carried a kerosene lamp toward the door, the shadow of her tiny figure appeared indomitable against the room's back wall.

"You're Emily?" Annie asked.

The woman behind the rusted screened door answered, "Ayuh."

Hurricane was right; Aunt Emily did have an up-East twang. "I'm Annie and this is Billy."

"Howdya-do?"

"We saw your sign and came to rent a boat."

As Billy stepped forward, the dog, hairs raised on the back of its neck, sprang, his front paws resting on the screen door's crossbar. "Is your dog friendly?" he asked nervously

"Can be. Depends."

The dog gave another deep-throated growl.

"I'm a friend," Billy managed, trying to appear calm.

"Friend?"

"Of Hurricane's."

The woman shaded her eyes and pressed against the screen, peering out. She was wearing a white sleeveless nightgown; loose flesh flapped from her upper arms.

"I got a note here from him."

"Well, come along then," Aunt Emily said, motioning him in. But as he moved, the dog's growl turned into a vicious snarl revealing two rows of sharp teeth.

"Tread easy. Rover and I aren't used to strangers arriving this early in the morning."

"Sorry about that," Annie told her, "but we needed to get an early start."

Unhooking the screen door, Aunt Emily opened it just far enough for Billy to slide the note through. As soon as it had been passed, she closed and locked the screen.

"Hurricane said that maybe you'd be willing to rent your boat," Billy explained.

"Hold on a minute," she called. She sat at the table, put on her glasses, and opened the note.

With his front paws resting firmly on the screen door's crossbar, Rover's green-gray eyes looked through the rusty screen directly into Billy's. It seemed that it took the old woman forever to read the note, but she finally lowered it and broke into a thin, high, cackle.

"What's the matter?"

"It's Hurricane's writing, all right," she chuckled.

Relieved to have his legitimacy established, Billy laughed. "You can tell by his handwriting?"

"No, it's not the handwriting," she said, coming back to the door. "It's the spelling. He takes after the men of his family. Neither Clyde, my husband, nor Hurricane's father could spell. Those Jackson boys were good-looking but they couldn't spell because they didn't speak the English language the way normal folks do."

Billy's attempt at a chortle was met with a savage growl from the dog.

"Shut up!" The old woman cuffed Rover on the rump, causing him to cower, turn, tail between his legs, and slide under the bed in the far corner of the room. Aunt Emily unhooked the screen door. "Come in," she said. "Proud to have you."

Billy held the screen for Annie and they cautiously entered the room.

"Sit," the old woman instructed.

Since there were only two chairs and she was already seated in one, Annie sat in the other. Billy stood.

The old woman looked at the note again, shook her head, and smiled. "Hurricane's my nephew," she mused, "born the night of the big hurricane in twenty-six. That's why they named him Hurricane, a family with real imagination."

Placing the note on the oilcloth she asked, "How far out you figure to go?"

"Ten miles," Billy said.

"Ayuh," she said, nodding approvingly. "Can't trust the fish caught in close to shore with all that rich sewage from Palm Beach."

"Well, I gotta be honest with you," Billy confessed, "we're not exactly going fishing."

Aunt Emily paused, "Pleasure?"

"Well, no, not that either." Billy squatted beside the table so he could look into the old woman's face. A menacing growl came from under the bed. "Hurricane said it would be all right to tell you, although we gotta keep this under our hats. That's why he didn't put it in the note."

"Sounds mysterious. You aren't running dope, are you?"

"No, nothing like that," Annie answered.

"Salvage operation?"

"No."

"Well, what is it then?"

How the hell were they going to explain the situation to this old woman who lived out here in the boonies?

"You see," Billy answered, "We have this friend who died, and he left a will saying he wanted to be buried at sea, ten miles off Jupiter Light."

"Why did he want to be buried there?" Aunt Emily questioned.

"There was this other writer, a poet," Annie explained. "He drowned when he jumped off the backside of a ship, in April, nineteen thirty-two."

"Are you talking about Hart Crane?" Aunt Emily asked.

Annie could not believe her ears. "You know?"

"Of course, I know. This friend of yours. He's with you?"

"Yup," Billy answered.

"Cremated?"

"No, he's just stretched out in the back seat."

Aunt Emily thought a moment. "Well, I've always believed a body should be buried where she wants to be buried. But unlike my nephew, Hurricane, who's got a soft side to him which tends to make him gullible, I have to have a little more proof to be certain of your bona fides." As she rose, Rover slid out from under the bed snarling and slathering, white foam on his dark lips as he slid on his belly across the room.

"I don't know what I can say to convince you," Billy said, looking apprehensively at the approaching dog.

"Who is this friend of yours anyway?" Aunt Emily asked.

"His name's Tennessee," Annie answered.

"Tennessee Williams?"

"You knew him?" Billy asked.

"Not personally, but who else is named Tennessee other then Ernie Ford?" Seeing Rover approaching, she barked, "Back off!" The dog turned and cowered back under the bed. "I always considered Tennessee a fellow poet who unfortunately got mixed up in show business. Thing I can't understand is how you got Hurricane to help you. He's only semiliterate and about as homophobic as anybody I know."

"We...we raised his consciousness," Billy said.

Aunt Emily gave a shrill one-note cackle, "Ha, what with, a fork lift?"

"He was ready to be gotten to," Annie said.

"When did Tennessee die?" the old woman asked.

"End of February."

"Well, I've been out of the loop. What did he die of?"

"He choked to death."

Aunt Emily shook her head, "Vachel Lindsay, Sarah Teasdale, Hart Crane, Randall Jarrell, Sylvia what's-her-name." She paused before adding, "Being a poet in this country can be brutal."

"That's the truth," Annie said.

"Come along. I'll show you the boat."

Rover slunk toward the old woman with a growl. "Oh, shut up. These are friends." She slapped him affectionately and she held his collar. "Just pet him. He'll be fine."

Annie patted Rover's rump, cooing in a low voice, "Good Rover," while Billy put his hand cautiously on the dog's head and scratched between his ears. Suddenly Rover's great pink tongue lapped out at Billy's hands.

"There, you see, he likes you," Aunt Emily announced triumphantly.

Rover rolled over on his back revealing an erection.

Annie moved toward the screen door. "Walt and I will bring Tennessee."

"Can I help?" Billy asked.

"You check out the boat."

As he fitted himself through a trap door and onto the rungs of a ladder that led beneath the shack, Emily cautioned him. "Look sharp! Sometimes there's a 'gator lying out here."

The motor boat was tied to a rotting wharf.

"I suppose the water in the bottom is from when it rained?" he said.

"No, we didn't have any rain over here," Aunt Emily responded. "*Folie* leaks just a little, nothing to worry about."

Rover bounded to meet Walt and Annie as they came into view carrying the sleeping bag.

"This is Hurricane's aunt, and that's Rover," Billy told Walt as he excused himself to help Annie bail water out of the boat.

"Pleased to make your acquaintance," Walt said with the hint of a bow.

"Ayuh, likewise, I'm sure. Emily's the name."

Walt put out his hand, "Walt here."

They shook firmly.

"She's a beauty, isn't she?" Emily said to Annie, pointing to the boat's bow where *Folie de Grandeur* was painted in faded cream-colored letters against the weather-beaten wood. "Charge will be thirty dollars an hour with a one hundred dollar deposit... refundable."

Annie was taken aback but didn't argue. "Walt can't swim. Are there life preservers?" she asked, pulling the deposit money from her strap bag.

"We never use those things." Emily answered. "Clyde always said going out in the water with one of those things on was like taking a shower in your raincoat." Turning to Walt and shaking her head she said, "Clyde always was one for the mixed metaphor."

Tucking the money under one of her droopy breasts in the bosom of her nightgown, she added, "There's a life preserver in the bow seat with a good long piece of hemp rope attached in case you need it."

Once most of the water had been bailed, they boarded, Annie in the bow, Walt sitting in the center, Billy in the stern, the sleeping bag on a tarp in the bottom of the boat. Billy looked over the side. "Is she sitting just a smidge low in the water?"

"Won't hurt," Emily told him. "Gives you ballast, stabilizes her."

"How do I get this thing started?"

"Just turn the knob to 'on' and pull the rope, like you'd start a lawn mower. You know how to steer, don't you?"

"Yup, don't worry."

When *Folie's* motor finally kicked in, an alarming puff of smoke came from the engine and the boat zigzagged across the water.

∽

Discouraged and frustrated, by being so close to the twenty-five thousand dollar reward and then losing sight of the Buick, Ezekiel was beside himself. Gun in one hand and steering with the other, he raced north along highway One looking for any possible turnoff, while getting farther and farther away from Jupiter. Seeing an all-night gas station, he slammed into the drive.

The Blonde barged ahead of him. "You got fountain Coke?" she breathlessly asked the clerk.

"Yes, ma'am," the girl answered.

"Give me a large one to go with plenty of chipped ice."

"Fresh lemon slice?"

"That'd be nice."

Ezekiel was furious as the girl slowly drew the Coke, cut the lemon slice, rang up the sale and gave the change. "Are you through with your transaction?" he snarled.

"I think so," the girl said, "unless you want some chips to go with your Coke?"

"No thanks, Hon," The Blonde replied sweetly.

"How many side roads are there that go anywhere between here and Jupiter?" Ezekiel asked.

The clerk was slow to answer. When she did, it was not what he wanted to hear. "I don't get what ya mean," she said.

"What part of the sentence don't you understand? You know what a side road is?"

"One that goes...to the side, that's not the main road?"

"You're a regular quiz kid," Ezekiel told her. "So, going back toward Jupiter, are there any side roads a car could turn off on."

The clerk took a moment. "Well...they couldn't turn left and go very far if they was headed back to Jupiter."

Ezekiel's eyeballs rolled back into his head, "Duh! Is that because if they did, they'd run into the ocean?"

The girl's face turned crimson as she realized that he was making fun of her. "There's a couple of roads where a car could turn right."

"Before they got back to Jupiter?"

"Yes, sir."

"That's what I thought." Wondering if she knew what she was talking about, he added, "I mean roads that go somewhere. We're not talking cul-de-sacs here."

"A 'call do....' who?"

It crossed Ezekiel's mind that she was deliberately taunting him. "One of those circle drives at the end of a street that means you can't go any farther because if you did keep going you'd go in a circle, a cul-de-sac," he said. "Like a circle drive?"

"Well, there is a road just after Hobe Sound that goes west. Its number is Seven Oh Eight. The sign's down but you can't miss it." Seeing the rage in his face she raced on. "It goes into Seventy-Six. That takes you over to Port Mayaca on Lake Okeechobee. I think you'd like it over there, if you're...fixin' to go...fishin' or somethin'?"

"You know, cracker, you give me a pain in the ass. You're so dumb you oughta have been twins, then you'd at least be a half-wit. Have a nice day," he said, storming out.

"What on earth...?" the teary eyed clerk asked The Blonde.

"Oh, he's a real first-class son-of-a-bitch. Don't listen to a thing he says because—and I know this is hard to believe—he was born without a single redeeming feature."

"Goddamn, hurry your ass up," Ezekiel yelled as she approached the Ford.

"Why did you have to be so mean to that girl?" she asked.

"Because she's too stupid to live, if I'd had my gun with me, I would have shot her fuckin' face off."

"You wouldn't!"

"Some people don't deserve to live," he snapped.

You got that right, she thought, taking a sip of her Coke.

The sun was just below the horizon as they motored slowly down the Loxahatchee between patches of saw grass, lily pads, and reeds that clung to the shore; vivid red streaked the sky. The brackish smell of the river reminded Billy of New York's East River beneath the Brooklyn Bridge. They passed under a drawbridge and saw two young men on the deck of a magnificent white yacht moored at the marina, next to which an old woman fished off the dock.

Approaching the waterway, between concrete piers that jutted into the ocean, the wind increased and the waves became higher. Billy steered directly into them. With the boat so low in the water, he knew that if they got sideways of a wave, they could swamp. Fortunately, Walt was heavy and the center seat was a little toward the stern so that the bow rode fairly high out of the water.

As they entered the causeway, Billy remembered he intended to check the odometer at the point where the shore met the ocean in order to tell exactly when they were ten miles out.Bending, he examined the motor. "Where's the odometer," he called out in sudden alarm, "to measure the miles?"

"Isn't it on the motor?" Annie asked.

"I don't see it." He looked again. "No. There ain't one. So how'll we know when we're ten miles out?"

"I haven't the vaguest idea," Annie said.

Now what! Billy thought. What are we going to do? "Okay," he said. "Let me think this through. What we gotta do is..." He lowered the throttle just enough to keep *Folie* moving forward into the oncoming waves. Remembering the two guys on the white yacht, he upped the power, waited for an interval between waves, then wheeled the boat around and headed back upstream to a small docking area.

∽

Billy and Annie walked toward the large white yacht with some trepidation. "Excuse us," Annie called. "Could we trouble you with a question?"

"Sure, come aboard."

Topside, the yacht was a dazzling display of luxurious perfection in navigational equipment and comfort.

"Our problem is this," Billy explained. "We need to go out in the ocean exactly ten miles and there's no odometer on the boat."

"There never is," the smaller of the two men said. "The solution is very simple, though. To measure distance at sea you have to have a loran."

"What's that?"

The man couldn't help but smile at Billy's naiveté.

"A loran," the taller of the two men spoke, "is a piece of electronic equipment that acts as a navigational device."

"How much would one cost?" Annie asked.

"Oh, somewhere between one and two thousand dollars."

Billy listened politely as the shorter man talked, but he could see the guy's growing impatience with his obvious lack of navigation knowledge. Finally, Billy nodded in order to make the guy feel like he was getting through even though he hadn't a clue of what he was talking about.

"Incidentally," the taller man addressed Annie, "would you be interested in auditioning for an independent film we're making down here?"

"Oh, I don't think so," she answered quickly.

"It wouldn't take much time. My name is Dick Keiley, and this is my co-author, and director, Harry Morganthau. We're down here from Harvard's Carpenter Center, filming our senior project. It's a version of Aeschylus' *Oresteia*."

"How interesting," Annie purred, "but I think not."

"Have you ever acted before?" he asked. "We're using some of the actors from the Burt Reynolds Dinner Theatre in town."

He didn't add that the young actress from the Bert Reynolds Theatre they had hired to play Athena in their senior thesis production had left town during the night. They would need to recast. The crew was on-call and the shoot was scheduled for early afternoon. They would have to find a replacement.

"The film will be a spectacular, break-out, production," the other man told her. "Your part would be Athena. In the classic she's the one the Oracle of Delphi advises Orestes to seek in Athens in the hope of getting some final justice and end the vendetta that the pursuing Furies are waging against him."

"I appreciate the offer," Annie said, "but I really can't."

"We've updated the story to modern times, of course. Athena is now represented by the sort of Florida marina we have here, and Athena heads the Florida Supreme Court which will try him, presiding over it herself and casting the decisive vote. We think the story has enormous resonance for today's audiences since it deals essentially with justice."

"Well, you're very kind to offer, but really, I can't." Annie turned to leave.

"Granted there's not much money in it, but without your sunglasses and your kerchief...what color is your hair?

"Red."

"That would be perfect. You would make a striking Athena. And there would be lots of publicity. My father is influential with some major critics."

Annie shook her head. "Terribly sorry."

"Thanks anyway," Billy said. "I think I understand more about navigation now. Sorry to be so dumb about all this." He backed away.

"It's really very simple," the taller man said. "Just buy a loran. The boat shop opens at ten. In the meantime there's a wonderful place to breakfast right over there. They serve a delightful *Les Oeufs au Caviar.*

༦ꙍ

Annie couldn't help but notice Billy's utter dejection as he stepped off the gangplank and they headed back to where *Folie* was moored. Heaving a sigh, he asked, "Now what are we gonna do?"

"Hey, Mister!"

It was the old fisherwoman.

"Yes ma'am?" Billy acknowledged.

"I couldn't help overhearing your conversation. Trouble with those poor little rich boys is they don't have a clue that anyone navigated prior to the time their Wall Street daddies bought them that multi-million dollar yacht. You need a Loran like I need more liver spots. Now listen here, it's impossible to figure exactly ten miles out even with the most expensive equipment. If you're searching for doubloons in a sunken Spanish galleon, you'd better do like that rich kid said, but if you're just interested in getting a mathematically correct approximation..."

"Ball park figure's fine," Annie said.

"Are you figuring nautical miles?"

"Well, I wasn't, but I am now," Billy answered.

"Do you have a compass and binoculars?"

"Yes." Annie patted her strap bag.

"Do you know in which direction you want to go?"

"Ten miles directly east of the light," Billy told her.

"That's easy then. Now look here, there's a big old white house south of here with a widow's walk..."

"We passed it."

"That's eleven and one half land miles from the Light, which would be about a close as you could get to ten nautical miles. So you can use that as your site. If you keep on an even course *due east* of the lighthouse, you'd be ten miles out when the white house is at forty-five degrees."

She drew a horizontal line in the dirt with a stick. "This line is the shore." In the center of the line she drew a L. "This is the lighthouse." At the right end of the line she drew an S. "This is the site which is that big old white house. Then she drew a perpendicular line from L and at the end of it made a P. "This is the point where you want to go." Then, drawing a diagonal line from P to S, she said, "When you get ten miles out the angle from P to S–point to site–will be at forty-five degrees."

A broad smile spread over Billy's face.

"You got it," the woman laughed. "I can see it in your face, you got it."

"First time I ever understood anything mathematical," Billy confessed. "But I'll need something to measure the angle."

"You're the something," the old woman chuckled.

"How do'ya mean?" Billy asked.

"Hold your right arm straight out in front of you toward the lighthouse, now your left arm straight out from your side. What's the degree of the angle?"

"Ninety degrees," Billy said with confidence.

"Now move the left arm halfway toward your right arm."

Billy understood immediately. "Halfway in would be forty-five degrees, thanks."

"As William James said, 'The union of the mathematician with the poet, fervor with measure, passion with correctness, this surely is the ideal' and you are most welcome."

♋

Driving at a ferocious rate of speed, the needle on Ezekiel's frustration barometer was at one hundred percent. Having tracked the side road and giving up after driving a few miles toward Port Mayaca, he now approached Jupiter's drawbridge. A guard came from the gatehouse and held up a stop sign.

Up river, a tall three mast schooner was heading out to sea. Ezekiel brought the Ford to a stop and turned off the motor. As he did, activity in the early morning light on the other side of the river caught his eye. Even at a distance, he could discern the hippy-looking guy and the girl with the dark glasses and kerchief over her head. And as he looked further up the river, in the direction they were running, he saw a boat with the old colored man in it.

He leaned out the window and called to the guard. "I've got to get across. It's an emergency. Can't you stop that goddamn boat?"

"No way!" the guard answered.

The moment the bridge's spans started to raise Ezekiel smiled at the thought of making the most mischief he had ever made. Actually, there was no decision; a lifetime of mischief-making had conditioned him to an automatic response. Turning the key, he shifted into drive and pressed down on the accelerator.

"Stop," the Guard yelled as the car sped past and up the incline of the rising span.

The span rose rapidly and the Ford's tires, worn thin from the abuse of too many fast starts, began to lose traction on the wet early-morning steel, slowing the rate of acceleration. Ahead, the gap between the two sections widened. Reaching the lip of the span, the Ford shot through the air and almost made it. It was at that moment that The Blonde, her seat belt already unfastened and her hand on the door's latch, leapt out, clutch bag in hand, to land on her knees on the angled concrete.

The Ford had struck midway on its underbelly, where it now teetered precariously as though unable to decide whether to slide forward down the span or slip backward. Held momentarily in a delicate balance, the span continued to rise, causing the Ford to slide backward until the lip of the steel bridge caught some part behind the front tires and it hung perpendicular, swaying slightly. The Blonde watched as a terrified Ezekiel tried not to move a muscle.

Below, the schooner sailed between the spans, the adults and children on its deck wide-eyed. When the boat had safely passed, The Blonde, balancing herself on the paved slope, reached out to where the Ford's underpinning clung so desperately, and with a surprisingly light touch, pushed just enough to change the balance. She watched in fascination as the Ford and Ezekiel plummeted into the Loxahatchee, sinking quickly out of sight.

Seeing the guard talking to another man on the other side of the river, Rosemary—and from now on her given name would be what she would be known by, and she would never again allow anyone to call her "The Blonde"—quickly made her way down the steeply raked span of bridge as fast as she could without soiling or ripping her silk flowered dress, losing her clutch bag, or breaking a high heel. She turned instinctively toward the sea at the bottom, and dazed made her way along the marina's walk.

ᘒ

The two rich, young fledgling film producers both knew that the red-haired woman with the sunglasses and kerchief would have been perfect for the goddess Athena, and they couldn't fathom how she could have refused their offer. After all, they were dealing with such an important subject as justice.

"I suppose you'd better call Jeff. Have him contact the crew and the extras and tell them the shoot is off. Maybe we can get one of the Equity actresses at the theater to—" His voice trailed off as he noticed Rosemary approaching.

"What a beauty," they said.

Rosemary was quite astonished when the two young men, obviously gentlemen, came down the gangplank of the yacht, and stood waiting for her. She had a sudden sense that somehow her young life was going to be changed. Her heartbeat quickened, the horror of the day vanished, and she smiled broadly.

⌒〜⌒

The sun was rising as *Folie de Grandeur* motored toward the concrete piers. As they passed between them Billy's vision included both the causeway and the land on either side. But halfway through, at the point where water met land, he saw the beach only in his peripheral vision and as the boat went further and further into the ocean, the shore became less visible until land vanished altogether and only the tips of the jutting-into-the-ocean concrete piers remained. They, too, vanished and soon there was nothing in the one hundred and eighty degrees of endlessness but the blue sky and the sledgehammer waves.

Overhead, a sky hawk taunted the little boat as gulls screamed and dove and pelicans flew low, skimming the water. Billy was gripped with fear as the waves hammered against the bow and sent spume flying. *Folie* was nothing, if not insignificant, to the sea's wild unpredictability. But he could not be afraid. This time, admittedly with a lot of help, he had thought the thing through. It was the end of the journey. Everything would be–*had to be*–all right.

The glory of early morning was preceded by an evenness of red across the horizon. As the color ascended, signaling the sun's rise from below the sea's surface, the sky grew redder and redder until quite suddenly the rim of the giant hot circle thrust its way up through the sea, growing in size as it surged upward out of the blue-green water until it had erected itself into the sky.

Later, after it had risen, there would be the sun's curious effect: a triangular shaft of reflection in the water with diamonds, millions of constantly changing diamonds, sparkling bright, and sometimes—rarely it is true, but sometimes—accompanied by a ripple of fire.

This endlessness brought openness, with no perimeters except the horizon. And occasionally even the horizon, where watery earth met sky, was blurred by the blueness of both with no perceived division between them, and *Folie* was lost in boundless space.

Suddenly, in this vastness, with the boat on the crest of a wave, he saw the dorsal fin of a shark cut through the water, followed by the wake of other smaller fins. But before the sharks surfaced, a dolphin broke the water's blue and, arching the horizon, made a distinction between earth and sky. As she cruised—he fantasized her searching for a school of groupers for Sunday breakfast— she surfaced every so often to breathe air into her lungs through her blowhole. The sight of this activity gave him a sudden and instantaneous feeling of connection, and his fear of the periscope-like movement of the fin was allayed. Only occasionally, when the fin neared the boat, did his mind return to the danger.

Annie kept her eye on the compass; Billy, wind blowing through his hair, held tight to the tiller, keeping *Folie* on course. "Can you keep a fix on the lighthouse?" he called to her.

"Yes," she answered.

"Can you see the widow's walk?"

"Yes," she called over the sound of wind and waves.

Walt now sat straddling the middle seat, facing neither fore nor aft and therefore, by a simple ninety degree turn, could take in both sea and the remnants of land. The old man's nostrils flared as he breathed in sea spray. Occasionally, he held the bottle of Old Grand-Dad aloft and took a long swallow. As the wind blew through his beard, he would raise his arms, as if to answer the swooping, crying gulls. While facing seaward, an extra large wave hit the boat's bow and the flying spume clung to his beard; his eyes peered out sparkling and as bright as the diamonded water.

"Walt, take the tiller for a second. Just hold it steady,"

They exchanged places and, removing his shirt and tying it around his waist, Billy stood in the boat's center and stretched out his right arm toward the lighthouse, his left arm at a ninety degree angle. Then, moving it toward the widow's walk which glittered in the early morning sun, he called out, "Not yet."

෨

Sometime later, when the boat was again high on the crest of a wave, far ahead, and slightly to his right, Billy saw the black and glossy periscope-like dorsal fin of the shark. But then, closer to *Folie,* and to the left, the dolphin leapt from the water and flew through the air, followed by two other dolphins. "Look!" Billy called. Walt let out a loud whoop, and the lead dolphin turned her head in Walt's direction.

A heavenly music ran through Billy's head and his fingers drummed on the weather-beaten gray wood of the seat. The rhythm ran through his left hand to his right that held the tiller as the big shark came so close that he could see its slate-blue back. As he grew accustomed to looking into the sea, he saw just below its surface the blue and silver, long pike-like bodies, pointed heads and menacing jaws of barracudas. Perhaps in former times, he thought, sharks followed boats in the same prescient way that vultures hovered over soldiers going into battle.

"You got that sack weighted good?" he yelled to Annie.

"I think so."

"He's gotta go down fast."

Annie was so busy navigating that she had no time to look into the sea. Walt, facing forward into the wind, or looking up at the gulls, was totally submerged in his own thoughts, unaware of the danger. Only occasionally, when the shark's fin came close to the boat did Billy allow himself to feel the terror. Then, when their little boat was once again high on the crest of its thousandth wave, his eye caught at some distance to his left the reassuring sight of the dolphin flying low, forming an arch with her body just above the water.

"We're getting close," he called.

"How far?" Annie asked.

He cut the motor. "Walt, you're gonna have to hold the tiller and keep *Folie* into the wind and waves."

With Walt at the helm, Billy stood tall with his right arm outstretched toward Jupiter's light and slowly brought his outstretched left arm toward the widow's walk. "Yes, we're there."

Annie stood and recited Blanche's line from *A Streetcar Named Desire*. "'I can smell the sea air and when I die, I'll be buried at sea, sewn up in a clean white sack and dropped overboard, at noon, in the blaze of summer, and into an ocean as blue as my first lover's eyes.'" She looked directly at Billy.

Walt intoned the Episcopal service. "'I am the resurrection and the life...he that believeth in me, though he were dead, yet shall he live...If I take the wings of the morning, and remain in the uttermost parts of the sea, even there also shall thy hand lead...and hold me. In sure and certain hope of the resurrection to eternal life...we commend to Almighty God our brother, Tennessee and commit his body to the deep.'"

Billy and Annie removed the clean white sack from the sleeping bag and he scanned the sea's surface for a sign of the shark. "Now!" he cried. They dropped the sack overboard, its whiteness suspended on the green blue water.

They silently looked into the water as Walt chanted over and over, "'This fabulous shadow only the sea keeps.'"

The white sack didn't sink. It bobbed in the water straight up and down, the weights at the bottom pulling it down, but pockets of air at the top keeping it afloat. It was during this interval, as they waited for the heavy woven cotton to absorb the sea water, that the shark surfaced and headed toward the bobbing sack containing Tennessee Williams's body. It was within feet when the dolphin suddenly sprang from the sea, followed by her pod, blocking the approaching shark along with his escort of barracudas. In the momentary confusion of the standoff, the sack, now fully saturated, sank quickly, plummeting into the sea's depths.

Letting go of the tiller, Walt stood on the seat, his head flung back, drinking from the bottle of Old Grand-Dad, and not hearing Billy's warning shout to sit down. Momentarily stymied, the enraged shark headed for *Folie* and bumped into its side. Walt's arms extended backward and the weight of his body shifted forward as he fell into the sea.

The boat was askew in the churning water. Annie felt it lurch, heard the splash and watched as Billy jumped, leaving her the boat's lone passenger. A wave came crashing over the side. She crawled to the stern, grasped the tiller and righted it, heading the boat into the next wave. Billy surfaced. "The life preserver," he shouted. "Get the life preserver."

She made her way back to the bow, opened the seat's lid, got the life preserver attached to the coil of rope, and threw it toward Walt, only to see it fall short.

She thought of leaping in after it but at that moment she saw the gigantic dorsal fin and the entire back of the blue shark. Almost as big as the boat, it swam toward Walt. She saw the jaws open, and past the sharp spine-like teeth, the fiery folds of its throat. She screamed. Having released the tiller, the boat once again was sideways to a wave and was struck with great force, throwing Annie to the deck.

Billy's two hands gripped the side of the boat. She reached over and, with the energy and strength of the moment, pulled him into her arms. Suddenly, everything seemed to stop. The sea was calm, and she felt the healing warmth of the sun against her skin. She lay there for some moments before raising her head. Far out she saw the great shark's fin gliding through the water.

As Billy tried to start the motor, she called, "What are you doing?"

"Going to find Walt."

"It's no use, he's gone. I saw...*saw*." She held her hands to her face.

"What?"

"The shark."

∽

Before going over the side, a Dionysian ecstasy had taken hold of Walt as he danced on the boat's seat, heaven before his eyes. Like Ahab, he believed himself to be immortal; he had eliminated all "explanatory relative clauses." And like Hart Crane's mentors— the visionary poets, Rimbaud and Baudelaire—he had touched fire that burned him alive.

But as the weight of his wet clothing pulled him downward and he saw rainbow colored fish with transparent clarity, the out-of-body experience quickly faded and his rational mind told him he had damn well better surface and draw a breath. It was now a life-giving panic through Apollonian understanding that caused the kicking of his legs and the flaying of his arms. He emerged through the foam of the crest of a wave and sucked life-giving air into his lungs.

Once surfaced he saw Billy's head at some distance bobbing in the water; saw the boat awash at the bottom of a trough, spray spewing over it; saw Annie, the rope of *Folie's* life preserver in hand, which she threw and had fallen short, screaming and pointing behind him. He turned and saw the huge open jaws, the gleaming rows of white teeth that framed the delicate pink shading into deeper rose of the throat, the red-black muscles in back where the jaw hinged, and the corkscrew shaft that led downward into darkness, and he realized that the hinges of the shark's jaw were about to clamp shut on his body.

Beneath the surface he saw the pike-like head of a barracuda about to take one of his feet. It was at that moment when he most wanted to live that he saw the eye. Although small for her body, it seemed to him to be filled with compassion, as though she understood his circumstance. The eye winked, and for one moment it crossed his mind that she was afflicted with an incurable *tic douloureux* as with some minor character in a story by Chekhov.

Then suddenly, quite unexpectedly, he felt the dolphin beneath him, her back between his legs which he instinctively tightened around her body. Leaning down, he put his arms around her neck, her skin slippery and warm.

Easy rider secured, she sprang from the sea, narrowly avoiding the shark's closing jaws, and her delights were dolphin-like: showing her back above the elements she lived in by making a great arch with her body she capered and cavorted, sometimes up, sometimes down, in a great circle while, like an escort at some distance, other dolphins did the same. Rhythmically, every twenty seconds or so, she went below the surface and then rose, expelling her breath in a low musical hissing sound as her blowhole broke the surface and he heard her music as in a mid-summer's dream: "Since once I sat upon a promontory, And heard a mermaid on a dolphin's back, Uttering such dulcet and harmonious breath, That the rude sea grew civil at her song, And certain stars shot madly from their spheres, To hear the sea-maid's music."

After what seemed an eternity of playful frolic, the Apollonian again overcome the Dionysian and seeing *Folie de Grandeur* in the distance with both Annie and Billy, mouths agape, looking toward him, he leaned over and whispered to the dolphin, "As much as I'm enjoying this, I'd better get back to my friends."

She turned, eye tic twitching out of control because of a short circuited comprehension until he pointed toward *Folie.*

Understanding instantly, she sprang through the sea while on either side, arching the horizon, the honor guard of porpoises leapt through the foam as though dancing to a drummer's crazy syncopated beat. As an explorer into another intensity, a deeper communion, he knew that "love is most nearly itself when here and now cease to matter" and he laughed to hear, "The wave cry, the wind cry, the vast waters of the petrel and the porpoise" and to know that "In my end is my beginning."

The dolphin snuggled up beside the boat's weathered boards, rolled over on her side and gently deposited him into the arms of his companions. Then, she speared the life preserver's hole, which was still attached to the rope, and the rope to the boat, with her snout, and swam.

Folie seemed to fly through the water, sometimes her bottom slapping hard against a wave. The trio could see land coming closer and closer and then they were through the concrete piers headed to Jupiter's marina where the dolphin, depositing the life preserver back into the boat, placed her head on its edge while they stroked her. She left them with a smile, swimming directly east from Jupiter Light to where she guarded Tennessee Williams's and Hart Crane's watery gravesite.

∽

In the upstairs apartment, Hurricane, wakened by the streaming late morning sun through the bedroom window, yawned and stretched languidly, then settled back, eyes closed, a satiated smile on his face. He hadn't slept this late in...well, he didn't think, ever.

Grace popped her head into the bedroom. "You finally awake?"

"Oh yeah."

"Hungry?" she asked.

"I guess," he said in a way that meant he was ravenous.

"Don't dress; just throw on Harry's old bathrobe."

They had almost finished brunch when she stroked the hair on his forearm. "Want some more coffee?" she asked, not waiting for his answer but crossing the room and looking out the window. "I got up early. Just love a day like this, don't you?"

"Yup," Hurricane said.

"It's so clear."

"Wind like that pretty much clears things away."

"By the look of that coconut palm," she said, indicating the torn branches of a tree down in the parking lot, "I'd say you were right."

"Never seen a storm like that one end so fast," Hurricane said.

Grace poured his coffee.

"Just half."

She poured a full cup.

"Whatdaya suppose Billy meant last night when he talked about 'being a kind of folk hero in a few arcade circles'?" he asked.

"Oh, I don't know, kids talk funny nowadays." She sat back down and patted the inside of his thigh, very high. "Get enough?" she whispered.

Hurricane grinned, loving her hand there, "For now, anyway."

Grace giggled.

"Great breakfast," he said. "I haven't had eggs and oysters in, well, ever, I guess."

"They go good together," Grace told him.

"I sure slept late," he said.

They were silent for a moment before she asked, "Why'd you do it?"

"What?"

"Help the kids out?"

"Oh, I don't know."

"Yes, you do!" She stamped her foot and smiled. "And it was lucky for Billy he had you to help figure out exactly where to dump that poet. I suppose Walt's right, that it's good to have those poet fellows around, but..." She patted his thigh. "but for getting the job done, give me a man who knows his arithmetic."

Hurricane couldn't help but laugh.

"When you think of your average American, pulling themselves up by their bootstraps, working all their lives, sending the kids through college, then when they finally retire what do they get, a bar on a two-lane highway that hardly anyone travels, swamp, hurricanes, snakes, wild pigs and social security."

"Not much in life is for certain," Hurricane said. He suddenly reached for his wallet and removed a piece of paper which he carefully unfolded.

Grace looked at the name, "Your son?"

Hurricane nodded.

"I didn't know..."

"It's a rubbing I made from that marker in D.C."

The sudden image in Grace's mind's eye of the Vietnam Memorial Wall brought instant tears to her eyes.

"Last November, they dedicated the Memorial by reading all fifty-eight thousand names. I listened on my car radio when they read the Js and when his name..."

She waited a moment out of respect for his feelings and then said simply, "What was he like?"

Hurricane took a moment before he answered. "A little like Billy, only I remember him younger. He had the same long hair until the army cut it off; he was a little wild, caught him smoking pot and raised hell and so he went and enlisted." He took a deep breath. "Annie got it right about me last night. She honed right in on it: 'All hat and no ranch.' I didn't have the...I didn't have the guts to be honest like the boy was."

"If Billy hadn't gone to Canada," Grace indicated the rubbing. "This could have been him."

"I know that...now. I hope they're okay, hope they got done what they set out to do."

∽

Because of various delays the film shoot did not commence until mid-afternoon. Apprentices from the Bert Reynolds Theatre, clad as huntresses and playing the three Furies, Alecto, Tisiphone, and Megaera, were dressed with "look real" rubber snakes in their hair and carried torches, scourges and sickles. They watched the lovely Rosemary, as Athena, make her entrance, clad in a long robe, wearing a breastplate which bore at its center the head of the Gorgon Medusa, a helmet on her head, holding lance and shield in one hand and a sword in the other.

All of them, along with the fisherwoman who had been recruited to play one of the hags from under the earth who comprised the Areopagus and whom Athena had to convince of Apollo's innocence of the sin of matricide, were too involved to notice the small boat with three people in it, that at that moment chugged up the Loxahatchee River.

൦౿

When they disembarked at Aunt Emily's wharf and had greeted Rover, Walt told Emily the "unbelievable" miracle: his being rescued by a dolphin who towed them back to the marina. Aunt Emily laughed and informed them that the rescue was not unbelievable or a miracle. The same had happened to her once and she was overjoyed to learn that her dolphin friend, Amélie, the five hundred pound bottlenose, had resurfaced after being absent for weeks.

There were quick thank-yous to Emily, a hasty goodbye to an excitable Rover, followed by a fast trip back across the state during which time, although Annie hesitated to say it, she did so because she feared that Walt's story, at least as he told it to Aunt Emily—with its poetic enhancements from Shakespeare and Eliot—might strain Hurricane's credulity and violate his willing suspension of disbelief, his new-found poetic faith.

Walt pointed out that there was any number of documented instances in which the highly intelligent Amélies of the world had come to the rescue of their fellow animals, but that he would remain silent about his rescue, acknowledging that Annie was right; there was no point in tampering with Hurricane's natural ignorance. This remark was quickly followed by a head shake, a smile and an acknowledgment: "How wrong I was about that guy's ability to understand the reasons for us undertaking this 'damn fool' escapade in the first place."

They stopped just south of Fort Myers where they vacuumed the Buick's interior and gave it a double wash to remove the mud.

Then quite suddenly they were back with Grace and Hurricane.

~

Annie called American Airlines and found there was no direct flight until morning from Ft. Myers to New York, but there was a puddle-jumper flight that would take them to Ft. Lauderdale where they could catch the eight o'clock to New York.

"You want to make reservations?" the representative asked.

She wanted assurance of a seat but would rather not use her credit card. "Is the flight full?"

"No," the guy answered. "This is September, there's plenty of space."

"I think we'll get the tickets at the airport, then. Thanks."

"We'd love to have you stay for a few days," Grace said.

"We have to get back. You don't know how much this has meant to us," Annie told her. "Thanks for all your help, and I know all this will be our little secret."

"It'd better be," Grace laughed. "I think what we did is called aiding and abetting. Well, you don't tell on us, we won't tell on you."

Annie hugged her. "Trust me!"

Hurricane, however, wondered if it was smart for the three to be seen together at the airport. "At least while the heat's on."

Grace smiled. "You think there'll be much heat?"

"Probably not," Hurricane admitted. "It'll all die down quick. Now, if it'd been Tennessee Ernie Ford you dug up, there'd be law enforcement officers crawling all over the place."

"Know what?" Grace said, "I've an idea that can help so no one will recognize you."

❧

Hurricane drove a beardless and short-haired Walt, now looking like a college professor, a brush-cut Billy looking like an Up-East college kid, and Annie with a kerchief over her hair and large smoked glasses, to the Ft. Myers airport after a tearful parting with Grace and a promise that they'd stay in touch.

"There may be a line at the ticket counter," Annie said. "I'll go in and get the tickets. Thanks for everything." She reached up and gave Hurricane a hug. She had a sense that Billy and Hurricane should say their good-byes in private so she added, "Walt, you come with me. Walt and Hurricane hurriedly shook hands and he and Annie were off inside the terminal.

"Well…" Hurricane said awkwardly.

"This is it," Billy said. "Did you know there was a twenty-five thousand dollar reward for the return of the body?"

"Yes, I knew that."

There was a pause before Billy asked, "Why'd you decide to help us? I mean, you were so against us when you came in last night. What changed your mind?"

Hurricane looked like he was reaching for his wallet and then decided not to. "Ah, I don't know," he muttered. "Just…I don't know."

"Anyway, thanks for all you've done."

"You're welcome. And son, it's none of my business, but you ought to get yourself squared away out there in Seattle. That Annie's a damn good woman and…well, you just ought to clear things up as soon as you can."

Billy reached out his hand to shake but Hurricane put his arms around the boy and hugged him tight. Billy slapped Hurricane on the back, hard, like men do when they show affection, and Hurricane slapped Billy on the back, released him and not looking at him directly mumbled, "I'll get a dang ticket if I stay parked here at the curb any longer." He walked away, drove the Plymouth down the boarding ramp, mingled with the stream of traffic and headed back to pick up Ruby at her mother's.

◌෨

Annie and Walt had worked their way to be the next customers in line when Billy joined them. Annie explained about the shuttle to Ft. Lauderdale to connect with the eight o'clock to New York."

"It's about to leave. How many?" the clerk asked.

"Three," she told him.

"Two," Billy said.

She turned and stared at him.

"Cut me some slack," he said, low, so the clerk couldn't hear.

"Sure," she said. Her mouth turned up in a smile but she wasn't smiling inside. He couldn't tell her what he was going to do because he didn't know what he was going to do. He wanted like the devil to reach out and bring her into him, but he didn't. "Take care of her, Walt," he told the old man.

The clerk was impatient. "Which is it, two or three?"

"Two."

"Coach or first class?"

"Coach."

"Smoking or non-smoking?"

"Non-smoking."

"Cash or credit card?"

"Cash."

She paid.

"That will be gate number..."

◌෨

Billy had walked away while she and the clerk were talking. He knew that when she turned it'd be better if he was gone because if he wasn't, then he'd probably not be able to go, he loved her that much. He was crying as he walked fast across the parking lot to the highway where he wiped his eyes and held up his thumb.

෧౨

Walt, who knew how much pain Annie was in, said, "About Billy..."

She responded by saying, "Please, Walt, not now."

They had made a hurried transfer from the puddle jumper's gate to the big plane in Fort Lauderdale and were seated together in the forward coach section, Annie on the aisle, Walt at the window. She had removed her sun glasses and was about to take off the head scarf when a big guy and an attractive brunette hurriedly boarded. She put her glasses back on and nudged Walt.

"What?"

"Isn't that Tracy Cole?"

"Where?"

"About to sit down in first class."

"It is!" Walt said, about to get up and greet her.

"Don't even think of it," she whispered, pulling him back in his seat.

"Why?"

"That's her boyfriend Jake Filler, a detective whose done work for June."

"You think maybe...?"

"And since she'll certainly remember you..."

"She got A's in my classes," Walt said defensively.

"That's the point. So when we deplane, pretend you dropped something on the floor and search for it. Remember, first class passengers get off first so when we land we'll just sit tight and let all the others in coach get off before us."

෧౨

As the plane flew out of Lauderdale and headed out to sea, the sun was just below the horizon. Walt looked down into the million sparkling diamonds of light "where the wanderers chose to rest, where marble clouds supported the sea and a dolphin arched the horizon."

∽

When the plane landed at LaGuardia, she and Walt waited until everyone else had deplaned before making their way through the crowd. Outside the terminal, she could not help but notice Jake and Tracy waiting in the taxi line where they would pay forty dollars while she and Walt would cross the street, catch the M40 bus, pay her token, put in the senior fare of seventy-five cents for Walt, and ask for two transfers. At Broadway and 116th Street they would transfer downtown on the 104, she to 76th Street and he to the West Village. And as soon as she got home she would remember to call Grace to tell her they made it home okay; then she would call June who would be royally pissed with her, but she would start crying and say she had to have an abortion and June would forgive her—that would be something June could understand—and she would get David Lesco to forgive her, and her friends Doug and Brian would want her back anyway, and then she would call her mother to see if she was back home from her Club Med trip, and then she would completely fall apart and...

No, she would not.

Chapter VIII
Monday, 19 September – Tuesday, 4 October, 1983

D uring the days that followed, the faces of the drivers of cars and trucks blended together as if they were one, as did all the days and nights and one cheap chow wagon after another, and sleeping in train stations and on bus terminal benches and sometimes just sleeping out in the country with his back against a tree.

Billy finally made it to Seattle. Going down a street of white bungalow look-alikes that were the same as when he'd left only now they were different somehow. It was evening as he walked along the street, his coat collar turned up against the chill coming off the Sound.

A car passed and he thought how strange it was to notice a single car driving along a deserted street; how strange to see a street with no cars at all. The car turned into the driveway of the white bungalow to which Billy was headed, a driveway that he once considered his own, the driveway that he and Clara and the kids drove in and out of countless times. But the truth was that it was never his driveway, never been his house. He'd never paid the rent.

He walked faster because he recognized the car as Clara's, only Clara wasn't driving.

A man got out of the driver's side. Clara exited the other side and the kids crawled out from in back. The man–big guy–put the boy on his shoulders and held the girl's hand, a sack of groceries in his other, and closed the door with his foot. Both kids were laughing. The man went toward the back porch, followed by Clara, who carried two more sacks of groceries. Billy had never met the guy but he liked him right then and there.

He waited to see the lights come on inside, first the kitchen in the back, then the hallway, and then the blue flickering light of the TV in the front room.

Clara was making a life for herself and the kids.

That was good.

～

Later that night, Maeve said, "Come in," to his knock. He could see that her room over the store looked just about the same. Maeve didn't. She looked beat laying there on the water bed, her face thin with dark shadows under the eyes. She sat up as soon as he entered and it was like a miracle the way she pulled herself together; as long as the miracle lasted she was the same old Maeve.

"Billy. Man! Where the hell you been?"

"I split for awhile."

"Yeah, I noticed."

"Came back," he said.

"I see."

Maeve rubbed her eyes and blinked. "What the hell happened to your hair?"

"Got a haircut."

"I see."

"I need a place to hang my hat."

"Hell, you ain't got a hat." She laughed.

"I know," he said, grinning.

She threw aside the quilt that covered her. "'I got a great big bed with two pillows for my head/ Hey, but lately I've been sleepin' alone...'"

He squatted beside her. "I got me a girl."

"You mean besides your wife?" Maeve asked.

"Yup, I came back to get things straightened out with Clara."

"Oh, shit!" Maeve said. "I'm never gonna get a chance to hop your bones. You're never in between."

"In between?"

"Women! In between my sheets."

"You ain't got no sheets."

"I know," she said, "takes too much effort to wash 'em."

He smiled. "You make me feel welcome."

"I could make you really feel welcome." She reached for him.

He shielded his crotch with his hands.

Maeve thought a minute. "Okay," she said, and that's when the miracle of her pulling herself together passed and she changed back into looking as beat as the street she lived on. "But would you mind, if I promise I won't try anything—and I promise I won't—would you mind just getting in under the covers and holding me? I swear I won't touch you."

Billy was exhausted. He took the pack off his back and removed his shoes that were pretty well shot and socks that smelled, and got in under the covers.

"Spoon up to my back," she said taking his arm and putting it around her.

She felt awfully thin.

"Tomorrow," she said, as though it was difficult for her to talk, "I'll see Lucy and we can get a gig going, man."

She was silent and he could hear the struggle her lungs were having providing breath. He started to remove his arm.

She held onto it and he put it back around her.

When she was asleep he withdrew his arm. Dead tired, he lay on his back for a long time looking at the dirty windows that looked out over the street and watching as the colored on-again, off-again, neon light cast its reflection into the room.

༄

He called Clara at work the next day after he got a room of his own.

"Where you calling from?" Clara asked.

"Here."

"Seattle?"

"Yup."

"Where are you?"

"Downtown."

"Well, don't come home," she warned.

"I know."

"What do you mean?"

"I came in last night just in time to see you and your guy and the kids come home from the store."

"Well, what'd you expect, never heard from you."

"I know. I think you did the right thing."

"I started the divorce last spring."

"I'll go along."

"All it takes is for you to sign the papers and it's final."

"I'll do that as soon as they're ready. Call me at Lucy's."

"All right."

"How are the kids?"

"The kids are fine," she said. "You're not to see them."

He did not answer. It was something he hadn't expected.

"Kids are resilient," she explained.

"What's that?"

"Kids forget quick. They snap back."

Kids remember. He remembered when his dad split.

"They just love Jack," Clara told him.

The new guy's name was Jack. "Do you?"

There was a pause. Then she said, "He's steady, got a steady income. Jack spends time with the kids and me."

"Do you love him?" Billy repeated.

"Oh, Billy, if you don't take your head out of your ass and stop looking back to the Sixties you'll be a loser all your life."

ᠭᠣᠣ

Lucy's night club was just about the same. The trap set had seen some hard wear and Billy had to get Lucy to replace the skins on one of the snares. Curtis, Morrese, and Rod were all there for rehearsal. They practiced hard but Maeve didn't sing much. When she did she sounded tired and sad.

They all knew that Maeve was high on Saturday night when she called them into her dressing room, the same three-fold greasy screen just off the kitchen, for the pep talk prior to going on.

"Girl, you outdone yourself," Curtis said. He felt the material of her Salvation Army finery. "Some threads." Maeve struggled to get into a black dress cut down to her ass in back, but high in front. The skirt layered with a series of black fringes that shimmied when she moved. She wore long black gloves that covered her arms, had put a black plume of ostrich feathers in her hair, and draped a red filmy boa around her shoulders.

"Out there tonight ain't no stadium full, like with Bette Midler in 'The Rose,'" she said, putting clown white make-up on her face to cover the dark shadows under the eyes. "And Time magazine hasn't taken back that slanderous shit they printed about rock and roll being dead. And the Reagans are still in the white, white, White House, man, and there's some kind of mysterious infection going around, but like the Duchess of Windsor said, 'you can never be too thin or too rich,' and we're goin' out there tonight with the same skimpy house, the same fuckin' indifference." She slashed her mouth with a red lipstick to punctuate the final word.

"Maybe we should change the repertoire," Morrese said.

"Whatdaya mean?" Maeve asked defensively.

"Different kinds of songs, more *now*."

"Whatdaya mean, 'now' for christsake?"

"More Eighties."

"Hell no," Maeve exploded. "We're keeping the Joplin repertory same as always. Why should I spread my legs for the Eighties? Anyway, it's all the same gig, man, and 'I never did understand why half of the world is cryin', man, when the other half the world is cryin' too, man, and they can't get it together.'"

Maeve opened with "Cry, Baby."

Then she sang "One Night Stand," and followed it with "Bobby McGee," "Down on Me," "Summertime," and "Get It While You Can." She sang with all her heart, like an amateur "lover in French" and Billy knew that's all anyone could do—just do the best you can—knowing within yourself that it is the best you can do, whether you were dealt a bad hand or not.

Maeve sang "Misery'n."

> "I been misery'n
> Ever since my Daddy gone, yeah."

It was then that Billy decided he would split right away. Things had wound down in Seattle. He'd signed the papers that morning.

It was when Maeve got to the part,

> "Why am I feelin' so strange?"

that she stumbled. Billy thought for a minute she was going to fall but Maeve grabbed onto the mike stand and finished.

At the break, backstage, she said, "You're gonna split ain't ya?"

"How'd you know?"

"I read minds." She paused a moment and pumped up her boobs. "Well, we don't always connect, man. Like sometimes the end of that arc you say your friend Walt talked about, ain't a beginning. Some tapes ain't on a loop, man, sometimes a tape just ends." She stumbled and grabbed on to the back of a chair.

"You feeling OK?"

"Oh sure. Next week I'm posing for Strength-and-Health."

"You wanna talk about it?"

Maeve shrugged. "Leave some threads untied, Billy. There's always gotta be some mystery left."

"Why is that?"

"Cause that's the way it is, man, join the complexity of the fuckin' human race." Then, sorry for yelling, she said, "Now get out of here while I get ready for the second half."

She reached for the needle and syringe.

Courage to go on was a hell of a lot in life, Billy thought, especially if you're doing something society doesn't seem to care a whole hell of a lot about in the first place.

༄

After the gig, it didn't take him long to get out on the street. He wanted to see the house just one last time.

He stood across from it and looked, than he turned away, drummed the sides of his jeans, hard, and started to walk. He needed to write his mother who had always supported whatever he wanted to do and had taught him to march to the rhythm that was right for him, regardless of how different the drum beat. Yeah, join the complexity of the human race, where there was always some mystery left.

A car approached. *Can you beat that for luck?* he thought, sticking up his thumb. The car passed, fast.

When he'd get to New York he'd go to the bridge. He'd gaze at the great awesome arc from the underside, and in the distance, high up, out of the sky, he'd hear the syncopated rhythm of drums and the plaintive sound of wind and he'd be filled with wonder.

> "Lo! Soul, seest thou not God's purpose from the first?
> The earth be spann'd, connected by network..."

He'd turn and see Walt. He'd throw his arms around the old man, dance him around in a circle, and Walt would bitch and moan about his middle ear. And later after he had bought the old man a quart of Old Grand-Dad he'd make his way across the bridge. As he did, he'd hear the sound, like the wind blowing down a chimney in winter, the constant and ever changing sound of wind, and as background to the wind, the sound of water lapping the shore and the river's traffic.

∽

He walked up Columbus Avenue. He passed the Columbian and saw Mrs. Trent through the window. He felt confident, even though he knew he couldn't count on Annie's being there, and it was then that he felt a hand on his arm. He turned. She was walking right along beside him, looking straight ahead, wearing her old leather jacket she always wore to work, her red hair blowing in the wind, and she was as beautiful as anything he'd ever seen and he almost lost it.

She gave him a moment to recover before she said, "How's Easy hanging these days?" She said it in her Mae West voice.

"A little to the left," he grinned.

Then, without breaking stride, she put her left hand in the left hip pocket of his jeans and he wrapped his right arm around her waist, tight, and they walked straight up Columbus to Diane's Uptown, ordered some ice cream and sat on the planter under the locust tree.

THE END

"We are all diminished by his death; lessened by his passing. If we had a culture that gave support and assistance to a man of his delicacy, perhaps he could have survived. There is no real solace or cultural support for artists who find it difficult to find root in this culture, which is so hard and fast and commercial."

**—Marlon Brando, on hearing that
Tennessee Williams had died.**

Author's Notes:

M y entry into the fertile world of Tennessee Williams began in the late winter of 1945. I'd just turned 19 and was on the USS Wyoming, which was in dry-dock for repairs at the Brooklyn Navy Yard. One day I walked across the Brooklyn Bridge and went uptown to the Stage Door Canteen where I got a free ticket to see Laurette Taylor, Eddie Dowling, Anthony Ross and Julie Hayden in *The Glass Menagerie.* The performance spoke to me like nothing I had ever experienced before. I've never forgotten it.

Taking Tennessee to Hart began as a play, which I wrote in 1985. It was titled *Cry, Baby* in which Tennessee Williams played a significant, albeit oblique role. A screenplay followed, and then I reworked it into novel. By that time it had become *Taking Tennessee to Hart*, the title suggested by my friend Stuart Howard.

I got to meet Tennessee in the spring of 1973 when he came to Purdue University for the annual literary banquet, bringing with him Olive Deering whom I had directed in *Private Lives,* and Alfred Rider who read Tennessee's *Two Character Play* (sometimes called *Out Cry*) at the event. A young man from my playwriting class invited Tennessee to the class party after the banquet and, of course, he came. The setting was familiar—student apartment with ruptured sofa springs and posters pretending to be art—which Tennessee describes so brilliantly in his essay, "Something Wild." I have a picture of Tennessee and Marge, a Kokomo Indiana student, towering over Williams with her red hair done up in a beehive so lacquered that a bullet shot from close range couldn't have penetrated it. Marge later sent me a copy with the inscription, "Me and a fellow playwright."

Although he was cordial, there was no significant exchange between us. I was shy at meeting the man, who in my opinion was our greatest playwright. And Tennessee was also shy. I often wonder, had we talked at length, if I would have learned a great deal more about him. As it is my knowledge of Tennessee Williams has been gained over a lifetime of reading his published, and many of his unpublished plays, and by directing multiple productions of *A Streetcar Named Desire, Suddenly Last Summer, The Glass Menagerie* and *Cat on a Hot Tin Roof.* I also read and taught his autobiography, *Memoirs;* his mother's *Remember Me to Tom;* Donald Spoto's *The Kindness of Strangers;* and much later Lyle Leverich's *Tom.* And there was Bill Prosser's unpublished *Voyages* which concerns Tennessee's later plays, as well as the playwright's published short stories (which I love), essays, poems and his novels in addition to all the published essays about him and interviews with him. My immersion in his world has been richly satisfying and has contributed, often subtly, to *Taking Tennessee to Hart.*

I term *Taking Tennessee To Hart* a "documentary novel" because it has fidelity to actual times, places, and events including the geography of New York City, the trip across the country, the cemetery in St. Louis; and the death of Tennessee Williams, his history and his relationships. All these elements are factual including the novel's premise that Tennessee had a codicil in his will requesting that his "bones...rest not too far from those of Hart Crane."

The basic story, however, and the major characters—Walt, Billy, Annie, Hurricane, and Grace—are fictional. But as in most fiction, the characters and dialogue are based on prototypes, or composites of prototypes, and actual conversations as selected and enhanced by the author's imagination. In short, characters and dialogue are backed by faithfulness to the actual, including not only time, place and the cost of a phone call, but interviews and world events including news, speeches, and even the content of TV commercials.

Acknowledgments

Throughout the many years as I worked on the play, the screenplay, and finally the novel a vast number of people—over 150 whose names readily come to mind—have made contributions for which I am indebted.

But the person who contributed most is my wife Robin. An excellent editor, she is especially good at cutting unnecessary words and phrases. She also took the research trip with me, following the route as described in the novel, taking notes and reading aloud Whitman's "Leaves of Grass." I need to *hear* the words I've written to know if my intent is clear. During the final cutting Robin read the manuscript aloud. I know from having directed so many plays that when I do not understand what is being read, the fault is with the writing, not the reader. We worked together at the kitchen table during a two-week period, pruning, changing and sharpening. It was an intensive, creative time, and it was wonderful to hear her laugh at some of my silliness and say, "Oh, I just love this part. You can't change a word here."

I'm deeply indebted to four other people whose professional opinions I treasure: friend and associate, Page Karling, who read and commented on the very first draft of the play; two former Purdue University colleagues, Erling "Gene" Kildahl and Burnham Carter whose insightful reactions to the novel were greatly appreciated; and former classmate Beverly H. Nichols.

Writers Donald Bain and Renée Paley, long-time friends, have championed *Taking Tennessee to Hart* from their first reading and have provided not only skilled editorial hands, their publishing company Hyphenates, Ltd., has given life to the novel.

In addition there is film maker Todd Baker; Tennessee's second agent Billy Barnes; editor and fan Paul Bernabeo; literary manager/dramaturge Mark Bly; literary manager of Circle in the Square; Nancy Bosco, literary manager of the Royal National Theatre; Jack Bradley, actor; Karlene Bradley; editor Sarah Burnes; editor Matthew Carnicelli; actor Linden Chiles; actor/writer Connie Clark; agent Hy Cohen; professional reader Candace Corrigan; actor/computer designer Matt de Ganon; editor Michael Denneny; Garrettsville chamber of commerce member Robert Farley; professional reader Chester Freeman; editor of *TheaterWeek* John Harris; artistic director of the York Theatre (NYC) and actor-singer Janet Hayes (Walker); actor John Newton; actor Stephen McKinley Henderson; actor and one time prison inmate "W 'B' H"; actor/teacher/ casting director Stuart Howard; voice teacher Chuck Jones; noted actor James Earl Jones; dancer Ryland Jordan; actor Melissa Leo; literary agent Katharine Kidde; actor Merle Louise; director Tom Moore; acting teacher George Morrison; literary agent Mary Nichols; literary agent Betsy Nolan; editor Griselda Ohannessian; actor Saxon Palmer; actor Joan Pape; fan of my *TheaterWeek* articles Richard Pasqual; actor Parker Posey; Pinder Lane literary agents Dick Duane and Robert Thixton; actor/ teacher Joan Potter; director/teacher William Prosser; director/ actor Larry Randolph; editor Ray Roberts; actor Tracy Sallows; literary manager/ artistic director of Playwright's Horizons Tim Sanford; producer Julian Schlossberg; former president of Walt Disney and head of animation Peter Schneider; screenwriter/ musician /composer David Stockdale; literary manager Robert Strane; actor/teacher Roxana Stuart; Pawling (NY) undertaker John Thomas; lawyer and theatre buff Betsy Turner; theatre architect John von Szeliski; director Robert Walker; director Joe Warik; gentleman producer Robert Whitehead; classmate/burial expert Rudy Whitney; literary manager Rob Zeller; and editor Kathy Zuckerman.

And author Philip Horton who graciously gave me permission to use material from his biography, *Hart Crane: The Life of an American Poet*, and his short story "There is the World Dimensional."

It is my hope that the reader will, with thanks to those acknowledged above, find the reading of *Taking Tennessee to Hart* both informative and entertaining.

About the Author

J oe Stockdale has had a long and distinguished career in theater, with a special emphasis on the works of Tennessee Williams. Dean emeritus of the Theatre & Film division, School of the Arts at SUNY, Purchase, N.Y. where he helped launch the careers of dozens of successful actors and actresses, he'd earlier been professor of theater at Purdue University, and artistic director of the LORT Purdue Professional Theatre. He's written extensively for such theater publications as *Dramatists*, *Equity*, *TheaterWeek*, and *Playbill*, and is the author of *The Man in the Spangled Pants* and co-author of *The Architecture of Drama*. *Taking Tennessee to Hart*, his first novel, was originally written as a play. He lives in Kalamazoo, Michigan, with his wife, Robin.

www.ingramcontent.com/pod-product-compliance
Lightning Source LLC
Chambersburg PA
CBHW072226190626
46809CB00017B/904

* 9 7 8 0 9 8 3 8 8 2 5 0 3 *